KEEPING IT
IN THE
FAMILY

Screen to Page
Los Angeles, CA
www.screentopage.com

Names: Regan, Kevin P., 1987— author
Title: Keeping it in the family : a novel / Kevin P. Regan
Description: First edition. | Screen to Page, 2025
Identifiers: ISBN 9798992262414 (hardcover) | ISBN 9798992262407 (paperback) | ISBN 9798992262421 (e-book)

First Edition 2025
Cover design by Ashley Santoro © 2025

For Mal, who reminds me every day that love is real. Even if it takes a few tries.

KEEPING IT
IN THE
FAMILY

a novel

KEVIN P. REGAN

1
FAKING FAMILY

C OLLIN RAN THROUGH THE halls of CBS Television Studios like a mad man. He passed framed
posters of some of the most successful sitcoms of all time.
When he approached a poster of *Young Sheldon,* Collin
stopped and groaned. He looked into the eyes of the literal
poster child of Hollywood's lack of originality and wondered what in the hell he was even doing here.

He was not excited about his upcoming meeting.
Collin had turned in six different concepts for development under the blind script deal he'd signed only a month
before. This was his first studio deal. It was no overall –
hell, it wasn't even a first look – but it was a start. They
knew his name now, and that was half the battle.

All six ideas were snubbed by the studio's executives,
so this meeting was for a "brainstorming session," which
meant they were going to *tell* him what he had to write.
They would try to make him think it was his idea—this
was the job of a creative executive. They were tasked with

talking indignant artists *out* of creating something original and *in* to making something marketable, while simultaneously espousing to the public their unwavering support for new and original voices they'd never actually distribute.

This mostly involved a lot of compliment sandwiches: good news, bad news, good news.

> *"The good news is we loved the world you've created. The bad news is we hated all the characters, the story, and your intended themes. The good news is we have a fix. Have you thought about aging everyone down and setting the show in an apartment no working-class human could afford, preferably in New York City? Maybe add in a wacky neighbor? We're really trying to find this generation's Kramer."*

Sweaty and out of breath, Collin startled a skittish receptionist bellowing out, "I'm late."

After recovering from the shock, she glared at Collin before taking a deep breath.

"And 'I'm Late's' agent," came a voice from the waiting area.

Sitting behind a magazine was Collin's well-tailored agent, Gene Berk. He was reading a tattered paper copy of *Variety* from the year 2022. He didn't deign to look away from his trade while he updated his client.

"They pushed us twenty minutes, like always. Have a seat."

Collin took a deep breath and sat down. Gene put down the outdated magazine and pulled out an iPad from his chestnut leather messenger bag. He checked some data; made a connection in his brain.

"Did you know post-apocalyptic thrillers made the most money in 2022?"

"Benefits of a global pandemic," Collin said.

"You should start thinking about features."

"Let's make sure the studio's not pulling the blind first."

"They are—" started the skittish receptionist. Collin's heart dropped.

"*What*?!" he screeched.

"—ready for you. Ms. Radler is ready for you."

"Jesus, you scared me."

The receptionist smiled politely as she showed Collin and Gene into the offices to meet with the studio executive. When they were out of earshot, she added, "One day, everyone will fear me."

C OLLIN SAT IN THE large conference room and tapped his fingers on the table in an attempt to calm himself. Gene could tell Collin would give anything to not be here right now, but he didn't give a shit. He had the calm confidence of an agent who believed in his client. If nothing else, Gene was Collin's absolute advocate. He knew how good Collin was, and he wouldn't let anyone, especially Collin, tell him otherwise.

Gene believed the ten percent he'd earn from Collin's career was worth making the drive to Radford from Beverly Hills. He wanted to personally make sure the studio executives knew they were idiots. Collin did not know this was what he was planning to do, and Gene was glad of it. Collin was too nice for his own good sometimes, which Gene thought was wild. He had read Collin's serial killer comedy scripts—that dude was able to conjure some dark but hilarious shit. Dead dick jokes were a hard tone to nail, but streaming paid dead dick. Gene knew he needed to get Collin into network if he wanted to make real money.

Gene and Collin perked up the moment Lana Radler walked in. Her assistant held the door open for her.

"Collin Cassidy here to see you, Lana." She coldly added, "Gene Berk, too."

Lana was a force of nature contained by a pantsuit. Old school Hollywood. She rose through the executive ranks in the nineties and waved a middle finger at her enemies as she broke glass ceiling after glass ceiling. Gene heard that she once told Bob Iger to suck her dick at a charity dinner. Some even said she made him get on his knees. She commanded every room she entered. Gene was shocked by the way she managed to do this today.

Lana pulled an I.V. drip full of bright yellow liquid into the room with her. The catheter hub was taped to her left hand, and she wheeled it in with her right.

"Thanks. Tell the doc I'm feeling pukey. Might need that vape pen."

"On it." And with that, the assistant was out of the room.

Lana walked over to shake Collin's hand and got light-headed. He caught her and helped her take a seat at the table.

"Lana, are you OK?"

"What, this?" She held up the hand with the catheter hub, "Oh, don't worry, just a little chemotherapy."

Gene cursed under his breath. He was impressed. Even if it wasn't an intentional power move, she was playing the role of nonchalant executive to perfection. How was he supposed to call out a cancer patient?

"Shouldn't you do that in a hospital?" Collin asked.

Lana held up the massive rock on her ring finger. "Benefits of being married to your oncologist. Plus, I don't want any of the sharks around here thinking I'm about to take any time off," she said as a long, thick, clump of hair fell off her head.

Collin, Gene, and Lana stared at the hair on the table for a long moment, none of them willing to mention it. Gene no longer thought this was a power move and that calmed him. Collin broke the silence.

"Are you sure you're—" Collin started.

"Let's get back to the matter at hand." Lana didn't want to hear any more about her circumstances. She was here to talk business.

"—I know I owe you a new pitch. I've got a few ideas . . ."

Gene tapped Collin on the shoulder and gave him a paternal *stop talking* look. Normally, agents did not attend these kinds of meetings. Pitching the network concepts to fulfil the requirements of this deal was Collin's job, not Gene's.

A blind script deal was simple: the studio paid Collin to write a pilot, and Gene had seen to it that they paid him well above scale for this deal. But because the deal was "blind," it meant the studio—and their network counterparts—got to develop the idea with Collin from scratch. They could take as long as they wanted to find an idea they would greenlight, and Collin would have to keep coming up with new ones until they sent him to script. It was development *hell*.

Gene knew that Collin had submitted more than enough A-plus concepts, yet Lana's team had rejected each one. Every log-line Collin had shared with Gene before he pitched the studio was solid. That's why Gene was here today. It wasn't his client's fault the studio executives didn't have good taste. It was time to call a spade a shovel.

"Lana, cut the shit," Gene said. "You knew what you were getting with this deal. Collin writes cable and streaming. You're network. You shot down all his premium ideas as 'not on brand,' whatever the fuck that means. I've already got two of the projects you passed on set up at Twentieth, but this deal is in first position so he can't work until you stop dicking us around. Let's just make this simple: What. The fuck. Do you want?"

Lana glared at Gene. It was a battle of wills. Agent versus studio executive. The battle ended when Lana's eyes widened, she ran to the trashcan and vomited into it. She dialed her cell phone and yelled, "Vape pen. Now!"

"Are you sure you're, OK?" Collin asked again. "We can do this another time . . ."

Lana continued to spit into the waste bin, until she got a hold of herself. "I'm fine. Cancer's a bitch, but so am I." She gathered herself, took a long deep breath then sat back down at the head of the conference table.

"All right. We want a family comedy. Something classic, but modern. Something we've all seen before, but that has never been on air. You know?"

Collin was a deer in headlights. He hadn't the slightest idea what in the fuck any of that meant. "I . . . I . . . Those are conflicting—" Gene interrupted him before he could say something honest and, therefore, stupid.

"We hear you loud and clear," Gene said.

"We do?" Collin said. Clear was not how he would describe the directive.

"We do." Gene said. He told Collin with his eyes not to say another word.

"Great," Lana said. "Send me a couple log-lines next week and we'll talk."

As Lana stood up to leave, her assistant entered with her THC vape pen. Lana took a long-ass hit and released a giant cloud of vapor. After a few grisly coughs, she relaxed.

"You guys want in on this?"

C OLLIN AND GENE WALKED out of the building, but not before imbibing on cancer-grade Californian cannabis. The sun and warmth immediately put them at ease and helped Collin remember the world wasn't ending. For the moment.

Gene felt accomplished. Any time he could get a studio executive to tell him what they wanted instead of playing round after round of an unnecessary guessing game that wasted everyone's time was a victory. Good clients were like reluctant soldiers—they hated being given orders, but executed faster than someone who did things by the book. Gene slapped Collin on the back and ordered him to enjoy the moment.

They walked around the lot giggling until they found a coffee shop. Gene bought Collin a coffee he would expense to his agency. That, Gene thought, was the best part of the job: free coffee. All he had to do was claim he was meeting a client, and any coffee he drank was free. If he was alone, he always got two and gave the extra to someone on the street. Homeless people needed to get their days going too, and asking them about their lives could be considered business—you never knew who had the next Oscar-winning story to tell. Alcohol was free too, but that, Gene learned, was not worth it. The clients who wanted to drink with you weren't the clients who would stick with you. Collin was a coffee client. A keeper.

The moment was fleeting. Collin's predisposition to anxiety was eventually exacerbated by the THC. After being told he had to come up with brand-new ideas, he was spinning out under the bright California sun as film executives, the stars who kept them in business, and the crews who did all the manual labor mingled on the massive campus getting their necessary caffeine fixes. He turned to Gene.

"I'm thirty-seven, single, and live in a one-bedroom apartment. What the fuck do I know about writing a family sitcom?"

"What the fuck did Stanley Kubrick know about being in the military? He still made *Full Metal Jacket.* Figure it out."

"He also made *Fear and Desire* . . . so . . ."

"Reconnect with what it means to be a part of a family. Join a cult or something."

"Do you know how expensive Scientology is?" Collin said.

Gene was sick of his high being stepped on. Coffee and cannabis made him proactive. Collin needed to chill out and it was his job to make him.

"Adopt a troubled teen for all I care. I pulled a lot of strings to get you this deal and I'm not going to let you self-sabotage your way out of it." He got an alert on his iWatch and remembered he had another meeting. He stood up.

"I've got a three o'clock with Christopher Nolan's long-lost sister."

"Think the Nolan's would adopt me?"

"Get to work." Gene slid on sunglasses to hide his bloodshot baby blues and walked away from his client without another word.

Collin was certain now that he was done for. This was it. He was going to die alone in an apartment in Little Armenia. Coffee and cannabis made him melodramatic.

"Is that Dolph Lundgren?" he said to himself, out loud, his brain still figuring out how to operate in public under medical grade influence.

It was.

C OLLIN WAS MID-STROKE WHEN the memory came into his mind. Fireworks exploded outside his window and he paused the vanilla porn.

Pants at his ankles, he sat in a dilapidated chair across from the poorly built Ikea desk where his laptop was camped. He'd hoped a good release would get him out of his own head, but somewhere out there a federal law enforcement program was logging any website he might choose to spend time on. Or, at least, Collin was convinced they were.

His Google search history could, at best, be described as alarming after his stint as a staff writer on a serial killer comedy series. His research into successful killers, their methods, and the government's countermeasures created his suspicion that his every online move was being tracked, this paranoia brought to life all for ten episodes of dead dick jokes. Thanks, Netflix.

Individual privacy was long dead, and Collin acted accordingly. This made for some bland choices in carnal content. Not that he had extreme tastes by any stretch of the imagination—he simply didn't want the government to know what got him off, which, if he was being honest, was low production quality and the belief that the performers were a genuine, loving, couple who had a long-established safe word.

The fantasy that true love equated to copious copulation was a wonderful escape from the reality that romantic love faded to platonic love. If you were lucky. Most of the time, you ended up with your dick in your hand. The performance was getting hot and heavy when Collin let himself go to pause it. He thought those sex workers in particular were better actors than any he'd worked with. Which wasn't saying much.

THE MEMORY WAS FAR more stimulating than poorly produced passion. It was the time he and Orla hooked up in the lifeguard shack. He'd like to pretend this was a random occurrence, but memories like this cropped up on a fairly regular basis. What you remember most is what affected you most. Memories are traumas and joys—you don't remember the blasé. At least, not when your dick is in your hand.

This memory was both trauma and joy, thus extremely prone to random recall. Collin hadn't seen or spoken to Orla in years. While he was trying to get himself off, the image of their younger bodies going at it in the small shack popped into his brain. Maybe it never left. It was a distinct memory, clear as the day it happened.

Collin had held Orla up against the wall as she dug her nails into his back—he missed having core strength—and there was a lot of grabbing and biting. Collin couldn't remember what initiated the throes, but he knew Orla was a little angry. Angry sex was the best sex. Another reason he didn't trust the government with his porn predilections.

"Don't you fucking stop," she had ordered him. Past-Collin knew better than to refuse a command from Orla. She said what she meant and meant what she said.

He kept going; it felt too good to stop, regardless. Collin remembered that he and Orla always had a good rhythm with one another. So, it wasn't a surprise when they came together. It was, however, a surprise when they realized the condom broke.

He remembered showing her the shredded scumbag. Orla darted to the first aid kit that sat at the nearby table. Collin thought she might have just had some Plan B stashed in there for emergencies—people made all kinds of mistakes in the ocean and a true lifeguard was prepared for any situation.

Instead, Orla had shoved hand sanitizer inside herself. Collin had tried to stop her the moment her hand moved to where *he* had been just moments before.

"You shouldn't—" But before he could get the thought out, she was past the point of no return. Orla's scream was terror-inducing. It had sounded like she was auditioning for a horror film. Collin had half-expected other lifeguards to come running. Luckily, no one had heard her over the fireworks. It had been the fourth of July. Maybe that was why he remembered—fourth of July was next weekend.

He'd gasped and then, after a moment of her screaming obscenities, collapsed into a fit of laughter. Which hadn't made Orla feel any better about the blend of liquid flames and semen inside her. She'd turned her verbal wrath on Collin. He took it, knowing full well she just needed to get through the burn. For a girl who grew up around sailors, it was mild fair. A couple of 'fucks', a few 'cunts', and just one 'asshole'.

She'd admitted it was, in fact, funny a half hour later when the pain finally subsided. Collin had calmed her down, and they'd both got dressed. They'd walked to the pharmacy together to find a better solution. Alcohol was good for a lot of things, but not preventing pregnancy. It more often had the opposite effect.

W HY THIS MEMORY GOT him off was something
Collin did not want to think too deeply about. It
was probably because, at the time, he and Orla had loved
each other. He was, if nothing else, a romantic. A romantic
with a disturbing Google search history, but a romantic,
nonetheless.

With his balls empty and his head clear, Collin sani-
tized his own hands and pulled up his pants. He shifted
programs and stared at the blinking cursor on his 'Final
Draft' document. Time to work.

He had nothing.

"Fuck," he said and tapped his fingers in a syncopated
rhythm.

His phone vibrated on the faux wood grain of the
IKEA desk. It startled him. Who could be calling? No
one called him, except Gene, and they'd already spent too
much time together today.

He checked the phone. His brother-in-law was starting an Instagram live. This notification made Collin smile.
He knew what Kip going live meant. Happy for a reason
to postpone work a little longer, Collin opened his phone.
His sister, Valerie, was on screen wearing her Temple University embroidered scrubs and a scowl.

"There are real media outlets covering the event, why
are you going live?" She crossed her arms. Collin could

tell she was exhausted from a long shift. She was far from camera-ready.

"If you knew anything about teenagers, you'd know they don't watch traditional media."

2
SKATING BY

AUDREY HAD VOMITED HER brains out in the bathroom. She still tasted it.

She was standing atop the drop-in to the street style course she had grown up on. Her father was hosting this year's East Coast Invitational at the family skate park. He knew it would be good marketing. If there was one thing her father was good at, it was getting the word out, which was why his cell phone was trained on his own face shooting the event—that was already being covered by ESPN+—on his Instagram live.

"Yo, listen up. This is your man, the Master Monteiro, coming to you live from my skate park here in the city of brotherly love. We hosting the east coast invitational and my baby girl about to knock some o' these mothafuckers down a peg or two. She gonna show all these bitch-ass boys how it's done. Ain't that right, baby?"

Audrey did not respond to her father's request for comment. She didn't even acknowledge the phone in her face. She was too busy visualizing the run in her head. She knew every inch of this park. She was skating it before she could walk. For that, she had her dad to thank.

Her father, Kip Monteiro, known professionally as *The Master Monteiro*, was a ten-time X-Games medalist. In the early aughts, he could be spotted on any episode of *Jackass* or *Viva la Bam* that was shot at the skate parks Bam Margera would frequent outside Philadelphia. He gave the camera crews some of the best reactions to failed stunts a producer could ask for. He was also the only black skateboarder on screen, so he was hard to miss.

Kip combined his skate skills, sponsorships, and the money he made from bigger events, with his inherent business acumen. He was able to pay his own way through a business degree at Temple University and eventually opened Master Monteiro's Skate Park and Shop in Center City, Philadelphia.

The park and shop provided a place for at-risk youth to focus on a skill set that kept them out of trouble and kept Kip's family fed. When Audrey was born, Kip put her on a skateboard and she never got off. He started promoting the park and shop on social media, when the platforms were in their infancy, by making adorable videos of his then-infant daughter skating better than some teenage skate rats. This marketing blew up and his little skate girl videos went viral.

Master Monteiro's became the go-to place for beginners and pros in the Philadelphia area. Baby Audrey became a mini-mascot.

As Audrey grew, so did her following. By the time she was eleven, she was a sponsored skateboarder traveling up and down the east coast to compete. She would almost always take gold.

Kip, ever the vigilant father and business manager, made sure that all the money she made stayed in trusts and investment accounts. Audrey knew what she was bringing in yearly, which was more than most adults with college degrees, but she had no idea that her father had been making sure compound interest was working for her as well.

With over two million followers on Instagram, Audrey made even more money doing affiliate marketing. She hocked Nike, Adidas, Vans—any company that made a product they wanted skaters to use, Audrey used them right back.

Audrey loved skating and the opportunities it created for her. What she did not love were the nerves she got before a competition. All week leading up to the invitational, she woke up and vomited out of pure anxiety. This had never happened before, so she brushed it off.

In the back of her mind, she knew the real reason for her weak stomach, but there was no the time to worry about that. It was time for action. She'd worked her ass off, and now she was about to go on a run she knew in her bones, the same way a composer knew the notes in their composition.

Audrey's favorite part about skating now was that, as young woman of color with a large following, she got to make decisions about her performances that others might not get to make. The most important of which, to her, was the choice of song during her run.

She was a teenage girl in the modern era with a social media platform. The music she picked would be heard in videos and clips plastered all over the internet. She typically gave local punk bands, whom she wanted to promote on a larger platform, her boost. When possible, she'd try to get the bands booked to play the event and skate to their live performances. Willow Smith reposted one of her stories and the band playing during her run got added to a national tour.

Today, however, Audrey made a slightly odd choice in music for her run: she chose 'We Didn't Start the Fire' by Billy Joel. Billy Joel was her maternal grandmother's favorite artist and she wanted to dedicate this run to her.

Audrey and her grandmother, Eliza, were thick as thieves. Eliza was the only one in the family that treated her like she was a kid and not a mascot for the family business.

She knew that playing her grandmother's favorite artist would let her know she had something important to share. Grandma Eliza always understood the secret signals Audrey would send subtly in her videos and performances to show she loved her.

Audrey was going to set this skate park on fire with a run dedicated to her grandmother. She wanted to go see her right this moment. Only Eliza would understand why she was having these stomach issues.

Talking to Grandma Eliza was Audrey's true focus. A plan she had been working on was finally coming to fruition and the first person she wanted to tell was her grandmother. Her parents were not going to understand—parents *never* understand—Grandma Eliza would.

The competition was simply something that had to be done first. So, Audrey prepared herself mentally to nail the run. She saw every move she would make and the precise timing of big tricks to high energy moments in Joel's anthem.

The instrumental open of 'We Didn't Start the Fire' blared from the speakers and Audrey dropped into the park.

The moment Joel's anthem blared out of the speakers, Audrey hit a five-forty kick-flip and landed on a rail, grinding until Marilyn Monroe let her know it was time to hop off with a kick-flip. She timed a three-sixty off one side of a mini ramp into an immediate seven-twenty off the other, just before the chorus kicked in.

Audrey hit every note.

She kept her stunts on pace with the quickly spat lyrics, which kept the audience enthralled as to how she could keep up this clip.

The climax of the run came while J.F.K was being blown away. Audrey hit a spine at high speed, launched herself into the air where she executed a perfect Backflip McTwist and stomped the landing.

The crowd went nuts.

Kip's social feed blew up with comments.

"That's my daughter!" Kip said to the hundreds of thousands watching on his live story. "She needs a ninety-six average to move on ... Let's see what the judges say." He flipped the lens to show the three judges making their deliberations on Audrey's run.

After a moment, the numerical scores were shown on a digital screen that rested in front of each judge. The first judge—an aging skateboarder who had really taken the time to analyze the run he just witnessed—gave Audrey a ninety-eight point nine. The second—a bearded man in his thirties who had the air of a tech bro trying too hard to fit in—gave her a ninety-nine point eight. The third judge—a woman in her forties who wanted nothing more than to be done with this—showed ninety-seven point nine.

The crowd applauded Audrey even more.

"My baby is going to nationals!" Kip screamed into his follower's ears. He tried to get some kind of emotional reaction out of Audrey, but she had moved on from the moment the way only a disaffected teen who had done this time and time again, could.

"Grandma's waiting for us in Cape May. Can we go?"

"Of course, baby girl! Right after you say hi." Kip said.

Audrey rolled her eyes, painted a faux smile on her face, and waved to the fans watching online.

COLLIN WATCHED AS HIS niece waved on his brother-in-law's story, still a little stoned. He was proud of her.

That pride quickly shifted into guilt: guilt for not being there in person for his niece's big competitions, guilt for not calling his parents enough. He knew he should call more, but he only wanted to call with good news.

He didn't want to burden his parents with the fears and anxieties that came with pursing your dreams while on the opposite end of the continent.

These were the thoughts that came to his mind while he tried to brainstorm ideas for family comedy projects to bring to Lana, still staring at a blank screen.

Guilt wasn't funny.

Looking for a way to procrastinate, Collin opened the drawers of his desk to find a pen. Maybe going old-school would get his creative juices flowing.

He dug through the cluttered drawer, moving batteries and paperclips in hopes of finding a ballpoint. What he found was a long-forgotten relic: a ring box that had gathered years of dust in the back of his desk drawer. He held the box, admiring it for a moment before sliding it back into its hiding place. Collin slammed the drawer shut and decided that his apartment was a mess.

Procrastination was imperative to Collin's creative process. He needed to distract his mind with his body so that, when he subconsciously came up with a solution or an idea, he could claim divine inspiration. The only reason Collin was in half-decent shape was that going to the gym helped him get out of his head. If he were to merely engage in the mental processes necessary to come up with ideas, and not be performing some other mundane task, he might have to consider writing as work and not just a creative passion. Magical thinking was necessary.

Collin's preferred method, outside of the gym, was procrasti-cleaning. While he brought about order to his physical surroundings, his mind was solving its current problem of what kind of family sitcom to pitch the studio. A family sitcom that, as his Lana had put it, was something "we've all seen before, but that has never been on air."

Fucking nonsensical bullshit.

While his subconscious worked on the conflicting directive, his body picked up dirty laundry from every nook and cranny, including the refrigerator. When you're a single man who lives alone, every surface can be used as storage.

He organized his books by color and size, vacuumed the floor, then realized that organizing books by color and size was psychotic. He then reorganized his books by category first, then alphabetically within each category. Like a normal, sane human being who wasn't influenced by organizational reality shows on Netflix.

After hours of cleaning and organizing to the point where he might feel confident having guests come to his home, he sat on the couch and opened a dating app. He unconsciously swiped left on everyone he came across. It wasn't that he didn't find the profiles attractive or interesting enough, he simply knew deep down that he didn't want to put the time or effort necessary into getting to know someone new. This was nothing more than window shopping for people. Another procrastination tactic.

While swiping left, his cell phone rang with a Face-Time request from his mother. He answered immediately, happy for another way to distract himself.

"Hey, Ma," he said.

Eliza was cooking in a massive kitchen. Collin could hear the onions sautéing in the pan while she chopped garlic. His mother could give Gordon Ramsey a run for his money, both in the kitchen and in cutting down people who didn't deserve to be there. No one wanted to get in the line of fire while she was preparing meals.

"Your niece is pregnant," she said. Something Collin loved about his mother was she didn't waste time with preamble prattle. She always got right to the point.

"Audrey's sixteen, she can't be pregnant."

Eliza tossed the garlic into the sauté pan and the sizzle made Collin's mouth water. She grabbed a bell pepper and started chopping away.

"Honey, I know you don't understand much about female anatomy, but sixteen-year-olds are quite capable of becoming pregnant."

"How did this happen?"

"Sex, I presume," Eliza said. "I didn't ask for the details. But these things usually happen in a fairly consistent manner."

"Jesus. How's Val taking it?" Collin's sister had always been a little high-strung, and becoming a grandmother, he thought, might kill her.

"Between you and me," Eliza said, while checking to make sure no one had entered her kitchen of solitude, "she and Kip are making this worse than it actually is. Come to Cape May. It's time for our fourth of July family vacation anyway, and your niece could use some comfort from the uncle she idolizes."

If Collin's life had been a cartoon, this is where the animators would have drawn a light bulb over top his head.

"That would be cheaper than Scientology," he mumbled to himself.

"What?"

"You know some family time might be good for me. I'll need to work while I'm there, though."

"You ever stop working?" Eliza said, concerned.

"Where do you think I get it from?"

"Your father."

"How many Airbnb reservations you make for the house next month, Mom?"

"Well, I've staggered the rooms, so we'll have twenty. The Jones's and the McCarthy's on Monday and—" Eliza realized her son had set her up. She stared at her offspring and pointed her knife at the camera, annoyed and proud that her sarcasm had been passed down properly.

"You're a little smart-ass, you know that?"

"That I do get from Dad." He winked. "I'll look at flights."

"Love you, honey." Eliza said. She got what she wanted. Better not to press the conversation and let her son get on with his day.

Collin would get what he needed, too: a quick refresher in family dynamics. The fact that his mother's cooking would come with the deal was a bonus.

"Love you too, Mom."

3
FAIL BETTER

ORLA RUANE SPENT A lifetime in the ocean with a mind that consistently went against the current. She was still wearing her red lifeguard bikini—the newest variation of a swimsuit she'd worn every summer since she was sixteen—despite being clocked out.

Her inky, wet hair blew in the wind while she paddle-boarded parallel with the shore to get some peace and quiet. She enjoyed the moments of Zen she got from being out on the waves alone. She let the sun tan her salted skin until a foam football hit her in the jaw, knocking her off the paddleboard, and Orla sank into the sea.

She resurfaced a moment later to find children were swimming toward her to retrieve their ball.

Orla realized the season was in full swing. Cape May was no longer her hometown, it belonged to the tourists or the . . .

"Fucking MERTs," as Orla and other locals referred to them.

Orla spat sea water as she climbed back atop her pad-dleboard, refusing to let the MERTs ruin her morning. She paddled back to shore, riding waves with expert ease as the surf did most of the work. Once ashore, a pregnant woman in a chic one-piece bathing suit, Saint Laurent sunglasses, and a massive sunhat waddled towards her.

"I'm sorry about them. They're not very coordinated . . . Orla? Orla Ruane?" The woman distinctly recognized her.

Orla took a beat. She couldn't place the woman. She squinted at her and the woman took off her sunglasses. With her weasel face in full view, Orla couldn't believe it.

"Becca McPherson?" she said. "Haven't seen you since our thesis defense, how are you?" Orla and Becca graduated from the same Ph.D. program. Becca was a romance scholar. Orla always thought that was hilarious because Becca could never commit to anyone.

"It's Cohen now," Becca said, held up a massive rock on her left hand, squealed, and pulled Orla into a hug she did not want. Orla had the breath squeezed out of her.

"Oh, my god. Congrats. What are you doing here in the Cape?" Orla said, trying to escape Becca's grasp.

"Saul's family has a beach house, we come down from the city when we can. What are you doing here?"

"I live here," Orla said. "Where are you now? Last we talked you got that fellowship at Northeastern."

"NYU! Full tenure position, but I'm on sabbatical next semester," she patted her very full uterus, "Where are you?"

It had been nearly a decade since they had graduated together. Orla looked down at her feet as she squished sand between her toes. Her current academic pursuits were not a topic she enjoyed discussing. Especially with more successful colleagues. She bit her bottom lip before giving in to Becca's interrogation.

"I'm working at the community college here, but I also adjunct at Stockton. And lifeguard, obviously." Becca forced an uncomfortable, toothy, smile. Orla could feel Becca's pity. She wanted to drown herself in the ocean.

"So nothing full time? Oh, that's great news! We have an opening in Brit-Lit. I know, I know, you're Irish lit, but just teach the Northern Irish books," she said with a wink. "You *have* to apply. Use me as a reference, it'll be like old times!" Orla looked at her old friend's stomach. "Well, OK, not exactly like old times, but we still get wild at office parties."

Orla was deeply touched. It was a very kind offer. NYU was exactly the kind of school she dreamed of teaching at.

She didn't believe for a second she'd get the job, but it was still nice to be thought of.

"Here," Becca said, shoving her phone into Orla's hands. "Put your email in your contact and I'll send you the details. You still have the same number? 609 area code?"

"That's me." Orla said.

"It's a new posting so it hasn't gone live yet. This is kismet!" Becca said, while Orla put her information into the phone.

"You really don't have to do this." Orla said.

"Oh, my god. Stop. Orla, you're amazing. NYU would be lucky to have you. I'm gonna look like a hero for head-hunting you. I can't believe I didn't think of you earlier. Pregnancy brain. You'd think after three I'd be used to it." Becca saw one of her kids picking up a horseshoe crab.

"Beckett Levi Cohen, you put that down!" She screamed.

Orla handed Becca's phone back.

"I should get back and make sure they don't kill themselves." Becca said.

"I'd help but," Orla indicated her lifeguard uniform, "off-duty, and I have to get to my seminar."

"Teaching summer semester?"

"Always." Orla sighed.

"Well, I have your info. We're heading back to the city tonight, but I'll be in touch. It was so good to see you! I'm sorry my kids are little shitheads."

"We call them MERTs."

"What's a MERT?"

"You don't want to know." Orla winked. Becca laughed, knowing better than to argue.

"Well, they get it from their father," Becca said and pulled Orla into another awkward hug. Orla tried not to press into Becca's baby bump.

When she finally let go, they waved goodbye and headed in opposite directions on the beach.

W HILE ORLA WAS IN the ocean and talking with Becca, her cell phone had been ringing non-stop. She had ten missed calls from her sister, Siobhan. Upon seeing that it was already eleven a.m., she knew she didn't have the time or the patience to deal with whatever overblown situation it was that her sister wanted to bitch about.

Siobhan liked to make little things into big things for the personal drama. She was like their mother in that way.

During the off season, there's not much to do in Cape May, so she kept herself entertained by believing that her social life was akin to a Bravo reality show. There had been a three-month-long mystery last winter as to whether or not one of her friend's husbands was cheating. It turned out he was just going to therapy. Which is what they talked about for the next three months.

Orla did not have time to speculate on what it might be that Blaine Verrastro wouldn't talk to his wife about, but would tell that therapist, whose gender still hadn't been confirmed. She had a class to teach and still needed to fight her way through her lifeguard colleagues to shower in time at headquarters.

Cape May Community College was situated west of the great sound and just north of the zoo. Occasionally, animals from the ill-funded zoo would find their way to graze on campus. One time, after teaching her Introduction to Irish Literature class, Orla came upon an elephant chowing down on Kentucky Blue. She ignored it, as one does with wild elephants that show up unannounced. She hoped the lionesses weren't on a hunt for food as well.

Orla had lived in Cape May her whole life, outside of a four-year stint in Philadelphia for her undergrad and six in Boston to get her Ph.D. Even then, she came home during the summers to work her lifeguard shifts and catch up with old friends.

Cape May was a great place to visit but, for those few who called it home, it could be difficult to make a living year-round. All jobs were seasonal and, therefore, so was the depression felt by many locals. The industry was essentially hospitality, real estate, fishing, and education. The latter receiving the least money and attention.

Orla considered herself lucky. While she had hoped to be a professor at a more well-funded university, having large lectures on the literary and political rivalries of Yeats and Joyce, she felt proud to be working with the local kids who wanted more than to work at their daddy's hotel or bar. But now that she knew about this position at NYU, she felt something she hadn't felt in a long time: *excitement*.

She could only accept another university job, otherwise her financial world would be thrown into chaos. As an educator, she still needed to work three years, four months, and twenty-five days more before she could wipe away her six-figure student loan debt under the public service loan forgiveness plan. While she taught classes every fall, spring, and summer, she barely made enough to get by sharing a home with her sister and brother-in-law.

She kept telling herself that, once that debt was off her back, she'd have the freedom to try to apply to larger programs at more prestigious campuses. And now that opportunity had literally hit her in the face. She didn't want to get ahead of herself, but the excitement had her giddy. She thought she was content to serve her community in the classroom as well as the ocean, but now that she had another option, she was torn between the safety of this world she knew so well and the opportunity for adventure in a big city.

O RLA MADE NO ATTEMPT to acknowledge the five students who were already in their seats. This was her seminar class and the one she most looked forward to because she got to teach what she had spent all that student loan money on. She wrote Samuel Beckett's immortal words on the blackboard:

Ever tried. Ever failed. No matter. Try again. Fail again. Fail better.

"So, what do you all make of this quote in particular from this week's reading?"

Kayden was a know it all, and cracked his neck as if the knowledge he was about to drop needed a warm-up. Orla took a deep breath, reminded herself it was good to have students who were interested in the material, and nodded at him to go ahead.

"Because of the stunted syntax and deliberate impoverishment of language, it's an attempt to take away agency or identity of both speaker and addressee. With the language stripped of its referential function, the only positivity that can be extracted from the text is through pushing failure to its limit in order to succeed."

The whole class stared at him blankly. Orla simply shook her head, having read those exact words many times before.

"We get it, you read the essays I assigned," Orla said. The class laughed as Kayden sulked, caught memorizing. Orla, ever the lifeguard at heart, threw the boy a lifeline to save him from the swirling seas of laughter.

"OK. OK. As long winded as that was, Kayden is on to something. Let's talk about the dichotomy between Beckett's intentional negativity and the piece's perceivable positivity."

A groan of exhaustion exited Michael, who was infected with an incurable case of senioritis.

"Dr. Ruane, come on. It's the last class before finals. Everyone's papers are in progress, and we all need a much-deserved mental health day."

Orla took a moment to consider this request. That would give her time to put materials together for this NYU position. The other faces, save Kayden, all acknowledged that this was the way they felt. As excited as Orla got from getting to discuss Beckett, she knew these kids had more than earned a break. Beckett would always be there. Unlike Godot.

"Thank Godot, someone said it." The room let out a relieved laugh. "Jesus, how much longer were you people going to let me go on?"

Just as Orla was about to dismiss them, the greatest sin one could commit in her classroom cut her off.

A cell phone rang.

Orla's jovial face melted into the angry scowl of an academic who had made it very clear at the beginning of the semester—and at regular intervals thereafter—that cell phones must be turned off in her classroom. It was her most petulant pet peeve. She would burn down a village of puppies to find the perpetrator.

"Whose phone is that?" No one fessed up. Orla began roving the classroom, following the sound as best she could. "You all know the rule: cell phone rings in class, you do not pass."

It wasn't Kayden or Michael, or the girl with green hair whose name she could never remember. The next ring moved her closer to the front of class until it was obvious who the culprit was.

Siobhan was calling again.

"Oh, God damn it. Of course it would be me . . ." Orla put her head in her hands, embarrassed.

"Does this mean we all get As?" Michael asked.

"All right. Get out of here, all of you. Papers are due in my email no later than noon on the thirtieth." And with that the students all escaped, leaving Orla alone with her still-ringing cell phone.

ORLA DECIDED NOT TO answer her sister's incessant calls and thought the best course of action was to simply return home and speak to her in person. She would give Siobhan a clear and unmitigated declaration that if she doesn't answer her phone, she's busy, and she would call back when she was able to.

Siobhan and Orla lived in the same home they grew up in. It had been left to both of them in their father's will and this was the only reason Orla felt comfortable living there with Siobhan, Siobhan's husband Jesse – who spent half the year on a ship as a merchant marine captain anyway – and her nephew Noah.

When Orla entered the home decorated with more nautical memorabilia than Orla thought necessary—her brother-in-law's doing—she found Noah sulking on the living room couch. This was a rare event. As a sixteen-year-old boy in a beach town at the height of tourist season, he was expected to be out causing mischief.

"What are you doing home?" she asked. "It's summer, shouldn't you be out scamming MERTs into buying you booze?"

"He's grounded!" Siobhan shouted from the kitchen.

"For what?" Orla shouted back.

"For life," Noah said. With no further explanation, he made a beeline for the stairs. He was not in the mood to rehash whatever conversation Orla was about to have with her sister.

"You can tell me later on the stand," she whispered to him as he bounded up the steps. Orla took a deep breath before walking into the kitchen.

There she found her sister, sans make-up. For a real estate agent who believed image was everything, this was fear-inducing in Orla.

Something was seriously wrong.

This fear was confirmed when she saw Siobhan filling her wine glass to the brim, with an already empty bottle sitting on the kitchen island. The lecture she had planned about not calling incessantly might need to be put on the back burner. This made two lectures she had planned and canceled today.

"Sorry I didn't call back, but I was on my way home anyway."

"Oh, it's cool," Siobhan said, sarcasm coating her words, "don't worry. I'm gonna be a grandmother. No big deal." Siobhan took a swig of what was left in the bottle before picking up her wine glass and sipping enough to release the surface tension.

"Wait. *What*?!" Orla could not process this information. How was this even possible? Then she remembered Noah was a sixteen-year-old boy. Sixteen-year-old boys were idiots, especially the smart ones like Noah.

"Noah knocked that girl up," Siobhan said, on the brink of tears.

"Jesus Christ. This is why boys should be sterilized at birth. Circumcise and sterilize. Boom, world peace."

"Oh, there's something worse," And this admission scared Orla more than the calls, or her sister's lack of make-up, or the bottles of two-buck-chuck she saw that still needed to be drunk in the fridge.

"What could possibly be worse?"

"When you didn't answer . . ." Siobhan said. "I called . . ."

"No . . ."

"I had to tell her," Siobhan said, pleading for forgiveness.

At the realization of what her sister had done, Orla simply opened the fridge, grabbed an already opened bottle of white, pulled out the cork, and started chugging before she could build up the courage to ask what she needed to ask. After downing half the bottle, Orla wiped her mouth, looked her sister in the eye, and asked with all sincerity and urgency, "Why would you tell *Mom*?!"

4
GHOSTS OF US

COLLIN FLEW INTO PHILADELPHIA and rented a basic sedan. The car wove its way south on the Garden State Parkway until the smell of saltwater filled the air. While zoning out listening to local radio stations, the Bluetooth speakers in his rental car rang aloud, breaking him out of his daze.

Gene was calling.

Collin accepted the call via the steering wheel button, and before he could say hello Gene was screaming through his speaker system.

"What the fuck are you doing in New Jersey!"

"How did you know I was in New Jersey?"

"You shared your location with me when we first met for coffee."

"That was like five years ago!"

"Regardless, I say again, what the fuck are you doing in New Jersey!" Collin had hoped he could avoid this call. Fortunately, he knew just how to reassure Gene.

"You told me to reconnect with family. I'm reconnecting." Collin checked the time on his dash—he should be at the exit soon. He had driven from Philadelphia to Cape May so many times the route was in his muscle memory. He knew exactly where he was in the world without the use of GPS, when he was back east. In Los Angeles, he needed his GPS to get to the grocery store.

"Since when do you listen to me?" Gene asked, almost amazed that his client had taken his advice.

"It's almost the fourth. No one in LA is working." Collin knew he was right and the sigh that came through his speaker let him know that Gene knew so too.

"Just make sure you are," Gene said. "There are only two weeks left in this development season. If you don't get something greenlit by then, Lana could keep you tied up until next year."

"I got it. Goodbye, Gene. Love you!" Collin ended the call with his thumb on the steering wheel. He thought for a moment.

"Hey, Siri?" His phone dinged in recognition of the voice command.

"Turn off location sharing for Gene Berk."

"I'm sorry, I can't do that," said the robotic voice.

"God damn it." Collin made a mental note to stop sharing his location once he got to Windward House.

He turned up the radio and let the pop-punk station play while he re-embraced the solitude that driving afforded him. He won't have it much longer—there would be no privacy and no peace once he was with his family.

When the DJ called Blink-182 *classic rock*, Collin wanted to jump out of the car. He was an elder millennial and not particularly fond of the *elder* addition to his generational label. The song ended and the cruel disk jockey did his best Stern impression while reading news copy.

Radio was fucking weird.

"Bummer news. This Independence Day weekend, Cape May County is on evacuation alert. Hurricane Constance is on track to become a category four by the time she makes landfall later this week."

Collin changed the station and found a catchy tune to clear his mind.

"Of course I come to town and everything goes to shit."

He turned on his blinker, got into the right lane, and merged off the highway via Exit Zero.

C OLLIN DROVE THROUGH THE vacation town filled with well-maintained Victorian homes. Cape May attracted a lot of wealthy and famous people during the summer, and that influx of cash into the local economy allowed the county to go all out for big holidays like the fourth. Independence Day decorations were in full swing. Red, white, and blue covered all the traffic lights, docks, and businesses. Collin saw children playing with sparklers in the shopping district, their parents barely paying attention. The burn ward would be busy soon.

When he stopped at a red light by the docks, he saw his younger self and Orla sitting by the water, holding hands, laughing. The ghosts of his past live on in this small town at the southernmost point in New Jersey.

The wave of anger that hit him when he saw the ring box collecting dust in his drawer found its way back into his heart. But this time it was tinged with something else, something more visceral.

Remorse.

He remembered all the good times he had with Orla here. Being lifeguards each summer together, sneaking into bars as twenty-year-olds because no one cared.

Collin's family hadn't bought their house here until he was already a teenager. Orla and her family called him a MERT the first year and a half they were together. They refused to explain what it meant. It was infuriating. When he finally learned what the acronym stood for, he couldn't help but laugh. Only patience was rewarded with understanding. He remembered the day he met Orla and was first called a MERT; he remembered the fake ID he got back in Philadelphia so he could go to the local's bar when he got down to Cape May; he remembered how no one checked it.

As he learned, only MERTs thought anyone cared about the legal limit. If some rich fuck's kids got caught drinking, the fines they paid helped the city. Why stop a cash cow? Rich kids got their records expunged anyway. If it was a local kid, most of the time they knew the cop and got off with a warning. Let the MERTs drink and pay the city's bills.

God, he had forgotten about the local slang for tourists; hadn't thought about MERTs in a long time. Being back after such a long time away, he was a MERT once more.

As he drove around town, Collin watched the ghosts of his romantic past enjoy their time together. He remembered all the fun he and Orla had as he passed landmarks he'd long forgotten. They had been regulars at the C-View, where they got wasted then walked home, laughing hand in hand. They had made out after sneaking into the lighthouse at night, avoiding security. He remembered all the joy he had when this town felt more like home than Los Angeles ever would.

His anger began to fade away and had fully morphed into millennial nostalgia by the time he pulled into the parking spot at Windward House and turned off location sharing.

Windward House was a massive Edwardian home built in 1905, when homes still had character. The house sat on prime real estate only half a block east of the beach and half a block west of the Washington Street Mall. Collin's father, Allan, had bought the property almost two decades ago and painstakingly renovated it while trying not to murder the heads of the Cape May Historical Society, who made that endeavor far more expensive than it ought to have been.

Allan was a union carpenter who started working when he was only sixteen years old. He had learned about real estate by being the manual labor on innumerable job sites; he eavesdropped on the developer's phone calls and figured out how the business worked; he learned that the skills he had honed from the time he was a teenager were immensely profitable, if he were willing to do most of the work himself.

When Allan and Eliza were young, he bought their first home in West Philadelphia for only nine thousand dollars. It was a shit hole. He spent another five thousand renovating it into a decent family home, then used the equity he had earned to purchase another fixer upper, did the same dance, and turned it into an income property.

By the time he was twenty-three, Allan Cassidy was a landlord known for being fair and actually fixing the problems his tenants had. He built a reputation that bankers, buyers, and builders all vouched for. This was how Allan learned that debt was good. Debt, it turned out, wasn't taxable. So, he bought more and more shit holes, turned them into beautiful homes, apartments, and commercial buildings. He turned a nice profit flipping some and renting others. He only up-charged the commercial buildings. Fuck the suits. Not bad for a kid who barely finished high school.

His apartments and single-family homes stayed affordable while making him a decent living doing nothing more than the carpentry and manual labor he had always enjoyed. Allan found himself at peace when he was renovating buildings. His favorite part was demolition. If he was ever having a bad day or needed to let off steam, any project in the demolition stage got his attention. Something about the fact that destruction was necessary before something better could be created, kept him humble.

That, and he loved smashing shit with a sledgehammer.

This was the outlet for any latent rage he might have in him. It allowed him to stay calm and levelheaded when dealing with his family. Allan may have worked a lot, but he did it out of a love for that family.

Windward House was an anniversary gift to Eliza, Collin's mother. She was in the beginning stages of empty nest syndrome—their youngest daughter had turned thirteen that year, so, naturally, she wanted nothing to do with her mother. Eliza wanted a project, so Allan bought the 4200-square-foot vacation home in order to give his wife a business to manage. One he knew she would enjoy.

Eliza needed to be needed. With her kids growing up, Allan knew the next best thing would be taking care of others. She would have been a nurse if she had gotten the chance to go to school. So, he bought her a four-floor, eight-bedroom, six-bathroom bed and breakfast instead.

She'd slapped him for saddling her with a job, then she'd thanked him in one of the massive bedrooms later that day.

She took to the job the way he knew she would. With obsessive reverence.

Eliza loved Windward House and she wanted anyone who stayed there to love it too. It had become more of a family home than the one in Philadelphia. The family spent major holidays at Windward House, especially Fourth of July and Christmas—summers and winters were meant for family.

Collin had been good about going home for Christmas. He enjoyed coming to Windward House in the winter. Cape May was a ghost town then and Collin found it invigorating to walk around a town that was currently crawling with tourists, when it felt more like a setting in a Stephen King novel: empty and haunted. That was how Collin preferred Cape May.

This summer, Windward House would not be empty, and Collin was unaware that he would soon meet a ghost within its walls.

I NSIDE WINDWARD HOUSE, NOAH sat wearing his lifeguard uniform, next to his mother, across from Eliza, Kip, and Audrey. No one spoke, or really, knew what to say. They all awkwardly ate the finger foods Eliza put out for her guests. She and Audrey traded glances, and Eliza did her best to reassure her granddaughter that everything would be all right, with a quick wink.

"We just wanted to say . . ." Noah said, before being quickly interrupted by the arrival of Valerie Monteiro, Audrey's mother, with a steaming cup of coffee in hand.

Valerie was the wild child of the Cassidy clan, and the sleeve of tattoos on her right arm told the tale of her misspent youth. The Temple University-embroidered scrubs she wore as pajamas reminded everyone that she'd grown since then. She had disappeared for a few years to follow hardcore bands on tour across the US when she was not much older than her daughter was now. A fact she was hoping her mother would not bring up.

Not today, she thought.

Valerie and Kip met at Temple, when she was doing her nursing rotations at the campus medical center. Kip overshot a gap he was trying to jump with his skateboard and had, as Valerie was to tell him, fucked his arm up royally.

"Sorry," she said. "Figured I'd need to caffeinate for this. Where's Dad?"

"You know your father," Eliza replied, and everyone sat back down in silence for another long moment. The stairs creaked as Allan Cassidy bounded down, rubbing his stomach. Allan's body had been carved by manual labor and weathered by time. He wore a tool belt around his waist, as his years as a union carpenter taught him that old Edwardian homes like Windward House needed constant upkeep.

"Allan, where have you been?!" Eliza shot at him as the front door opened at the other end of the house.

"I was fixing the third-floor toilet. Took about ten minutes. Then I used it," he said. "That took about forty-five."

"Classic Dad," a female voice from down the hall rang out. It was Casey Cassidy. The youngest of the Cassidy clan was dolled up in a L'Agence suit, Jimmy Choos, and pulled Coach luggage behind her. Casey was a shark in investment-and-wealth-management waters. She had the psychopathic tendencies necessary to not only succeed on Wall Street, but to thrive.

She let go of her luggage and embraced her captive audience. "Sup, fam," she said. "The successful one is home."

"You fix my I.R.A?" Allan asked.

"About as well as the IRA fixed Ireland," she deadpanned.

Sick of all the interruptions, Audrey finally decided it was time to make herself heard.

"Noah and I have something to say," she squeaked out, barely audible. "*Hello*?" No one was listening to her. The family kept the conversation with the new arrival going instead.

"Casey," Eliza said. "You take the room on the second floor next to Audrey. Then come back down here."

"Big bro here yet?" Casey asked.

"I have seven-to-one odds he doesn't show," Valerie added.

"Mom? Will you listen?" Audrey tried once again to be heard, to no avail.

"I'll take those odds. One thousand dollars says he shows."

And as if on cue Collin entered, still wearing his Wayfarers, with his cell phone glued to his head.

Gene had called him about one of the other deals he was trying to get set up, despite Collin no longer being in town. "Gene, I told you, everything will be fine."

He raised a finger in apology to his family, mouthed, "*Sorry*," then looked to Casey, while covering the microphone on his cell, "You get her to make the bet?"

"She owes me seven thousand dollars," Casey said, looking at her sister. Collin and Casey high-fived. Teaming up against Valerie had been their favorite game since Collin had taught Casey to steal her toys as a toddler.

"You're always wrong, Val," he said, then heard Gene react. "No, not you . . ."

"You saw him parking!" Val protested.

"You made the bet, bitch. Better have my money when I get back."

With that declaration, Casey dragged her luggage up the staircase, mean-mugging her sister in jest. Val flipped her back the bird.

"All right, all right. Goodbye," Collin said, and hung up on his agent. Upon hanging up, Collin realized that one more person had entered while he was on the phone, and the whole room was staring at him.

"Sorry I'm late," a voice Collin recognized all too well said to Siobhan.

It was at that point that Collin realized it was Siobhan sitting on the Cape May Historical Society-approved couch, but hadn't *yet* realized who was walking right up to him.

That recognition sent a tinge of fear into his heart.
Orla.

"Why are there so many people here?" The voice continued.

"Catholics don't believe in prophylactics," Collin replied as he turned to face Orla, dressed in her lifeguard uniform.

It was real. Red alert! This was happening. The woman who, a few days ago, had been nothing but a conjured-up memory in his spank bank was standing right in front of him. Oddly, still wearing the same lifeguard uniform from his fantasy. He had to be having a stroke.

Upon hearing the voice and seeing the face of her former lover, she too hoped her brain was sending sudden and synchronized bursts of electricity affecting her consciousness and sensations.

"What the fuck?" he said.

"You've got to be shitting me," she said.

At the same time, they both said to one another, "What the fuck are you doing here?"

E IGHTEEN YEARS AGO, ALMOST to the day, Collin and Orla had moved in to a small one-bedroom apartment together in the Roxborough section of Philadelphia.

It was the summer before their final year at Penn. They had been dating for almost four years and were sick of sharing space with roommates. Collin and Orla had wanted nothing more than to be the "real adult" couple who had a place off campus. They'd worked as a team to lift all their furniture up to the third-floor apartment in the blistering summer sun.

After finally getting their couch in, concluding their arduous move, they'd collapsed on it, covered in sweat and dust. Despite the heat, sweat, and dirt, they'd cuddled close. After grabbing beers from their thrift store score of a fridge, they'd celebrated their first apartment sans roommates with a quickie in the living room. That passion had led to a much longer session in the shower.

A few months into the school year, they'd both received letters from their respective top choices for graduate school. They'd sat on the same couch they had labored to hoist up to the third floor, and had held the letters in their hands. Collin's was a large envelope with a return address for the University of Southern California. Orla's was just as large; however, its return address was for Boston College.

"On three," Orla had said, and she'd begun the countdown, holding two for a long moment.

"Dear God, woman, say three!"

"Two and a half . . ." she'd smiled at him, before finally saying, "three!"

They'd ravenously tore at their envelopes and exclaimed at the same time "I got in!"

The joy they'd shared lasted only a moment. The reality that they had both gotten into their dream schools—and that those schools were on opposing coasts—set in.

Joy had become fear. Fear that a hard conversation was inevitable, and neither one of them wanted to have it.

They'd decided to fuck on the couch again instead.

T HE SAME FEAR AND inability to talk about what needed to be said was shared the moment Collin and Orla saw one another again in Windward House. The couch being full of their respective families meant their old avoidance tactics would not work this time around.

Before either of them could address it any further, Audrey decided to take matters into her own hands. She stood up on the table, which finally wrestled everyone's attention away from her uncle and Noah's aunt.

"Noah asked me to marry him and I said yes!" She screamed to the room, making sure they all heard.

After a stunned moment of silence, her father simply said "Hell, no!" as her mother exclaimed, "Are you *kidding* me?!"

"How could this day get any worse," Siobhan sighed.

Two loud knocks were heard coming from the front door.

"Oh, my God, *what*?!" Valerie yelled as she slammed her coffee on the table, got up, and opened the front door to reveal Beth Ruane-Cousineau.

Orla and Siobhan's mother had the leathery skin of someone who sunbathed without protection. That leathery, sun-kissed skin housed a wolf in sheep's clothing. She was a woman who took charge and did not care who she had to step on to get what she wanted.

"So, what did I miss?"

5
YOUNG LOVE

AFTER THE SITUATION HAD been explained to her, Beth sat in Windward House with a look of judgement Orla and Siobhan had seen more than a few times in their lives. It was a combination of disappointment and contempt.

"How could you let this happen?" she said to Siobhan. "Didn't you raise this boy to have some standards?"

The Cassidy clan bristled at Beth's words. Siobhan, used to her mother's bluntness, rolled her eyes and ignored the question. She took deep, calming breaths.

Orla knew her mother's presence was Siobhan's fault. Orla had successfully gone no-contact with her mother for nearly a decade. The psychology professors she spoke to said that was the only way with narcissists.

Despite knowing their mother could never be satisfied, Siobhan still wanted to be the golden daughter. She included Beth in big family moments like birthdays and Christmas. This normally meant Siobhan, Jesse, and Noah would travel to Florida, leaving Orla with the house to herself. Beth becoming a great-grandmother fit the category of life event Siobhan would want her to be part of. Maybe if Siobhan got therapy, instead of gossiping about her friend's husbands, she'd see their mother for what she truly was.

"I'm sorry, are you trying to say my daughter isn't up to your standards?" Kip asked, standing to tower over the new guest. Beth returned a rictus smile rather than responding.

This, Orla thought, was exactly like her mother. The same mother who'd cheated on and divorced their father, left them to move in with the French fuck who was technically their stepfather, and moved to Florida.

Orla wanted to scream, '*Go back to Florida with your French fuck of a husband,*' the moment she saw that look. It took all her tact to bite her tongue.

A S A MOTHER, BETH was a charlatan. She painted on a kind smile and watched her words, but she was raised never to trust anyone. That meant no one should trust her either, and she lived up to that substandard.

Beth believed that most people were idiots. She also believed she was not most people.

She was wrong on both accounts.

Beth did what was necessary to make her life simpler, more pleasant, and devoid of drudgery. She'd married Siobhan and Orla's father when she was in her early twenties. He was a firefighter and a lifeguard, and to a twenty-year-old girl who thought *Baywatch* was the height of excitement, she'd believed she had caught herself a winner. He would work, she could stay at home and live the easy life. But her reality was far from glamorous and he was no David Hasselhoff. Though her daughters would beg to differ.

The Cape May Fire Company was perpetually understaffed. This meant the girl's father was working eighty-hour weeks, essentially living at the firehouse like a full grow frat boy. He spent his days shooting the shit with the boys, washing the fire truck, and only occasionally making it home to see the two infant girls she was raising alone. He was also responding to emergency situations and saving lives as the only EMT-certified member of the brigade, but Beth didn't think that mattered much.

Raising children was far more work than Beth had been led to believe. Her mother had taught her that the only way to get by in life was to find a man worth a damn and trap him with children. Following this advice, Beth had instead found herself trapped with crying, ravenous monsters. Thanks, Mom.

Postpartum, Beth never fully bonded with either of her girls. She saw them for what they were: loud, selfish, unsatisfiable creatures of pure consumption. They cried constantly. They were either hungry, thirsty or had shit and pissed from the last time she'd fed them. But she'd learned if she didn't feed them, the crying was worse than the shitting or the pissing.

Beth found—because her husband was never home—she was often able to entertain other virile young men in order to keep her mind and body occupied with non-maternal tasks. Orla and Siobhan were the first ones to tell their father about their mother's constant visitors. They were small children and their father had asked them what they had done all day.

They had no reason not to tell him the truth. At the time, those four and five-year-old Irish twins didn't understand that telling Daddy, "Mommy makes weird noises when Uncle Tommy comes over," was wrong. They'd had no idea that they didn't *have* an Uncle Tommy. When they told their father, "she gets all sweaty and never wears clothes," they'd had no idea it would have such a profound impact on their daily lives.

The girls' father did nothing with this information for years. He didn't want the girls to think badly of their mother. He still loved her and wanted to maintain the semblance of a perfect family unit. Beth was doing everything in her power to push him away and he would not give her the satisfaction. He even had the gall to get a couple's counselor.

Beth rewarded him for his patience and belief in their relationship by filing for divorce the same week he was first diagnosed with a brain tumor. She had no way of knowing this, of course. The girls were teenagers, however, and assumed the mother they had grown up watching cheat on their father was just piling on. They didn't know she had wanted out for years.

She wasn't sure if that was better or worse.

Beth had found herself divorced and one of the rare women who lost their custody battle. She didn't want the girls as much as she wanted the child support payments. She had been banking on child support as a part of her exit plan.

Her firefighting, lifeguarding, soon-to-be ex-husband was so well regarded around town, he may as well have been the mayor. When the details of his divorce counter-complaint were made public, and the couple's counselor he had hired all those years ago testified in open court, Beth was no longer looked upon as the first lady of Cape May County. It's hard to win a PR battle when you're divorcing a local legend who might be dying. It didn't help that his sister was a county judge.

Alone with no alimony, thanks to her piss-poor divorce timing, Beth had worked as a cabana girl at Congress Hall, the high-end hotel in town, where she'd met a lonely Florida real-estate developer that summer. Guillaume Cousineau was French by birth, but grew up in the swamps of the panhandle. Gilly, as he preferred to be called, overcompensated for the circumstances of his birth by portraying himself as more American than any man ought to be.

Beth gave him a stay he was not able to forget.

When he'd told her he never wanted children, and he'd already had a vasectomy, she knew she had found the one.

He took her back to Florida with him and made her his swamp queen.

THIS WAS THE FIRST time either of her daughters had called outside of Christmas, which she knew was borne out of guilt and not want. She saw these sub-par circumstances as a way to remind the girls that, while she may not have been the best mother, wife, or, well, *person* while they were growing up, she could still be counted on to show up when she was needed.

That, and her husband had been annoying her lately, and she needed a vacation.

"Married? Are you kidding me?" Beth said. "You two can't even see R-rated movies without a guardian and you want to get *married*? No!"

To Beth, the matter was settled. This was simply out of the question.

"It's not up to you, Grandma," Noah said with authority. He was too young to form a real opinion on the woman, but he knew the effect his grandmother had on his mother, and he did not like it.

Siobhan, while upset with her son's current predicament, was proud that he had no problem standing up to his grandmother. That was something he got from Orla. Siobhan, as the first born, felt obligated to try to keep the peace. Orla and, now it would seem, Noah had no such compunction.

"The women in your family like to make decisions without consulting the people they affect," Collin said. His words were bitter and angry and came from a place of deep resentment. He immediately felt guilty having said them.

Beth looked at him. She kept her mouth tight and wanted very much to match Collin's vitriol, but saw that he was already acknowledging to himself that he was wrong.

"Is this really the time?" Orla asked.

"No. That would have been about sixteen years ago," Collin said.

Beth saw where this was going and was not about to let this conversation go off the rails. "No. It's up to your mothers and fathers. Children cannot get married without parental permission, so let's just stop this nonsense here and now."

"I'm with her," Kip said. Beth was not expecting the dreadlocked man-child to be her ally in this fight, but she took the support nonetheless.

"Dad!" Audrey cried.

"Don't 'dad' me. How are you supposed to compete in your . . . condition?"

And there it was. Audrey's heart filled with the resentment of a child who had bared the weight of her family's financial success for years.

"That's all you care about, isn't it?! Whether or not I skate at nationals. Can't waste a good marketing opportunity, right, Dad? Well, guess what? I'm not going to. I'm taking this season off from skating."

Kip looked like he had been slapped in the face. He couldn't form words. All those years of preparation and she was going to take a year off?

"Do you know what I would have given to be where you are at your age?!"

"Well, I'm not you, Dad!"

"Audrey, go to your room," Valerie said, knowing the adults were losing control of the situation and needed a breather. She put a calming hand on her husband's lower back.

"You can't just send me to my room until I'm not pregnant anymore."

"Wanna bet? Go." It was an order. A command. And that command got the response it typically got.

"Ugh!" Audrey stormed up the stairs, angrier than she'd ever been in her life. At the top of the stairs, she yelled "Fucking fascists," before slamming her bedroom door closed.

Noah stood up and went to follow her.

"Oh, no. No. You go wait for me on the front porch. You two alone is how we got here," Siobhan said.

"What do you think is gonna happen? I get her double pregnant?" He ignored his mother's directive and went to check on Audrey.

"Noah! Get back down—"

Eliza cut her off with a calming whisper, "Let him go, honey. He's just trying to be there for her. We should be glad they at least want to figure this out together."

"I'll come stay with you to keep an eye on things," Beth said to Siobhan.

"Mom, you know we don't have room," Siobhan said. "I thought you were getting a hotel?"

"I'll take Orla's room. She can sleep on the couch."

Before Orla could claw her own mother's voice box from her throat, Eliza inserted herself between them.

"Beth, please stay with us. We have an apartment downstairs available. We're all family now."

Beth's disgusted look upon hearing Eliza's attempt at comfort made it clear she was not keen on being added to this family. Despite her reservations, having a basement apartment to herself was far more agreeable than dealing with the near-constant passive aggression she was sure to find at the home her ex-husband had left to her daughters.

"Well, if you insist." She painted on her rictus smile and that was that.

"Why don't you head down there and get settled? The rest of you, I've got snacks in the dining room. We're not gonna figure all this out today."

Orla and Collin looked at one another. Neither wanted to continue the conversation that had been put on hold for more than a decade. Collin tried to apologize with his eyes, and it seemed Orla accepted this. She knew his micro-expressions better than most. Orla understood Collin was acknowledging that he'd let his anger get the best of him and he regretted it. She nodded his way to indicate this before heading upstairs to get Noah.

Collin, Kip, and Val walked Orla, Siobhan, and Noah out to the front porch. Kip, Val, and Siobhan spoke a little more in hushed tones while Orla got Noah situated in the car. She took her place in the passenger seat. Kip and Val hugged Siobhan goodbye and went inside.

Collin stayed on the porch, and he and Orla both attempted to avoid eye contact with one another unsuccessfully. He watched Siobhan drive their car as the sun began to set.

When they were no more than a speck in the distance, Collin sat down on one of the ancient rocking chairs that adorned the porch.

S MALL SETS OF FIREWORKS went off in the distant night sky while Collin continued to sit in the same rocking chair nursing a beer. He wondered whether coming here was a good idea. He came to spend time with his family, and now all he could think about were the most tragic aspects of his and Orla's relationship.

The yellow of the porch lights and lamps gave Windward House's turquoise exterior a warm blue luminescence. Waves crashing on the nearby beach and the laughter of drunk tourists could be heard from blocks away.

"Beer me," Casey said. She exited the house wearing pajamas, wrapped in a light blanket.

The screen door slammed behind her. She winced, worried she might have woken her parents. Collin handed her a beer from the cooler he had placed next to his rocking chair.

A particularly loud firework popped as Casey slammed the bottle cap into the porch's handrail to release it from the bottle. A trick she assumed everyone learned in college.

"Where is everyone?" Casey said, taking her first sip.

"It's three am. All the procreators are in bed."

"I heard yelling earlier, but my bed was so comfy. What did I miss?"

"Not only are the teenagers pregnant, they want to get married."

"Classic," Casey said with a sardonic laugh. "Young love. Fucking morons."

"Oh, and my ex is Audrey's new Aunt-in-law."

"The one who had the abo-bo before you knew she was pregnant?"

Collin chugged his beer, which was still half-full, before answering. "The very same."

He burped.

"Mom and Dad?"

"They don't know. I only told you."

Collin and Casey had always been close, despite their significant age gap. They have the same unique lack of respect for authority and love for learning. Collin preferred the arts, Casey preferred math. Based on their very different bank account balances, Collin would freely admit his brain fixated on the wrong subjects.

They told each other everything. Casey came out to Collin when she was twelve. She came out to him again when she was sixteen and realized she was actually bisexual. And a third time at twenty-one when she realized she was pansexual. He was the only one who believed her back when bi-erasure was the norm. Her parents thought dating men again meant she was finally over her *phase*. She was the only member of his family he talked to about what happened between him and Orla. Casey also gave him great material from her exploits in the New York City singles scene.

"Shit," Casey said. The full weight of the moment sitting with her.

"Yeah."

Collin opened another beer with the bottle opener affixed to the cooler. Casey was a great listener, but never really knew what to say to make people feel better in times like these. She had decided long ago it was better to simply say exactly what she was thinking, so that even if people hated what she had to say, at least she knew they hated the real her and not some character she'd created for their benefit.

"Well, the past only hurts if you remember it. That's why we have alcohol." She took a big sip and watched the smile grow on her brother's face. She'd nailed it.

Collin held his beer out. Casey brought hers to meet his. They clinked bottles, drank, and watched cheap explosions in the sky.

6
MERTS IN
MORTAL DANGER

O RLA SAT ATOP THE lifeguard stand overseeing a
wide swath of beach and the ever-increasing number of MERTs whose lives she was responsible for. The
responsibility made her think of her father. He had always
made it clear that, while the tourists could be obnoxious,
annoying, and downright unlikable as human beings, it
was still a lifeguard's duty to protect them from their own
stupidity and arrogance.

In addition to being a member of the fire brigade, he
had also been the chief of the Cape May Beach Patrol
since before she could walk. He took pride in making sure
that the people who came to his town could swim safely
because he had trained his cadets properly. The Chief of
Police could barely go a season without an incident where
one of his officers got overzealous with a tourist. The cops
beat the shit out of drunks without cause. Those drunks
would turn out to be a senator's son or daughter, or the

senator themselves, and cost the community good will. Unlike the police chief, the Beach Patrol Chief was revered in Cape May, and in New Jersey at large, as a bastion of leadership.

Thinking about her father's life always made Orla think about his death. She usually thought about the nights she spent alone in the hospital, or the anxiety she felt while waiting for him to get out of surgeries. This time a different memory, one she hadn't thought about in years, invaded her mind.

O RLA BROUGHT COLLIN TO the hospital to meet her father for the first time. Her father – who had been a large, muscular, man for as far back as she could remember – was now emaciated and frail. The large, unhealed scar went all the way around his freshly shaven head as he laid unconscious after what would end up being his last surgery. She held on tight to Collin's hand. Thinking that, if she let him go, he'd run away, never come back, and another man in her life was going to disappear on her. Something that, in the moment, she could not handle.

"Dad. This is my boyfriend, Collin," she said, while tears streamed down her cheeks. She reluctantly let go of Collin to hold onto her father's hand. To her great relief, Collin sat down next to her and comforted her quietly while she broke down.

"It's a pleasure to meet you, sir," he said. "Please know that my intentions are anything but honorable."

The laugh burst through all Orla's tears. She was surprised at herself. She didn't know she could laugh in a moment like this.

"Keep making her laugh, and I won't take you with me," her father said. His voice was as weak as the squeeze he gave her hand before passing back out.

That was what she fell in love with. Collin knew how to make her laugh, even in the most uncomfortable of times. He kissed her on the cheek and stayed with her until she was ready to go.

Collin held her throughout her father's funeral as well.

She wasn't sure if she would have remained standing while the casket was lowered into the ground if Collin hadn't been there to hold her upright. She felt as though she were in a constant state of collapse. Every muscle in her body was unable to perform its mandated function and she swore that her bones had turned to Jell-O.

She stained his white oxford with a mixture of tears, mascara, and foundation that Siobhan insisted she wear.

Collin held her tight as he whispered to her "It could be worse. Your mother could have shown up."

This made Orla full on snort in the middle of the Priest's rite of committal. The idea of her mother showing up was absurd and, therefore, hilarious to Orla. Only Collin would have understood this about her. She remembered thinking how lucky she was to be with someone who knew her so well.

What would she have done if her mother showed up that day? She imagined herself mauling her mother and throwing her into the ground alongside her father's casket. She imagined her sister kicking her mother in the ribs while she was down, and the entire funeral party ganging up on her until they would all have to agree to bury her with him. Which seemed like a cruel fate for her father.

The wounds of her mother's betrayal were still open and festering then. While those wounds would eventually scar over, the scar itself was plainly visible and a constant reminder that her mother was not to be trusted.

O RLA SHOOK THE MEMORIES from her head as if they were water stuck in her ears. She lathered herself with sunscreen and passed the protective liquid to her stand partner, Noah. Noah hadn't said a word about the other day to her yet, and she'd been too in her own head to broach the topic. She pulled the binoculars from their perch and checked out the surf.

A toddler face-planted the shallow water and it took a moment for the child's mother to pick him up. When she did, the child's face was covered in silt.

"God, I hope some MERT gets stuck in an undertow. I get so bored up here," she said, trying to break the ice with her nephew.

"Is Mom pissed at me?" Noah asked in earnest. He worried about his mother. His father was gone so much he felt like he was duty-bound to watch over her.

"I'm sure she can't wait to be called Grandma." Her words hit a nerve. She got him talking, which was a win, so she may as well play the cool aunt card to get some real answers out of him. "How the fuck are you gonna raise a baby?"

"Figure it out as I go along."

"That's bullshit, Noah. Married or not, you're about to become a father. How are you going to take care of a kid when you can barely take care of yourself?"

"We have a plan," Noah said. Orla saw he was full of unearned confidence.

"What? Live together in sunshiny happiness made with love? I got news for you kid . . . Life doesn't work that way."

While Orla felt like her sarcasm was getting through to him, she, unfortunately, got what she wished for. About thirty yards out into the surf a man was struggling to keep his head above water. He seemed exhausted. Orla immediately recognized he was caught in a riptide and was trying to swim into shore instead of parallel to escape it.

"I have enough in savings to get us a place near her family in Philly."

"Hold that thought," Orla said. "We've got a MERT in mortal danger."

She grabbed her rescue can, jumped off the stand and sprinted to the surf. Noah followed suit. He was not going to be interrupted again.

Noah swam faster than his aunt and caught up to her quickly. While they both glided through the water and dove beneath bigger waves, he continued to expound on his parental preparations.

"I'll go to school first. I'm gonna major in software engineering."

"You're a secret nerd?!" Orla spat out the salt water that filled her mouth, before the two of them made it to the drowning man.

"You know most future jobs will be in tech, right?" Noah said, as he expertly secured the man to his flotation can and took his right arm. Orla situated herself on the left, and the two of them started swimming, keeping the drowning man parallel with the shore, to make sure they escaped the riptide. As they swam, they continued their conversation as if there weren't a man between them who, a moment ago, thought he was dying.

"Don't hold your breath . . ." Orla said, regarding their being tech jobs in the future.

"I wasn't planning on it," said the drowning man before getting a mouthful of sea water.

"Sir, just kick with us and we'll have you back to the shore in no time," Orla said. The drowning man smiled to thank them, too tired for any more communication.

"By the time I'm done with school—and that may be longer than expected—the baby will be old enough for daycare or even kindergarten," Noah said, refusing to be drowned out by the ocean's attempts at drowning them.

"Why can't Audrey go to school first?"

"Well, for one, she still has another year of high school."

"OK. Fair. I forgot to factor in age."

"But she wants to be there for the baby, regardless. The first few years are the most important."

"That's true," the drowning man gasped out. "The first . . . the first five years of a child's development are crucial. I'm a—" he got another mouthful of ocean before finishing his sentence. "I'm a pediatrician."

"You're not helping, doc," Orla said.

"After that, Audrey can go to school while I pay the bills, and she can study whatever she wants. So, in about ten years we'll be a double-income household."

"That plan doesn't factor in student loans, which, I hate to tell you, are a bitch." They were close enough to shore now that they could all stand in the waist-high water. Orla and Noah walked the drowning doctor slowly back to shore, careful to keep him upright when the surf crashed into them.

"If we get married, we won't have any," Noah said.

"You vastly overestimate the power of marriage."

"No. Listen. Her mother is a nurse in Temple's medical building. She's a university employee."

"I'm a university employee, too, it doesn't give me special childcare powers," she said.

"At Temple, children of university employees go to school tuition-*free*. As her son-in-law, so would I."

It was in that moment Orla understood how much smarter her nephew was than she had given him credit for. That was a thorough ten-year plan. Hell, it was better than *hers*, which was to live with her sister until her loans were forgiven.

"Does her mother know this?" Orla asked.

"We tried to explain it all yesterday, but none of you would listen to us."

"That's a pretty solid plan," the drowning doctor said. "You've really thought this through. You're gonna be a great father."

Noah nodded to his aunt. *See?*

"Don't listen to the MERTs," she said.

"He's a doctor!"

"So am I!"

"Of Irish literature . . ." Noah reminded her. Orla huffed at her nephew belittling her doctorate. The real doctor was vexed.

"What's a MERT?"

7
RESEARCH

COLLIN PACED IN HIS room at Windward House while he tried to spot the micro-expressions of Lana's face through his cell phone screen. Her hair was now falling out in patches, leaving only Charlie Brown squiggles where her long locks used to be. This made it difficult for Collin to focus on her face. His eyes kept veering to the last strands making their last stand. Despite the chemo side effects, Lana seemed her normal, blunt self. She read the description of one of the titles he'd submitted and raised a drawn-on eyebrow in shock and dismay.

"Moronic, egotistical, *retarded* tourists," she read aloud from the log-line Collin had titled after the Cape May slang. "I'm high as fuck right now and even I know that's an awful title for a show."

"It's kind of a Cape May locals thing . . . it's authentic."

"You know you can't say *that* anymore, right?"

"That's why they call them MERTs."

"Are you trying to get cancelled?" Lana said as her assistant entered the Zoom frame with clippers in hand. The assistant, without any preamble, began to shave what was left of Lana's hair. In the middle of the meeting with Collin.

"What's that?" Collin said.

"Just getting a little makeover. Don't worry about it."

The assistant continued to perform her coiffeuse chores, the buzz and hum of the clippers scoring the meeting. Collin wasn't sure if he should say anything about Lana's hair care, so he simply acted as if it wasn't happening.

"How'd you feel about the other log-lines?"

"My cancer is funnier than the shit you sent me. I mean *really*."

She read off the printed paper her assistant—and functional friseur—had put in front of her before the meeting started. "Workplace comedies one through four—I said we wanted a family comedy, so why even send those? Standard former athlete taking care of his family, warring neighbors . . ."

While Lana continued her tirade about the unoriginal ideas Collin had put in front of her, Audrey knocked at her uncle's door. She looked in and saw it was a bad time, but Collin nodded to her and waved her inside. He mouthed *just a second* while Lana continued to belittle his boring ideas. When she finally stopped, Audrey got to see how her uncle worked.

"You said you wanted something classic!"

"But *fresh*! You got anything with a little kick to it?"

Collin looked at Audrey, grasping at straws. Then he realized *she* was the story.

Audrey.

There was no time to consider; no time to feel guilty. The best stories were mined from reality and exaggerated to provide entertainment value. He knew exactly how to take Audrey's predicament and turn it into a four-camera comedy with a minimum of three jokes per page. He could see the audience laughing at prat falls over leaking amniotic fluid. The concept came to him fully formed in the moment.

He had no other choice. He covered the microphone at the bottom of his phone and in a hushed tone addressed his niece.

"Please don't hate me."

He released his grasp on the microphone and Audrey watched as he spoke to the bald woman on his screen. "OK. I have this idea about a single dad who's teenage daughter just got pregnant."

THUNDERSTRUCK, AUDREY FROZE. SHE was unsure whether she should be angry or flattered. Her uncle was using her as a muse. Which meant he was *using* her. The same way her father used her skills to promote the skate park. She was sick of being the family mascot, but somehow this felt different. It wasn't going to be *her* doing anything. Her uncle simply felt that her situation was comedic enough to turn into a television show. If she was being honest with herself, Audrey knew this was true. She was a pregnant, sixteen-year-old professional skateboarder. How had she not thought of turning this into a reality show herself? She could upload clips of what it was like to YouTube. Once the views came in, so would the advertisers. She could make a killing on the marketing alone.

She couldn't be mad at her uncle. He was just like her. He knew a good opportunity when he saw it. Audrey had always felt a kinship with her uncle Collin because he was never around. Despite not being present, his presents, both birthday and holiday, showed he stayed as up to date as he could with her life.

Her favorite was still the gift he gave her as an infant: a stuffed horse head. She kept that ratty old toy on her bed to this day. Collin was her godfather and it wasn't until she was thirteen and saw *The Godfather*, that she finally understood the joke. He was a gift she couldn't refuse. Mainly because she was an infant. That made horsey all the more endearing.

All uncle Collin's gifts made it clear he was trying. He watched all her Instagram stories and congratulated her on every competition. He had also done what she'd always wanted to: escape. He got out. Which was now what she was trying desperately to accomplish and needed his expertise.

The buzzing sound that had been emanating from the speaker finally abated and the woman's voice was much clearer.

"OK. I like that. But what's the new spin on it?"

"The spin," Collin said, looking at Audrey with a knowing smile, "is that the guy who impregnated his daughter is the son of the one that got away. So, when these two kids bring their parents together to become grandparents, the parents have to deal with all their unresolved bullshit."

Audrey smiled. He wasn't just stealing her life, he was melding their lives together. Was this her uncle's way of trying to get closer to her? Telling their stories in tandem. Or was it just good material? She had brought him into his own story through hers. He had just as much of a right to it as she did.

She nodded her approval as her uncle waited for a response from his phone.

Lana pondered on the idea for a minute, she rubbed her now-shaven head as its fuzzy feel delighted her stoned senses. The idea was going through an in-depth subconscious analysis. Was it funny? Was it clear enough for the under-educated masses to follow? Was it marketable? Was it easy to produce? Could she get the president of the network to back this idea? Could she get the advertisers to buy spots on a series like this?

She let the idea—and Collin—marinate in silence for a long moment before an impish smile crept across her face.

"Daddy wants to fuck my mother-in-law. Ha! I knew you weren't a complete waste of money! Write that shit. *Now.* I want a story area ASAP."

"Great!" Collin said as Lana began to look at her newly bald reflection on her side of the conversation. She laughed and said to her assistant, "You know, this is the first time in years the carpet really does match the drapes."

"What?" Collin said, not knowing if he was meant to hear that. Lana had already hung up. The bad soldier had his marching orders.

He took a moment to breathe before remembering Audrey was patiently waiting for him.

"You hate me don't you?"

"Are you kidding?" she said. "You're writing a show about me! That's awesome."

This helped Collin abate the typical guilt that accompanied taking parts of his life and turning them into his work.

"I kind of just spit it out when I saw you."

"It's chill. At least someone is getting something good out of all this."

Collin could tell his niece needed him. She was never down on herself like this. Or maybe she was, often, and he simply wasn't around enough to see it. Like most of the world, Collin got to know his niece over social media, so he could not trust what he thought was her personality when it could merely be a persona.

"What's going on?" he asked. "You having second thoughts?"

"Oh no. Not at all. I want to marry Noah and I definitely want to have the baby. I'm just sick of Mom and Dad telling me what to do."

"I hate to tell you this, but that's kind of their job."

"Yeah, well, we're on vacation, aren't we?"

"You're sixteen and pregnant. If a situation your child is in has an MTV reality show named after it, the parents are allowed to be upset."

"Touché," Audrey admitted.

"So, what's up?" Collin could tell there was more to the story than simple *parents-just-don't-understand* teen angst.

"Huh?" Audrey wasn't following.

"You came to my room. Reason?"

"Oh, yeah. I uh . . ." she wasn't sure how to phrase this, so she just said it. Something she had learned from her aunt Casey.

"Can you meet up with Noah tomorrow night? I want someone who doesn't want to murder him for impregnating me to get to know him. Potentially report back to the parental units that he's not a monster. You know?"

Collin was flattered. He loved that his niece saw him as the rational adult in the room, even if he saw himself as an overgrown child.

"Sure. I have no horse in this race. But you gotta tell me why," he said.

"Why what?"

"Why are you so willing to give up on your best years to raise a baby with this guy? If I'm gonna write a show about it, I need to understand it. For . . . research."

He was trying to connect honestly with Audrey. She felt that. He wanted her to have an out for ironic detachment via the writing excuse so that she could feel safe expressing herself. She appreciated this out and took it.

"I love him. What the fuck else do you need?" She was so earnest and forthright with this answer that it shocked Collin. He was not expecting this level of emotional intelligence from a sixteen-year-old who sold skateboards on the internet. He really let her words sink in before he scrambled for a pen.

"I need to write that down," he said. He found a pen in the bedside table and began jotting down Audrey's quote, along with the ideas it generated in his brain.

"But, the real answer to '*what the fuck else do you need*,'" he said, "is money. You need money. If you're doing it on your own."

Audrey took that advice in. It was the first time anyone in her family was being honest with her about this situation, save her grandmother.

Audrey watched as her uncle wrote longhand in a Moleskine. She wondered if this was what he always did when he got an idea, or if it was just for emergencies. Did he not know about the notes app on his phone?

"You know what else you need to find out?" she said.

"What?" Collin muttered, trying not to lose his thought.

"Why the one that got away left in the first place."

Audrey's words were like a hammer to the head. They rung his bell. She wasn't going to let him get away with only attacking one aspect of the concept he'd just sold. He had to deal with all his new characters.

He knew she was right. He had to find a way to reconnect with Orla. Not as lovers or exes or even friends, but as two people with a shared history who needed closure.

"For research?"

"For research." Audrey confirmed.

"Think you might be able to give me a hand with that? She might actually talk to you."

"Have *you* tried talking to her?"

He had not.

8
THE ELEPHANT IN THE ROOM

COLLIN HAD NOT BEEN to the C-View Inn in over a decade. His heart rate rose, making his way into the old haunt—and haunt was exactly what the C-View was. There were ghosts here Collin would prefer not to visit; there might be a few worth getting reacquainted with, though. He took a deep breath and readied himself to face whatever ghastly apparitions might greet him.

The smell of hops and cigar smoke hit him in the face.

The Inn was a locals' bar, even at the height of tourist season. Anyone without a Cape May address who stepped foot on the sawdust-covered floors or tried to sit at the bar carved from oak and adorned in subway tile regretted it immediately.

The bottle display was functional. The most-wanted spirits were front and center while the rest gathered dust. The beers on tap never changed: Guinness, Yuengling, Pabst, and a seasonal Sam Adams.

There was no need for extravagant design, decor, or brand identity here. The Inn's brand was pay, don't puke. Patrons came here to drink, kick back, and talk shit. No one here was networking like in Los Angeles.

Collin felt much more comfortable remembering that he was now in a bar where nothing was expected of him.

Two types of customers frequented the Inn: grizzled old timers who had put their time in, season after season, drinking away their retirement funds; and, off-shift lifeguards. Siobhan worked as a bartender during the summer to make extra cash between selling houses. The market was slow during tourist season. Most buyers wanted move-in ready retreats prior to the spring solstice.

Collin watched as Siobhan brought a beer over to Orla and noticed there was an open seat next to her.

Collin had a familiar enough face to the patrons that he didn't get any stares for being there. They recognized him as someone who'd been here when snow stuck to the sand. No one was going to give him a hard time. Well, almost no one.

He approached the seat next to Orla. "Mind if I—"

"Just sit," she said. She refused to look at him while she nursed her Guinness.

Collin examined her while she drank. She seemed colder than he remembered. Though this may have something to do with the fact that he was intruding in what she considered to be her territory. He had the rest of the world, she was allowed to have her hometown.

Orla came to the Inn to get away from her problems and here was Collin walking right back into her life because her stupid fucking nephew couldn't keep it in his pants.

"What?" she sniped. His staring unnerved her.

"Nothing," Collin said.

Collin remembered the first time he saw Orla in this very bar eighteen years ago. His parents had bought the house in Cape May years before, but it often needed work. Collin and his father would travel down to do renovations. He had recently gotten a fake ID from a friend who knew a guy that knew a guy in Philadelphia, and had finally built up the courage to use it. Collin hadn't known that no one at the C-View Inn cared how old the federal government—or the state of New Jersey—thought their customers should be. Money was money in the off season, and all the cops turned the other way because they were drinking on shift.

Collin had spotted her from a table about twenty feet from the bar. She was with friends who were more than aware of the owner's disdain for drinking-age limitations. Orla had caught him looking over and had smiled at him.

She'd made her way over to Collin's empty table and said, "Excuse me?"

Collin had thought she was making a move, but then she'd asked, "Can I borrow this chair, sir?" She'd pulled a chair out for a friend who had just arrived. Collin rolled his eyes, but Orla had still smiled at him.

She couldn't help but smile when she saw him back then.

Now, Orla gave him dead eyes. She could barely stand to be this close to him. She felt angry, even though she knew she had no real rationale for not wanting him to be here. They hadn't spoken in a decade. If anything, it was like she was *supposed* to not want him there.

This would be a whole lot easier if their relationship hadn't ended so suddenly. That was both their faults. He had every right to be here for his sibling's offspring who also couldn't keep it in their pants.

The truth was, she didn't want him to leave. Or did she?

The alcohol was mixing her brain's neuro-receptive messages: angry, guilty, understanding, annoyed. Which was it?

As much as Orla hated to admit it, feeling multiple emotions simultaneously was possible.

Stupid biology.

Orla kept vacillating between anger at how she and Collin had left things years ago, and the odd excitement she felt at seeing him again. She hadn't expected all her repressed feelings—and attraction—to remain.

She was a few beers in and warming up to the idea that he was in her town. She knew it would happen eventually. His family owned property. Prime real estate, as Siobhan had put it after leaving Windward House.

Orla was surprised it had taken this long for him to return. Was that what she was mad about? Had she wanted him to come back sooner? Had she wanted him to fight for her when she was the one who had pushed him away in the first place?

Orla chugged her beer.

"Those kids have a plan," she said, wiping away a Guinness mustache. "A way better plan than you'd expect."

"I blame the internet," Collin said, trying to get Siobhan's attention so he too could confound his senses with alcohol.

Orla agreed with him. She waved a hand to her sister, who was at the other end of the bar, and put up two fingers to indicate she and Collin needed another round. Siobhan acknowledged this with a nod while pouring a flight of beers.

"She'll get us once she's got them," Orla said.

"Thanks."

The awkward silence was deafening. Collin knew what he wanted to talk to Orla about, but he wanted to bring it up naturally. Though he *also* knew there was no natural way to bring this conversation up. It had been buried for too long.

They were both relieved when the Elephant Man forced his way between their chairs. They were initially startled when the obese, bearded man, who smelled of sweat and stale tobacco, popped in. He was wearing an elephant suit that had the words '*CAPE MAY ZOO*' embroidered on the front.

"The fuck you looking at?" he spat at Collin and Orla, then yelled across the bar to get Siobhan's attention.

"Don't avoid the elephant in the room, doll! He needs a drink."

The Elephant Man put a cigarette in his mouth, but could not find his lighter. Elephants didn't have pockets.

"Got a light?" he said.

"Nah, man," Collin said. "Don't smoke."

"Fucking pussy-ass generation."

And with that, the Elephant Man wandered to the other side of the bar to confront the bartenders. The absurdity of a literal elephant in the room broke the ice between Collin and Orla. Now was as good a time as any, Collin thought.

"Huh. Wasn't expecting a literal elephant in the room," Collin said.

"The metaphorical one's much bigger," Orla said, then pointed at the Elephant Man, "he's regular."

"What's his real name?"

"No idea," She smiled.

"OK, I have to ask. I know I gave up my right to by leaving, but why didn't you tell me," Collin tried to clarify, "Before you—"

"Can I at least get my beer first?" Orla cut him off.

"I was too angry to talk to you back then. So I left. But I'm here now," he said.

Orla let Collin's words pickle in her head. She took a deep breath before replying.

"What do you want me to say? I was twenty-one. My dad was dead, you were leaving. My sister had a new baby of her own to look after and my mom was hundreds of miles away with that French fuck. I was alone. So, I made a decision. Alone."

"I wasn't gone yet. I could have, we could have—"

"What? You were gonna give up on your dreams for a child neither of us were ready to raise?"

"I wanted to—"

"Stop." She interrupted, over this interrogation. If he wanted her to explain herself, he should have asked her back then. Right now, she honestly couldn't say what was going through her mind at the time. She barely knew what was going through her mind even now as she spoke.

"OK? Just stop. You hate me. I'm indifferent to you. Can we just ignore each other and drink?"

Collin didn't know what to say. There wasn't much else *to* say. There was *too* much else to say. So, he just said OK.

"OK. For now."

After a moment of silence, he added, "I don't hate you."

Siobhan arrived with their beers and they both stared straight ahead, neither one of them capable of making eye contact, neither one of them exactly sure what emotions were being held in their hearts or minds. But they drank together, and that was a start.

A restart.

9
NAVIGATING THE STORM

NOAH CLOSED THE DOOR to his bedroom and opened his laptop. He navigated to FaceTime, took a deep breath, and clicked on the contact labeled DAD. The call connected and Captain Jesse Comstock appeared on screen, heavily pixelated, on the bridge of his ship.

Noah saw his father pixelated more often than in the flesh. Like the world was trying to censor him from Noah.

Jesse, a Merchant Marine, was always away at sea. Waves crashed and thunder cracked, but it was distorted through Noah's speakers. Calls with his father often sounded like robots trying to surf.

Jesse spoke with the calm, reserved nature of a man who had battled mother nature and won time and time again. Despite the chaos that surrounded him, Jesse stayed steady. He was the calm in the storm.

"Noah," he said with genuine excitement. "You taking care of your mother?"

"Doing my best, sir," Noah lied.

"Make sure you two are ready. A nasty hurricane is headed towards the northeast. We're doing our best to avoid it, but she's a mighty bitch."

"Sounds a lot like grandma," Noah said, and got a rare laugh out of his father. He took a deep breath, ready to come clean.

"Dad. There's something I've got to tell you."

Noah checked the screen. His father's image had frozen. He could no longer hear the sounds of the storm raging behind him.

"Dad?"

Nothing. The connection dropped a moment later and Noah's anger rose inside him.

"Damn it. Every time!"

He slammed the laptop closed and considered throwing it, but decided he'd regret that later. He took a deep breath to calm himself.

Noah had to meet Audrey's uncle in Wildwood soon. He was sick of everyone treating him as if he didn't understand the gravity of his and Audrey's situation. He knew there would be bills, and diapers, and no sleep. He knew this from watching Teen Mom on MTV.

He knew there would be constant crying and that he'd never know if the cries were from hunger or boredom or gas. And those were just Audrey's. The baby would be crying too. At first he'd have no idea why. Soon, though, he'd have those cries categorized.

He wanted to see if there was a difference between hungry cries and gassy cries. Did thirsty cries sound the same as diaper-rash cries? Once he'd figured out the exact pitch of each kind, he'd know exactly what the baby needed.

He was excited to analyze all the baby's cries on Pro Tools. Ever since watching YouTube videos as a kid about how sound made patterns in sand, Noah had been obsessed. Music in particular fascinated him. Music could change a person's mood instantly. Music was magic to Noah.

He loved mixing and playing with audio editing to really push the limits of what you could do with sound. He wanted to understand how the software that captured the sound worked. In fact, Noah wanted to understand how *everything* worked. If money wasn't a concern, Noah would have chosen to study everything he could. Student loans never come due if you never leave school.

He'd started by learning as much as he could about audio engineering software. He'd studied every line of code in Pro Tools—he could write the whole thing from scratch in his virtual machine if he ever needed to. Noah didn't care about playing in his band as much as he cared about recording and mixing.

Noah sat back down at his desk and looked over his application to Temple's computer engineering program on the laptop he'd stopped himself from destroying. Noah was always fascinated by how lines of code could make complex software programs run and he could always find a job as a software engineer. Who knows, he might design the next audio engineering program that became the industry standard.

As much as he wanted to focus on his future, Noah's thoughts kept going back to having to tell his father about the baby.

Noah knew exactly how his life was going to change. He wasn't going to be able to play in Amish Electricity, his three-piece punk cover band, anymore. Their lack of original material made it easier to let go of. He wouldn't be sentimental when he told the guys he was done.

They played pop-punk from the early aughts. Mostly The Movielife. Noah thought The Movielife was niche enough to make them seem like they were real connoisseurs of punk rock. He had stolen *Forty Hour Train Back to Penn* from his aunt Orla and felt like he had found a hidden treasure.

The band was how he'd met Audrey in the first place, so it had already given him everything he could have wanted out of it. No one got into music to make money anymore. Everyone who got into music wanted to meet girls. Or guys. Or whoever they were into. Most to their own detriment.

Noah knew he wasn't ever going to do better than meeting Audrey.

T WO YEARS AGO, AT North Wildwood Skate Park, Noah was doing his best to keep up with Travis Barker's tempos while Amish Electricity covered Blink-182's, 'Dumpweed'. He was distracted watching the cute skater girl. He couldn't shake the feeling that he recognized her from somewhere. She winked at him while grinding down a rail.

Noah hammered out the last beats of the song and their set was finally over. His arms were exhausted. He tossed his drumsticks into the holder attached to his cymbals. The crowd cheering made him feel better. He jumped off the stage and snagged a water out of the cooler set aside for the bands.

Tom and Rob, Noah's bandmates, joined him and lit up a joint. Tom always had weed on him because his older brother worked at a dispensary and wasn't very good at inventory.

"We fucking ripped, man!" Tom said, taking a deep drag and offering it to Noah.

"My timing felt off," Noah said as he passed the joint to Rob.

"You're crazy dude. You fucking nailed those fills," Rob said, then started hacking up his lungs. "Man, why do you always have flower? Gank a vape pen. Do it for my lungs." He held the joint out for Tom to take while keeping his head down.

"Baby lungs," Tom said, inhaling deeply with no impediment.

"Hey, could I get a hit?" a voice they didn't recognize called out. The cute skater girl rolled up on her skateboard and kicked it into her hand in an intimidatingly cool move. Noah was sure he had seen this girl somewhere before, but she had to be a MERT.

"For sure." Tom handed her the joint and Audrey took a nice long hit.

"You guys sounded dope. Especially you," she said, looking at Noah, expecting him to introduce himself.

"Noah," he finally said. "You look really familiar?"

"I get that a lot. I'm Audrey."

She handed Noah the joint and he took a hit.

"Oh, shit!" Rob said, "You're @little_skater_girl, aren't you? I follow you!"

Audrey grimaced. Noah could tell whoever his friends thought she was, she didn't like the label.

"You are! Oh fuck, can we get a pic?" Tom said, pulling out his phone and not waiting for an answer before snapping a selfie. Audrey's eyebrows lifted and her eyes rolled. Noah could tell she was uncomfortable.

"Guys, the event manager's grabbing your guitar and bass. Remember what happened last time?"

"Oh, fuck," Tom said, as Rob said, "Shit."

The two of them ran off to stop anyone from touching their prized possessions, leaving Noah and Audrey alone with the remnants of the joint.

"What happened last time?" Audrey asked.

"Nothing," Noah said. "They're just high enough to think something did."

Audrey snort laughed.

Noah was smitten.

"Wanna go grab some pizza?" Noah asked.

Audrey hit the last of the joint and tossed the roach. "What do you think?"

"Let's go," Noah said.

They walked to a shitty stall on the boardwalk that sold giant slices of pizza, and each got two. Stoned out of their minds, they laughed while trying to figure out how best to force the massive slices down their throats. They were both giggling and covered in grease when Noah couldn't hold back his curiosity any longer.

"OK, seriously, I recognize you from somewhere. Noah saw Audrey's smile fade and clarified, "And it's not whatever my idiot friends were talking about before. Are you from Cape May?"

Her smile came back.

"No, but my grandparents own a house by the beach. I spend most of my summers here."

Recognition hit Noah's face. "Did you learn to swim here?"

"Yes!" Audrey squealed.

"With the Beach Patrol, right?"

"OK. What is happening?" Audrey said. Noah could tell she hadn't figured it out yet. He couldn't help but fall into a cannabis-induced laughing fit.

"What?!" Audrey yelled, "What am I missing?"

"You got attacked by a school of jellyfish one class. When you were like, five or six years old. Right?" Noah said, smiling and trying to stifle his own laughter.

"No way," Audrey recognized him now. "*No way*. Are you—?"

"I'm the little boy who peed on you to stop the sting," Noah said.

They fell to the planks of the boardwalk in hysterics. Tourists stared at them as they passed.

"Oh. My. God," Audrey said, "Yours was the first penis I ever saw!"

She let out more guttural laughs before wiping tears from her eyes. They got to their feet, holding one another for purchase.

"I hope you liked it."

"Only one way to be sure," Audrey said, and moved closer to Noah pressing his hips into hers. She put her hand on his cheek and kissed him right there in the middle of the boardwalk, forcing the world to go around them. They were a world unto themselves.

W HILE NOAH GOT READY to meet Audrey's uncle, he wondered what it would be like not playing in the band anymore.

It wasn't as if Amish Electricity had written any original material that would never make its way into the world. The only original material Noah had coming out was the child gestating in his fiancé. He loved that Audrey was now his fiancé. He was more than happy to throw away band practice to be with her.

Ever since they connected that night on the beach, it was like they were meant to be. They spent nights on the phone just talking about their mundane teenage days while she was in Philadelphia during the school year. Despite having never met anyone Audrey went to school with, Noah knew all the details of the social hierarchy at The Baldwin School. Most of the mainline matriculations were rich kids with classic rich-kid problems: easy access to drugs and alcohol, little to no access to their parents. Audrey told Noah she did her best to stay out of the private-school drama. She just wanted to skate and chill. That was another thing he loved about her. She knew who she was.

Noah was a public-school student. *Star-crossed lovers*, he thought, laughing to himself as he put deodorant on. Being in public school made it easier for him to stand out.

By simply paying attention and doing his work, he was technically in the top of his class. Though that wasn't saying much compared to the other students at Lower Cape May Regional. Especially Tom and Rob. He was able to put being in the top five percent of his class on his college applications. Statistics were the best lies.

Noah calmed himself as he brushed his teeth. Remembering how he got here helped. He was ready to leave the house, but was, technically, still grounded. Despite this, his situation gave him a newfound courage to take on authority he never had before.

He no longer feared punishment. He was going to be responsible for another life, so getting yelled at or disappointing his parents wasn't a big motivator.

Noah left his room and moved down the hall. He couldn't hear anyone else in the house, which meant his mother and his aunt were likely at the C-View. He was free to go.

WHILE TEENAGERS DRANK VODKA out of water bottles, and carnies conned kids out of money with rigged games, Collin and Noah walked along the

Wildwood boardwalk eating pretzels and drinking fountain sodas. They avoided Jersey Shore rejects and all their drunken guido brethren. The lights and sounds of the amusement park on the pier reminded everyone that summer was here, and the best way to celebrate was by taking a chance on shoddily built carny rides close enough to the ocean that factoring in rust was a major aspect of the design plans.

Collin and Noah had a good time getting to know each other. They had spoken about how he and Audrey met, and Collin loved that he was a drummer and she was a skater. They were a gender swapped Avril Lavigne song. While he thought Noah was a good kid and could tell why his niece cared for him so much, it was time for him to give the kid some harsh reality.

"Here's the thing. Love isn't enough. And anyone who says it is, probably got shot by a deranged J.D. Salinger fan."

"What?" Noah said, confused.

"John Lennon? Killed by Mark David Chapman?"

"You need to update your references. That was before your time too."

Collin considered the ramifications of slapping a teenager in full view of the denizens of the boardwalk: *not worth it.*

"Anyway. He was a dreamer. Dreamers sound like they know what they're talking about, but in reality they're full of shit and LSD. Plus, they beat their wives. No one ever talks about that."

"Everyone talks about it. Have you not been on the internet, *ever*?" Noah said.

"Not once. I grew up with landlines and played outside before Al Gore ruined the world," Collin deadpanned.

"Whatever," Noah said. "I still love Audrey. And I have no intention of taking hallucinogens."

"You're a teenager. Your frontal lobe hasn't fully developed. You're basically brain dead by adult standards."

"You're not a doctor."

"And you're not in love!" Collin countered. "I'm sure you think you are. But no matter how true you think your feelings are now, the world has a way of changing people. For better or worse, you will change. And so will she. How you both feel about each other now is just hormones fucking with you."

Collin took a moment. He felt bad about being so blunt. He saw the fear on Noah's face. This wasn't why Audrey wanted him here.

"Plus, mushrooms are, like, so fun."

They sat in silence for a moment.

"I didn't tell you that," Collin said.

Before Noah had the time to formulate a counterargument, a voice startled the both of them.

"BABY DADDY!" Casey shouted from ten yards away. She was hammered. She hugged Noah, then sniffed him like a dog that had found something interesting.

"You reek of innocence," she said. "Gross."

Collin pulled his sister off the teenage boy. "See what time turns teenage girls into?" he said.

"Successful stockbrokers?" Casey countered.

"I thought you managed a hedge fund?" Collin said.

"Like you know the difference," Casey said, before her stomach audibly turned. "Uh-oh. Shouldn't have invested in boardwalk sushi."

She rushed to the railing of the boardwalk, slinked over the side, and spilled her dividends into the sand below. After feeding the crabs and seagulls, she wiped her mouth, ready to rally.

"I need bar buddies. Going alone is getting sad."

"Getting?" Collin said.

"I'm seventeen," Noah reminded her.

"This is Jersey, no one cares," Casey said.

She walked backwards, beckoning her brother and Noah to follow her to the bar. Collin looked over at Noah, trying to figure out if he could survive a night with Casey.

Then he realized, if Noah wanted to join their family, he would have to learn to socialize with them.

"You really want to marry into our family? Let's go." Collin said.

"Go where?"

"To do what my family does best." He shouted after Casey, "Wait up, we're coming!" Casey ran back over to the boys and picked Noah up in an embrace.

"We're gonna get you drunk!"

ORLA RELAXED IN THE lifeguard shack at CMBP headquarters. She liked to come here at night to clear her head. No one was around and being a captain meant she had keys. She would often come here to grade papers when Jesse was home on shore leave and she wanted to give her sister some private time with her husband. This was hallowed ground to Orla. The headquarters was a shrine to all lifeguards, past and present.

Pictures of every season going back to the fifties adorned the walls. Orla stared at a particularly well-framed action shot of her father during the lifeguard championships of '98. He was paddleboarding for the win. The photographer caught him wearing a smile as a wave was about to knock him over.

She remembered being a kid then, watching him, seeing how excited everyone was. That was when she decided she was going to be a lifeguard, too. Now, she was wondering if she had made the right decision.

She sighed, took a seat and attempted to enjoy the tranquil solitude.

Orla took the small pocket knife her father had given her when she first passed her lifeguard trials out of her pocket. It was a small clip-point her grandfather had given him when he did the same. The knife had her father's and grandfather's names engraved into the wooden handle. She spun the unopened handle in her hand watching *Rian* come and go. She kept the knife on her at all times. A good lifeguard was prepared for anything.

Her quiet contemplation was interrupted when Audrey walked in. She put the knife back in her pocket.

"Noah wanted me to come check on you; said you were reading a lot of Sylvia Plath." Audrey sat down next to Orla on the large couch.

"That's where your uncle and I fucked the first time," Orla said, pointing to the exact spot Audrey sat in. Audrey stood up.

"Really, was that necessary information?" Audrey shook away the heebie-jeebies and found another seat.

"No. But it made you as uncomfortable as I am."

"Well done," Audrey admitted. She was thoroughly grossed out thinking of her uncle and her fiancé's aunt getting it on in this small shack full of lifeguard memorabilia. Who would get turned on in what amounted to a nautically themed Fuddruckers? Gross.

Orla got up and began to pace the room.

"You know," Orla said. "I started here when I was sixteen. I've been a lifeguard every summer since."

"That's pretty cool," Audrey said.

"No, it's not. It's sad. I'm still in the same place I was when I was a teenager. Is that what you want? To be stuck in the same place you are now, doing the same things you've always done."

Audrey smiled at Orla. She was expecting this tact.

"I'm a sponsored skateboarder," Audrey said. "I made, like, 60k last year—not counting my endorsements—having fun."

"OK. Bad example," Orla admitted.

Audrey wandered around the headquarters. There were pictures of all the different lifeguard classes and events the CMBP had hosted over the years. She found a photo of her uncle and Orla, much younger, covered in shaving cream on the beach. They looked happier than any couple should be.

"So, you stayed here and my uncle went to California?"

"I went to Boston for my Ph.D. He was going to USC for film."

"But now you're here?" Audrey didn't understand. "Why didn't you stay in Boston?"

"The thing they don't tell you about academia," Orla said. "Is there are, like, no jobs. The only one I could find was here at the local community college. So, I came back home. Moved in with my sister and her husband. And I am slowly trying to pay off a six-figure student loan."

"Wow. You gave up on love for an expensive book club?"

"I got an education. I expanded my mind."

"And your debt," Audrey countered. "You should have just gone with Uncle Collin."

"That's what you're getting out of this?!" Orla was exasperated. How could this girl not understand? "Not to make your own way? Be a strong, independent woman?"

Audrey laughed in Orla's face.

"What's so funny?"

"I mean, girl power and all for following your own path. But, like, let's be real. If you actually believed half the crap you rail against, you would have gotten a degree in mechanical engineering, not book reading."

"I have a Ph.D. in Irish Literature."

"So, you read books about alcoholics by alcoholics?"

"They're not all . . . that's actually pretty much it, yeah."

"I might just be some dumb, pregnant teen to you, but at least I know what I want. You hate it here, but you don't leave. That's on you."

Audrey's words hit Orla hard. They knocked the wind out of her. At the same time, she was impressed by Audrey's audacity.

"Why are you really here?" Orla said.

"Didn't buy the Sylvia Plath bit, eh?"

"Noah knows that when I'm sad I read *Dubliners*, not a big *Bell Jar* fan."

"I wanted to know about you and my uncle. What happened between you two?"

"Time," Orla said. "Time kills everything, even love."

"Yeah. But what happened before all that time passed?" Audrey pressed.

"We were going to opposite ends of the country. We had different dreams. Sometimes people just drift apart," Orla lied.

"You look pretty happy here," Audrey handed Orla the shaving cream picture. Orla smiled, remembering the day.

It was the end of summer party. The day lifeguards, hotel staff, and the hospitality industry as a whole celebrate the fleeing of the MERTs with a citywide beach party.

They'd covered themselves in shaving cream after drinking too much. Orla remembered how they'd showered off, snuck in here, and went at it. That was the time Collin's condom broke and, in a drunken attempt at birth control, Orla had shoved hand sanitizer all the way into her cervix. The reminder of that pain wiped the smile from her face.

"We were, now we aren't. That's life," Orla said with a shrug. She placed the photo back in its spot.

"You should try reading some books written by stoners. Much more optimism," Audrey quipped.

Orla smirked. She liked this girl. "Noah knocked up a good one," she said, and placed a hand on Audrey's shoulder.

T HE RHYTHMIC BEAT OF bad electronica, embell-
ished by a mediocre DJ, blasted out of the sound
system at the Stardust nightclub. Collin couldn't help but
think he was in a bad episode of *Jersey Shore*. The smell of
sweat, spray tans, and desperation permeated his nostrils
and made him gag.

So many guidos fist-pumped while they downed Irish
car bombs, that he had lost track of his sister on the
dance floor. He scanned the half-naked bodies of those
less rhythmically challenged than him, and found Casey
grinding on a muscular man whose face was obscured by
the strobe lights and other patrons.

"Should we stop her?"

"She's an adult," Noah slurred.

Casey had been true to her word: they'd got Noah
drunk. *Too* drunk. To his credit, Noah tried not to give into
peer pressure, but Casey can be persuasive and pushy.

He was in the danger stages and Collin told Casey to
give him a break. Orla was already unhappy to see him—if
he let her nephew die of alcohol poisoning, there would be
no chance of reconciliation.

"Welp," Collin said. "I'm done watching that."

He turned back to the bar where Noah was struggling
to keep his head upright. He vomited in his mouth, but
had the wherewithal to swallow it back down.

Collin noted this. He could hang—an important factor for anyone attempting to join the Cassidy clan.

"Did you just swallow that?" Collin said.

Noah simply nodded, trying not to let it happen again.

"Not bad, Baby Daddy."

"Don't—" Noah struggled to not puke and talk. "Don't call me that. It's not like it was an accident or anything."

Collin choked on the drink he was sipping. Did he hear that right? Did Noah just admit that he and Audrey *planned* to have a child? That couldn't possibly be it. He must be drunk.

"Wait. *What*?" Collin said while wiping his mouth.

"We figured our parents would be cool with us getting married with a baby on the way." Noah said. "Did not see this reaction coming."

He took a deep breath, trying to keep the contents of his stomach where they were. "People love babies. They have those little fingers . . . they're little poop monsters. Who doesn't love babies?"

Noah spilled his guts, figuratively to Collin and, shortly after, literally all over the bar. The bartenders were busy hitting on drunk college girls, so Collin took this opportunity to move Noah to another table and avoid getting kicked out for besmirching the bar.

Collin couldn't concern himself with the puke. That's what bar backs are for. He was just given game changing information that made everything about this situation far more complicated, and he had no idea what to do with it.

These two children—who seemed fairly intelligent by every measure he could think of—had chosen to get pregnant.

They wanted to be married. They loved each other.

And because they were teenagers, they knew no one would believe that their love was real. So, they chose to do the one thing that would tie them to one another for life, whether or not their parents approved.

They were fucking idiots. Or, maybe, they were geniuses.

This was an effective strategy—ill-conceived, but effective, nonetheless.

No. They were fucking idiots.

10
PEOPLE YOU MADE

T HE NEXT MORNING, CASEY awoke in a state she
had become all too accustomed to: not remembering how or when she'd got home. The sound of her
phone's alarm being too far out of reach forced her to join
the world of the waking sooner than she'd have liked.

She'd forgotten to turn it off, even though she was
technically on vacation.

It was 6am. Normally, she'd have already made coffee,
packed a gym bag with the three P's—panties, pantsuit,
pumps—showered and dressed after the fourth P—pi-
lates—and been at her desk ten trades deep.

Now, she was still drunk and awake after what could
only have been about two to three hours of sleep. Work
hard, play hard. Then she realized the man she had been
dancing with at the club was in her bed.

"Forgot about that," she groaned.

She peaked under the covers to confirm: he was naked,
and he looked *good* naked.

A double check confirmed.

"Good dick," she said, sotto voce.

The balls looked a little weird, all balls did. *Was that a scar or just his scrotal raphe?* Despite the odd balls, he was a solid specimen. Even when she was black-out drunk, she had good taste. She'd have preferred to have a woman next to her too, but you can't bat a thousand every game.

Casey grinned to herself, proud of the pull she had. Unlike her parents and siblings, she was not one for monogamy. She hated the idea that she should waste her life trying to make one person happy. If she was going to do that, that one person would be herself.

The sight of a naked man or woman in her bed, whose name she couldn't remember, was not an uncommon one. Explaining this to Eliza and Allan, the poster children for a perfect marriage, was not an activity she felt compelled to engage in. She was, as a principle, anti-engagement. Her family could not find out about the man in her bed.

She had to get rid of him. Beyond not wanting to explain the complexities of her sex life to her parents, there was no way she was going to deal with her brother and sister ribbing her about her one-night stand. She was too drunk—and would soon be too hungover—to come up with good comebacks.

Can't have that.

Casey shook the man awake. He slowly opened his eyes and smiled when he woke up to her looking down at him. Casey was sure that, from his perspective, she seemed angelic.

"You need to go," Casey said. "That way."

She pointed to the French doors that opened onto the second-floor sun porch. The man did not argue or put up a fight. This made her like him even more. She'd spent too many hours explaining to finance bros she'd used and abused that, no, she did not want to get breakfast with them. Or coffee. Or tea. *Especially* not tea. The tea guys were the only ones Casey ever felt shame about having had.

She'd got what she wanted. Fed a biological urge. She didn't need them in her presence anymore. Casey presumed, with a body like that, this one was used to sneaking out of girl's bedrooms.

He got out of bed and put his clothes on with the urgency she had made clear was necessary. Without so much as a word, he made his way to the sun porch. He adeptly climbed over the railing and hopped down to the alleyway with the skill and grace of a parkour runner.

She was impressed. He had definitely done this before. Possibly even here.

Windward House was a bed and breakfast, and he was a local. Any number of guests could have hosted him over the years.

How did she remember he was a local? Oh no, the night was coming back to her. Collin might still be able to give her shit. He was with her at the club. So was Audrey's baby daddy. *What was his name? Ned?* Fuck. She needed coffee.

A moment later, her cell phone buzzed. The text was from an unsaved number.

> **My Name's Dale. I assume you forgot.**

Casey smiled. Dale. Good moves, Dale.

He'd left her with a smile, and she left him on read.

C ASEY, FREE FROM THE evidence of her dalliance, put on pajama pants and a T-shirt. She craved the coffee for the ritual of it, not the caffeine. Even if she wanted to go back to sleep, her body wouldn't let her. She was too used to getting up early.

While Casey worked out of New York, most of the accounts she managed were based in London. So she was based in London, timewise. Six a.m. was her vacation alarm. She was normally awake by three a.m. Or hadn't gone to sleep yet. The markets wait for no one.

Casey liked numbers more than people. But numbers didn't have good dicks, facsimiles thereof, or skilled hands, and thus she forced herself to do the bare minimum necessary to engage with society. People were exhausting. Alcohol made people more tolerable.

She remained staunchly anti-engagement as she tiptoed down the stairs, careful not to wake anyone up. When she arrived in the kitchen, however, she found her attempt at stealth to be in vain: her mother, father, and Baby Daddy's grandma were all in there.

Thankfully, a second pot of coffee was already brewing. Casey moved to the pot and started tapping on the counter trying to will it to brew faster than physics would allow.

"You're up early," Beth said, sipping from her coffee.

"Late actually," Casey said. "I have a few trades I need to get done."

"Trades?" Beth said.

"Casey works on Wall Street," Eliza said, proud.

"Well, la-ti-da," Beth said. "I've got a real-estate-agent-slash-bartender and a teacher-slash-life-guard."

"We've also got the television writer, the nurse, and the professional skateboarder-slash-small-business-owner."

"We're not Pokémon cards," Casey said, annoyed the coffee wasn't ready yet. "We're people you made."

"It's true. She came from my balls," Allan added.

"I had a little something to do with it," Eliza said.

"Does a baker credit the oven?" Allan said.

"Can you bake without one?" Eliza narrowed her eyes. Allan studied his right hand thoughtfully before showing it to her.

"I can, and the bread is much less expensive." This made Eliza giggle. They still had the same childish sense of humor.

"I like to think I yielded a nice R.O.I." Casey said, finally deciding to replace the half-filled pot with her own coffee mug. She willed the stream to fill the mug so she could escape this interaction.

"As much as I love this metaphor, what is the breakfast situation?" Beth interrupted.

Casey could tell Beth felt threatened by her parents. She may not like people, but she could read them like a profit and loss statement. The benefit of having to learn to fit in was that, once you did, you understood they were pretty boring. Petty, childish, insecure, needy—Beth was all these things tied together with inadequacy.

Allan nudged Eliza with a knowing smile. Casey was sure that made it worse for Beth. Her parents were sickeningly in love, even after all their years together. Casey was fairly certain she got her high sex drive from her mother.

"This is a bed and breakfast, correct? Shouldn't there be . . . breakfast?" Beth continued.

"Technically, yes. But we're on vacation." Eliza clarified. She and Allan clinked their coffee mugs and sipped their coffee.

"There's coffee," Allan added.

"Not enough," Casey said, with only a quarter-full cup.

"So, am I to just fend for myself? You won't even send the boy to the store?"

Casey could tell from Beth's tone of voice she thought this to be a great insult. How dare Allan and Eliza not wait on her as if she were a paying guest and not a freeloader whose own children didn't want her staying with them.

"I think you'll find a way to survive," Allan said.

The mug was finally full enough that Casey Indiana Jones idol-swapped her mug for the pot before a drop could fall on the hotplate. She took her mug and ran back up to the comfort and solitude of her room.

Casey made a few trades that equated to hundreds of millions in profits to her fund. Just another Tuesday.

The best thing that ever happened to her was the COVID-19 pandemic. Sure, millions of people died, but Casey was able to prove that she could effectively work from home whenever she needed too. A most worthy sacrifice. She didn't even need to make these trades, she was on vacation. She just enjoyed her work. And the money it made her.

With her work for the day done and her hangover abated, it was time to figure out what to do with the rest of her day. She could see what Kip and Valerie were doing, but she already knew the answer: fighting about their pregnant teen daughter.

There was no way she was willingly entering *that* war zone.

She was with Collin last night, so no need for that again. She was thankful he wasn't blowing up her phone with Jersey Shore memes about her hookup last night. Collin was too busy trying to figure out how to talk to his almost baby momma anyway.

Casey remembered when Collin finally told her what had happened. He was a mess. She had never seen him that simultaneously mad and hurt. It was a strange feeling. There's not much anyone can do to make a situation like that better. At the time, Casey felt like beating up Orla would help. Collin told her that wouldn't be necessary.

Casey had to let her brother get his feelings out. Thankfully, he was already moving to Los Angeles. When you're trying to avoid an ex, being three thousand miles away helps. And help it did, for like a decade. Before fate forced them together again. Fate was also a stripper Casey had hooked up with in the city. Fate was a bitch.

Casey considered seeing if Audrey wanted to go shopping, but didn't know if that was the best tact with a teenage girl who was pregnant and wanted to be engaged. Casey remained anti-engagement in this case as well. She saw marriage for the legal contract that it was: a property exchange. She didn't like any woman, or man, or person being considered chattel. There was no reason to bring god or the government—both distinctly little "g's" to Casey—into any non-business relationship.

Casey's phone buzzed. Dale was texting. He had waited a few hours and was shooting his shot again.

Want to forget me all over again?

Swish.

Casey typed. She considered for a moment. *Fuck it*, she thought, and hit send.

You know just what I want to hear.

Game on.

B ETH HADN'T BEEN IN the old house in almost twenty years. Siobhan opened the door with her key and watched as Beth stepped through the threshold. Siobhan could have sworn she saw a chill run through her mother, like she'd seen a ghost. She felt herself perform a Kegel clench unconsciously.

Siobhan wanted to squeeze herself into nothingness. Being around her mother always made her feel like she was a little girl again. Like, if she did even the slightest thing wrong, her mother would take away the only thing Siobhan wanted from her: attention.

After opening a bottle of pinot noir and pouring two glasses, Siobhan and Beth sat at the empty kitchen table.

Siobhan took a swig of her wine—she needed it to calm her racing mind. Her mother always made her nervous. The pinot warmed her gullet and gave her some relief, but really Siobhan's nerves were shot. She had a husband away at sea, a son growing up too fast, and ever since Beth arrived, Orla had been giving her the silent treatment.

She felt totally isolated.

Siobhan needed her mom. She wished she could be more like her sister, but something deep within Siobhan craved her mother's comfort and approval.

"Are you OK, honey? This is a lot to deal with. I remember when you told me I was going to be a grandmother, I nearly killed you," Beth said, sipping her pinot.

Siobhan smiled to hide her unease. This was another thing her mother would always do: make any situation all about *her*. Siobhan knew the reason her mother had shown up without being asked was because it was a chance to do just that; it's what she had done when Siobhan got pregnant with Noah.

"Mom, I . . . I don't. It's all just . . ." Siobhan couldn't get the words out. The same stammer she had in elementary school came right back to her in her mother's presence. Not that it mattered. Her mother wasn't going to let her get a word in anyway.

"Now you tell me I'm going to be a *great*-grand-mother—"

The front door opened and slammed shut. Siobhan could hear her sister's footsteps, and she contracted her pelvic floor once more.

"Jesus Christ," Orla said, entering the kitchen in her lifeguard uniform, "Why is she here?"

"I'm here to escape that family you imprisoned me with. They're cretons. We cannot let Noah marry that girl. What would people say?"

"What people, Mom? You haven't lived in Cape May for years," Siobhan reminded her.

"People here love the Cassidys," Orla said. "They run one of the best bed-and-breakfasts in town."

"People always talk. Especially when teenage girls get pregnant. That's why I'm here, my dear—"

Orla snorted. This was rich—her mother really thought she was the savior here.

Beth glared at her while she finished what she was about to say. "We will not let this little . . . skate rat . . . drag our family's name through the mud."

Siobhan contracted her groin for a long ten-count. She knew what her mother was. The gaslighting, the savior complex, the self-aggrandizement. Beth was only here to make Beth look good. To make Beth feel good. She didn't give a shit about what was going on with Noah and Audrey. She just wanted to rewrite history, play the victim, and make herself the center of attention. She wanted Siobhan to go along with it. She wanted her to be what she was growing up: the mediator; the one who tried to make everyone else happy.

Siobhan wanted to cuss her mother out. To yell and scream at her. She wanted to call her on her bullshit. But she couldn't make herself. She knew that if she did she'd regret it moments later when her mother took her on a guilt trip. Orla got the rebel gene, Siobhan thought. She felt she'd got the coward gene. She just looked at the floor, ashamed of herself.

"Mom, you dragged our family's name through the mud more than Noah or that beautiful girl ever could," Orla said. "Siobhan called you because you deserved to know that you were going to be a great-grandmother. She did not ask you to come here. Did you?" Orla looked at her sister.

She had not. But at the same time, she hadn't told her not to. She knew her mother couldn't resist a situation that would allow her to become the center of attention. Was this all her fault?

Siobhan began to stammer, but couldn't get the words out. She hated when her sister and mother fought. It was all too much for her; too much like being a kid again. She just wanted to have a glass of wine with her mom.

"You're only here for you, not those kids . . ."

"You will not talk to me that way, young lady!"

"Or what, Mom? What are you going to do?" Orla opened the fridge and grabbed a water bottle. "Leave? Oh no. I'm so scared. I'll have to live my life the same way I have since we were kids: without a mother."

"Orla, can you not—" Siobhan started to say before being cut off.

"Stop defending her," Orla said. "Nothing you do or say is going to be good enough, haven't you figured that out yet? She wants this attention, and you know what, I'm done giving it to her." Orla slammed the fridge closed and left the kitchen.

"I'm sorry, mom, I just wanted . . ."

"It's OK, honey. I can tell when I'm not wanted," Beth said.

"Can you?" Orla shouted from the other room.

"These are the people I made," Beth said as she gathered her things and marched to the front door.

"Mom. Stay," Siobhan pleaded.

But Beth was already out the door.

11
Bombing History

Nᴏʀᴛʜ ᴏꜰ Pʜɪʟᴀᴅᴇʟᴘʜɪᴀ, ᴛʜᴇʀᴇ is a clearing in the forest just before one might hit the Poconos. A gathering takes place there during the summer months. A gathering of illegal fireworks sellers.

The clearing in the woods is tented up and turned into a farmer's market of fire power. Anything a budding pyromaniac could want, that would otherwise need a license to be handled under the confines of society, is sold there at a massive discount. In the days leading up to the fourth of July, where there is a surplus of supply and the knowledge that demand in the legal market will soon dramatically decrease, someone in the know could get what is the civilian equivalent of a bomb for a few hundred dollars.

Collin knew this place well.

Having grown up in Philadelphia and spent most of his time in the basement parties where the city's punk rock scene grew to prominence, he was well connected in the underground fireworks market, despite not having lived in the area for over a decade.

If you know, you know.

His sister would not be happy that he brought Audrey along to what was essentially an arms deal, but he knew that Audrey needed to get away.

"We drove three hours out to bum-fuck Pennsylvania for *fireworks*?"

"For the good shit," Collin corrected. He found a sky-rocket and checked it for quality. He grabbed a nearby basket and put the pyrotechnic in it.

"How'd you know about this place?" Audrey asked.

"You don't have a monopoly on misspent youth."

Collin grabbed some M-eighties, aerial shells, and bottle rockets as he and Audrey wandered the market stalls.

Confederate flags hung in various tents. Some even sold them. This put Audrey on edge, despite being deep within Union territory. The sellers and the buyers, it seemed, were from different worlds. Or at least different Americas.

The buyers were city folk who had made the trek out to the middle of nowhere to do business away from the prying eyes of government regulation. The sellers were not from the city. Though there did seem to be a uniform of sorts the sellers all agreed to: jeans, steel-toed boots, and a mildly offensive T-shirt offering up their political leanings for all to see. Audrey decided it would be best to leave dealing with the vendors to her uncle.

"Thanks for getting me out of the house," Audrey said.

"Believe me," Collin said, "I needed out too. Orla's mom is . . . a lot."

Beth had only been staying at Windward House for a few days, but those days had felt like years to the Cassidy clan. She assumed that because this was a bed and breakfast she was to be treated like a royal dignitary and not like what she was: an unwanted woman being given shelter out of charity and the tenuous link shared via grandchildren.

She referred to Kip as "The Boy" and the fact that she used the article *the* was the only thing keeping her from getting punched in the face. She kept saying it was a common expression in Florida. If that were true, then Florida folk don't seem to know when they're being racist.

Probably because they almost always are.

Ignorance is a learned skill that keeps a flawed mind in a state of equilibrium. Beth would fit in quite well with the fireworks vendors. At least based on their fashion sense.

She had asked if "The Boy" could bring breakfast down to her apartment one too many times, and Eliza had decided her meal privileges were revoked. When Beth had a meal request, Eliza would simply state that the oven was busted. This allowed Allan to sit around with his tool belt on, pretending to fix it, while he fixed himself sandwiches. If the family was going to eat, they would wait until Beth either left the house or locked herself away in the basement, before preparations were made. It was an exhausting rouse, but she was a more exhausting woman.

Collin brought the haul from their current tent to the vendor and handed him cash.

"I want to smash her face in with my skateboard," Audrey said while waiting for the transaction to complete. The vendor pulled out a wad of cash to make change for Collin.

"She only gets worse," Collin quipped.

"That can't be possible."

"Just be glad she didn't bring the frog. Imagine the snootiness of a French asshole combined with the ignorance of an arrogant American conservative, who just happens to have the money and power to think he's right, but none of the education."

"Sounds like my kinda guy," the vendor said, handing Collin cash. He had a long white beard and wire rimmed glasses. One might confuse him with Santa Claus. If Santa Claus wore a T-shirt that read: *I may not be a gynecologist, but I know a CUNT when I see one.*

Collin took the money, faked a smile and moved on to another tent with Audrey.

"He's the perfect pissant," Collin whispered, now clear of the vendor's earshot.

"They sound meant to be. How do you know Noah's family so well?"

Audrey knew that Orla and Collin had dated, but she needed more intel. Orla had played her cards close to her vest. Audrey wanted her uncle to open up to her, and she'd learned as a young child with a mass of internet fans who demanded her attention, that the best way to do that was to ask open-ended questions. People loved to talk about themselves if you gave them the chance.

"Orla and I . . . have a history," Collin said.

"Lucky you, history's my favorite subject."

A massive explosion startled both Collin and Audrey. Collin instinctively grabbed Audrey and covered her body with his.

"The fuck was that?!" Audrey asked.

After taking a beat to get his bearings—and make sure neither of them had been hit by shrapnel—Collin surveyed the area. A few yards away, a meth-head wearing only overalls was running towards them. As he got closer, they saw that the man had wrapped a bloodstained T-shirt around what used to be his thumb. The meth-head ran past them, hyperventilating from the shock and adrenaline dump. Collin faux saluted the man as he passed them.

"Freedom. God bless America," he said.

"Should we, like, *help*?"

"You got a medical degree? It's just a thumb, happens all the time."

The meth-head made his way to his ATV. He struggled to rev the engine with his thumbless hand. After gritting his teeth and bearing down on the throttle, he got it going and disappeared down a trail in the forest.

"See. He's fine," Collin said, not so sure.

"Come on," Audrey said, not letting the explosion distract her from the question she had asked earlier. "We're getting to know each other. Consider it more 'research.'"

Collin chortled.

"I do need all the Gen Z trends," he said. "Like, I heard some teens think it's cool to get pregnant on purpose."

Audrey was caught. She put a hand to her chest, trying to stave off the anxiety rising within.

"You're not going to tell my parents, are you?" she said.

"Nah. Not my kid, not my problem."

She took a few deep, calming, breaths. "Thanks, Uncle Collin."

"But . . ." Collin said.

"Damn it." Audrey awaited the dreaded continuation.

"You have to explain it to me. For research," Collin said.

Audrey took another deep breath, trying to calm herself and find a way to communicate her rationale as adeptly as she could.

"I just . . . I don't know. Everyone's always asking us kids what we want to do with our lives. What we're doing to make the world better, you know? And becoming a mindless capitalist drone doesn't interest me. No offense."

"None taken. I sold out. *Hard*. Well, not hard enough. Casey, though, fucking nailed it."

"I honestly can't think of anything more beneficial than raising a kid with the person I love. Bringing someone into the world and making sure they know they're loved. Our family's pretty lucky—most kids I know, their parents are divorced. I know my parents love each other. I know they love me, even if they are pains in the ass. I know I love Noah and I don't see any sense in waiting to pass that love on."

Collin stared blankly at his niece for a long moment before he put his basket down and pulled his cell phone out of his pocket.

"What are you doing?" Audrey asked.

"Writing that down," Collin said as he typed.

He did know about the notes app.

12
COMING TOGETHER

THE END OF THE summer semester was always busy for Orla. Her classes were all finished, but she still had six sections worth of papers to grade while working a full-time lifeguarding schedule. She had just finished grading papers and was inputting the grades into the school's grading software when her cell phone rang.

She was shocked to find Collin's name on the caller ID. More for the simple fact that he hadn't changed his number in a decade, than the fact that he was calling.

She always assumed if she'd ever try to reach out she'd end up talking to some rando who had been assigned his number after he gave it up to embrace Southern California area codes. But there it was, the same contact she'd had transferred from the cloud in multiple iterations of phone upgrades.

Orla wondered what might have happened if she had been the one to call that long-saved number first. Collin had beat her to the punch.

After seeing Noah come home barely able to make it up the steps, she had some thoughts for him. She took a deep breath and answered.

"What did you do to my nephew last night?"

"Can we talk?" he said. His voice was full of angst.

"Ugh . . ." she said, not wanting to rehash their interaction from the C-View. "Collin, I don't think—"

"Not about us."

The tone of his voice, the confidence he had in cutting her off, made her believe him. Orla thought he wanted to rehash the past, but maybe *she* was the one fixating on the past, now that it had been dredged up. She didn't like being reminded of that time in her life—Collin was a living breathing reminder.

"I'm at my office finishing up grades. Can you meet me at the bar off campus? I'll text you the address."

"Already on my way," he said and hung up.

The brevity gave her anxiety. The Collin she remembered had patience and never rushed conversations. The anxiety grew until she remembered the last time she felt this way.

It was when she'd found out she was pregnant.

O RLA LOOKED AT THE double line on the pregnancy test she had covered in urine. She checked the box to be sure. She was, in fact, harboring a fugitive.

She carried the pee stick around the apartment she shared with Collin until she found her way to the kitchen where her letter from BU and his from USC were magnetically linked to one another on the fridge. She touched the letters as if that might magically change what they said.

The reality of the situation hit her like a freight train: she was pregnant, about to start grad school, and her boyfriend was moving three thousand miles away.

They had talked about how they would deal with the long distance, but in the back of her mind Orla always knew they were going to have to face reality and break up. Long distance never worked.

Her eyes welled up with tears she couldn't hold back. Were they from the impending loss of the life she loved, or the hormones that were now ransacking her nervous system?

She knew this wasn't something she wanted. Even if Collin were coming with her to Boston, she did not want a child. She also did not want to deal with the emotional fallout of telling her friends and family.

Orla wanted to deal with this alone. It was no one else's business. Not even Collin's. It's not like he knew much about her cycle anyway.

Stop. She needed to stop justifying things to herself. What needed to happen now was action. Swift and decisive. The first thing would be making an appointment at planned parenthood. She needed to know all her options.

She went on her laptop and booked an appointment for the next day. There. An action was taken. She was in control. That was what was most important. Everything would be OK. That's what she had to keep telling herself.

Everything will be OK.

Everything was not OK. Orla felt like she was dying. She couldn't catch her breath. Her chest heaved while her brain thought it needed more and more oxygen. Her heart raced so fast she was sure it was going to give out completely. She knew the symptoms from helping Collin when he had one, but had never had one herself. This was her first panic attack. It really did feel like she was dying.

You need to control this. You're not dying. Breathe.

She knew she needed to slow down her breathing. She could do this. She would remain in control.

Breathe. Breathe. In. Out. In. Out.

Orla called her sister with tears in her eyes. She could barely get it all out between sobs. She needed to tell someone what was happening. Siobhan knew what she was going through. She was nursing Noah and happy for the distraction.

"I'll meet you there tomorrow. It'll be OK," Siobhan said. Nothing else. No judgement, no pity, no assumptions. Her sister was going to take her to her appointment, and she could make a rational, informed decision there.

Orla let herself breathe. She felt like her lungs were working now. She took some time to wash her face in the bathroom sink and took a deep breath. She repeated to herself in the mirror, *'Everything will be OK.'*

The apartment door opened. Orla's heart dropped.

"Or, you home? I got us pizza and beer."

Everything is not OK.

Orla opened the bathroom window and threw the pregnancy test, box and all, out the window into the alley behind their house. No evidence. She would talk to him after.

C OLLIN SPOTTED ORLA AT the end of the college bar. Fledgling twenty-one-year-olds were celebrating the end of summer session. There was a beer pong station, a game of flip-cup going on, while others played corn hole and drank on the patio outside.

Collin sat down next to Orla. She wore jeans and a T-shirt with a form-fitting blazer over it. Collin was instantly taken aback by Orla in her professorial attire: she was approachable yet chic. The kind of professor teenage boys have all sorts of fantasies about.

He might need to update the lifeguard memories in his own fantastical musings with this new outfit.

Collin ordered a beer. He turned to Orla, not sure how to start this conversation.

"OK," he said. "I promised Audrey I wouldn't tell her parents about this. So, before I say anything, I need you to promise me you won't tell your sister or Jesse."

Orla could see the sincerity in his eyes. He really did not want to break his niece's confidence. "Telling Siobhan more bad news won't make my life any easier," she said. "I won't rat the little brats out. Girl Scout's honor"

"On Thin Mint's honor?" Collin smirked.

"Wow. You're serious. Damn. This must be juicy."

"I need your word," he said. "You tell, you can never have a thin mint again."

"OK. OK. I swear. On the best of all Girl Scout Cookies."

"Audrey and Noah got pregnant on purpose. So they could get married."

Orla downed her drink and ordered another upon hearing this. What the fuck?

"But Noah's usually so . . ." she thought how best to describe her nephew, landing on "responsible." She took another long sip from her fresh beer. "Why would they *want* to get pregnant?"

"Not everyone is devoid of parental instincts," Collin said, in jest. His smile bought some of her patience.

"Oh my god, you're so funny," she said.

"It's not like it changes anything," he said.

"Of course it does. They did this on purpose! It wasn't just some . . ." She trailed off, trying to find the right words.

"Accident? Mistake? Disaster?" Collin said.

The words sat in the air for a long moment before Orla put her beer down, looked him in the eyes, and with all sincerity said, "Fuck you."

"That tends to end poorly for both of us."

Across the bar, a group of fraternity brothers shotgunned their beers, while Orla and Collin sat in awkward silence. They chanted "Chug" and they chugged. Collin and Orla watched this, instead of continuing with their trip down memory lane.

"Dr. Ruane?!" a voice from behind them yelled over the sound system. It was the girl with green hair from Orla's seminar class, whose name she could never remember. "Oh my god," she said, "it *is* you! You have to let us buy you a beer."

The green haired girl pointed to a booth where the rest of Orla's seminar class was sitting, drinking, and beckoning her over.

"It's not really the best time," Orla said.

"Come on, it's my twenty-first birthday. We're all here!"

"I don't think—" Orla started, only to be cut off by Collin.

"How do you know Orla?" he said.

"Dr. Ruane's our seminar professor. Beckett!"

"We'll be right over," Collin said, a mischievous smile on his face.

"Yes! I'll grab us a pitcher," and with that, the green-haired girl moved to get the bartender's attention.

"What are you doing?" Orla protested.

"You won't talk to me about your life. Might as well talk to someone who will."

Collin got up and moved to the booth, shaking hands with the students and compelling Orla to join him. He watched as she reluctantly left her spot at the bar and walked towards them.

Seeing this group of kids so excited to see Orla outside of the classroom reminded Collin about the day he'd decided he wanted to marry Orla. The ring he bought shortly after was currently sitting in the drawer of his computer desk back in Los Angeles.

C OLLIN AND ORLA WERE naked under the blanket they kept on the sex-stained couch in their small apartment. The graduate school acceptance letters they'd just received were tossed aside to the floor. Collin stretched, he was spent. He gave Orla a kiss on the forehead, slid off the edge of the couch and stood up. Orla slapped his ass.

"Well done, sir."

"I told you, don't call me sir," he said with a wink.

They both smiled at the inside joke. Collin marched his toned and hairy ass over to the kitchen and grabbed two blue Gatorades out of the fridge. He tossed one to Orla.

"My hero," she said. Collin chugged his down in seconds.

Orla took a long gulp and sat up to grab the remote from the coffee table. She turned on the TV and the 'Casino Night' episode of *The Office* was on. Pam was about to break Jim's heart.

"Are we gonna talk about it?" Collin said.

"Seven-point-five out of ten. You had the pacing, but your power wasn't there. I could tell you were holding back," Orla deadpanned.

"I mean about the fact that we're going to be in different states next year."

"Opposite coasts," Orla corrected.

"It's gonna be fine," Collin said. He sat down next to her, pulled her head to his chest and kissed her crown.

"I know. I know," Orla said. "We've got all year to figure it out. Let's just be here. Together. Now."

"OK," he said.

They watched as Jim told Pam he was in love with her, and Pam said "What?!"

They both teared up. Like they did every time. All Collin could think was how, one day, he'd write a scene like this, one that would affect everyone who saw it this deeply. And he knew he'd be writing about Orla when he did.

Orla fell asleep on Collin's chest. He held her head while shifting himself off the couch and laid her down. Orla could sleep through a bombing raid.

Collin ran to their bedroom and rummaged through Orla's desk until he found her fashion ruler.

He took the ruler back into the living room, gently wrapped it around Orla's left ring-finger. He smiled while he noted the measurement and committed it to memory.

As he pulled the ruler away from her finger, Orla ripped a rancid fart while she slept.

Collin thought her unconscious expression was angelic. But the smell was demonic.

"For better or worse," Collin said, covering his nose with his hand.

"DRINK, BITCH!" ORLA SCREAMED at the green-haired girl as she sunk another ping pong ball into the opposing team's cup. The whole bar was watching the game. The crowd was rapt and roared with applause. Orla was drunker than she had planned on getting.

Collin had a way of making things she'd normally overthink seem fun. She knew it was unethical to play drinking games with her students, but the semester was over. They were all adults of legal age. Technically, as Collin had pointed out, she was doing nothing wrong.

Orla never cut loose like this on her own, outside of the C-View. Those were her people. She felt safe around her people. But Collin always made her feel safe, whenever she was with him. He had this odd charisma that made the people around him feel like he would take care of them.

"All right. One more and we win," Collin said. "We got this."

Green Hair and Michael took a moment with their pong balls. They whispered strategy with one another. They had one cup left. Collin and Orla still had four on the field, albeit in a haphazard shape.

"Diamond," Michael called out.

Collin smirked as he moved the four loose cups into the shape of a diamond. The rerack meant they were afraid. They needed the best shot they could get in order to make back-to-backs and keep possession. Collin wasn't worried. Green Hair and Michael, however, took it one step further.

At the same time, Michael took a normal shot while Green Hair made a bounce shot—worth two cups if it landed—and both hit their mark. Three cups down on one shot and they got both balls back.

"That was fucking beautiful," Collin slurred, as he threw the pong balls back to his opponents. He wasn't even mad. "You taught these kids right."

"I didn't teach them that," Orla said. "I don't need a bounce to win."

She glared at Green Hair. The student and the teacher stared one another down in a show of dominance.

"As Samuel Beckett once said, Professor, *Fail better*," Green Hair said as she landed her shot in the only remaining cup. The crowd roared.

Everyone was on the edge of their seats.

"Fuck!" Collin said.

"It's OK," Orla said. "Michael can't perform under pressure. I gave them a pop quiz once, to make sure they'd done the reading, little baby had a panic attack."

The crowd jeered at Michael.

"You gonna let her do you like that, Mike?" Kayden said from the sidelines.

"Shut up. I got this." Michael lined up his shot. Let it fly.

It circled the rim and . . . flew out onto the table. The crowd sighed, disappointed.

"Redemption!" Collin called out. He pulled Orla aside and solemnly handed her a pong ball.

"We both have to make this. Clean," he said. "Then we win. Otherwise, it's overtime."

He put his hand on Orla's shoulder. The intensity of a coach at the Olympics shown through his baby blues. "Are you with me?"

"I'm with you," Orla said.

"Together?" Collin said.

"Together," Orla answered.

They both released their shots one after the other.

Collin's arc was low and tight, Orla's high and long. Collin's ball hit the water in the cup first and settled. Orla's hit Collin's ball and bounced from side to side on the edge of the solo cup.

It took four full bounces before it finally fell . . . in the cup.

They won.

The crowd screamed. Drinks were thrown. It was chaos. The bartenders tried but failed to get their customers under control. Fledging twenty-one-year-old's can't be controlled.

All Collin and Orla could do was smile while they looked into each other's eyes. They inched closer to one another, lips pursed; that old tension right where they left it now that alcohol coursed through their veins.

The crowd lifted each of them into the air. Before they knew it, they were being crowd-surfed by the whole bar in opposite directions, as if this world couldn't risk letting them get any closer.

They couldn't help but laugh.

C OLLIN WAS DRUNK AS he took his first steps into Orla's office. It was small and packed with papers, books, and a desktop computer that was sorely in need of an update. They were both in far more jovial a mood than they had been at the beginning of the night. Collin learned how beloved Orla was by her students and Orla was outed as the campus playwright and director of the small, underfunded, theater program.

"I can't believe you're still writing," Collin said. "If you want, I can get you paid!"

"I haven't finished anything creative in a long time. Tons of criticism, though. Publish or perish, you know?"

"A writer and a critic. *'For never was a story of more woe.'*"

"Dodged a bullet, didn't we?" Orla smiled. She had fun.

"Those kids really love you," Collin said. He grinned at her the way she remembered him doing when they were younger, happier, and drunker. She avoided acknowledging the compliment.

"You cannot drive," she said.

"I'm fine," Collin said before falling into her desk, trying to regain composure, and then crashing to the floor. Laid out on his back, he decided he agreed with her.

"I don't think I should drive," he said.

"I really have to pee. My phone's dead. I'll call us a ride on the office line once I get back."

"Can I use your computer?" Collin asked, still laying on the floor. He held up his blank-screened cell phone. "Mine's dead too and I have to check my email."

"The password's on a Post-it. I'm about to piss myself. If you can stand, you can use the computer."

She turned on her heels and ran to the nearest restroom, leaving Collin alone on the floor.

Laying on the carpeted office floor, Collin felt the Auntie Em's coming on. The world started to spin and distort, his stomach churned in rhythm with the mental tornado he was the center of. Seeing threes of everything, he knew he needed to get up off the ground.

He sat up with what felt like a herculean effort. Grabbing the desk for support, he stumbled to his feet and crashed into the computer chair.

After booting up Orla's computer, he tried to read the password, but the characters all merged and floated in separate directions in front of his face. He slapped himself to force his eyes to focus, input the password, and navigated to the internet icon, which had a file labeled PLAYS below it and another labeled NYU APP next to it.

He considered the ramifications of going through Orla's personal files, but his drunken brain decided *why not?*

He double-clicked the NYU APP file open. There were several documents, too many to go through at the moment. She was applying for a job in New York. *Good*, he thought. She needed to get out of here. He closed that file and moved to the one that actually piqued his interest.

"For research," he said to himself as he clicked through the numerous plays. He checked to make sure Orla wasn't coming and, in his drunken haze, Collin opened his Gmail account and copied the PLAYS file into his google drive. He closed the file just as Orla returned to the office.

Orla grabbed the office line and dialed a phone number from memory.

"Hey," she said, into the phone. "Can you come pick me up at my office. Me and my . . . friend. OK. See you soon."

"Who's coming to get us?" Collin asked.

"My boyfriend," Orla said.

13
CARNIVAL FRIENDS

C OLLIN HAD NEVER SAT in the back of a police car before. It was a new, unnerving sensation. For all his misspent youth, he was able to keep himself from ever having the experience Orla had just provided for him.

He would have preferred an Uber. This was why he needed to keep a charger on him at all times. Charge your phone or end up riding in the back of a cop car.

The upholstery felt coarse and he was having trouble keeping his equilibrium, despite the shock of Orla having a cop for a boyfriend sobering him up. Rain started to fall on the windshield, creating a rhythm that distracted Collin's alcohol-addled brain for the briefest of moments.

The officer turned back to Collin. His chiseled features and thick hairline housed the naïve face of a man, or perhaps a boy, more than a decade Collin's junior. He was about to say something when Orla slid into the passenger seat and kissed him.

Collin sat trapped in the car while they made out, Orla drunk and feeling revelry, the cop a child who mistook her intoxication for gratification. They finished swapping spit and Dale turned again to look at Collin, remembering the *friend* of Orla's in the backseat, to say, "Storm's getting close."

Dale's voice irritated Collin. It was high pitched, cocksure, and full of false bravado. Collin realized he wasn't so much a cop as a child actor playing the role of officer. He wore the uniform and had the gun, but there was no sense that this man-child had any understanding of the gravity of his position.

"Dale," Orla said, "This is Collin."

Dale opened the glass divider to extend his arm for a handshake.

"Just got off my shift. How do you know this sexy lady?"

Collin took the officer's hand in his and shook. He could feel in the shake that he was the stronger man, and that inference combined with the alcohol coursing through his blood gave him the confidence to be obnoxious.

"Carnally," Collin said. Orla glared at him, angry, but he didn't care. He stared directly into Dale's eyes as he took his arm back over to the front of the car.

"Oh, sweet," Dale said. "What carnival did you guys meet at?"

Collin stifled a laugh as he looked into Orla's formerly angry eyes. The emotion shifted to embarrassment. Collin could tell this was a relationship of physical connection, not mental.

"Oh, you're lucky you're pretty," she said, giving Dale another quick kiss then looking back at Collin to shut him up with a stare.

"She tells me that all the time."

"I'll bet," Collin said.

"I'm gonna turn on the siren," Dale said, before throwing the switch that turned the blue and reds—as well as the annoying emergency vehicle siren—on.

"It's loud as fuck, but we'll get back in, like, five minutes, tops!"

Dale slammed on the gas, forcing Collin deeper into the backseat of the cruiser. While the tires hydroplaned, Orla turned to meet Collin's aled-up eyes. She'd had a great night with him, she really hoped that this wouldn't change that.

He tried to silently tell her she could do a lot better than this guy. The look she returned to his disappointed gaze told Collin that she was very aware of that fact, but enjoyed the thrill of the occasional five-minute drive, sirens blaring, with no real destination in mind.

Collin understood this all too well. He'd had his fair share of Dales back in LA.

The two of them came to a silent détente as the sirens blared and the cruiser sped through back roads.

Collin stumbled back into his room at Windward House. It was late and he avoided anyone else being awake. He thought it was odd when Dale dropped him off that he mentioned he had been here recently. Collin assumed that some tenant of his parents had a wild night and the local police had to make sure he got home all right. This was the reality of running a bed and breakfast in a resort town.

Having had time in the car, he was now at that most spectacular level of drunkenness, where inhibition had drowned, but thought flowed freely. He knew what he had to do and moved directly to his laptop.

He booted up a Final Draft document. Lana had asked for a story area, but the story was clear in his mind. He was going to write a fully fleshed-out outline. The characters were easily defined because their real-life avatars were all around him.

He typed away, lost in the fury of creative tunnel vision. He built sets in his head, acts, act-outs, buttons-on jokes, callbacks. He developed his characters as best one could in a twenty-two-minute pilot format; gave them idiosyncrasies that would make them pop off the page; brought their backstories to the foreground through light-hearted jokes and seemingly throwaway lines that would come back in the penultimate scenes to have more weight than the audience would have originally given them.

While his body and conscious mind were occupied with the task of writing, Collin's subconscious was dealing with its own origin stories.

C OLLIN USED TO WALK down the streets of Philadelphia with the idiotic smile of a man who had everything he could ever want: he'd gotten in to his dream school and he had a ring in his pocket that he was going to use to propose to his dream girl. His life was a dream.

Little did he know, it was one he was about to wake up from.

His phone rang while he was walking with that idiotic smile painted across his face. He checked the ID: Jesse was calling him. Collin thought nothing of it. He and

Siobhan's husband had become close. Dating sisters made you brothers.

"J, what's up?" he said into the phone. He was confused when Jesse asked him if he was OK. "Yeah, I'm fine, why?"

As he listened to what Jesse was telling him, that smile faded. He became horrified and bewildered.

"What are you talking about, she's not pregnant. . ."

"That's impossible," he said before listening to Jesse some more. "You're sure?" He listened while Jesse confirmed.

"No. She didn't tell me. . ." Jesse realized in that moment that he'd fucked up by saying anything to Collin. He tried to backtrack. Maybe he was mistaken. Collin knew he wasn't.

"Where?" he asked, with curt anger. Jesse sighed and told him and Collin hung up without another word. Collin pulled the ring box out of his pocket and, if he had had the strength, he would have crumpled it up like a ball of paper. Instead, he took a deep breath, placed it back in his pocket, and ran to get to his car.

Collin drove to the Planned Parenthood parking lot. The spot that Jesse told him Orla had gone to with her sister. He said she was there to have an abortion for a pregnancy Collin was not aware of. Collin was hopeful that

Jesse was mistaken, but he knew that hope to be in vain. Jesse, a man of few words and direct action, was never one to make any kind of statement without complete proof of the statement's veracity.

Collin found a parking spot that gave him vantage of the building's entrance. It was two o'clock.

He could not believe that Orla would not only keep a pregnancy secret from him, but also terminate it without even consulting him. He would have supported her no matter her decision, but the fact that she hadn't even told him . . . that was unforgivable.

Collin and Orla told each other everything. If she could do this, what else was she hiding from him? How could he ever believe anything she said? Trust would be gone. Trust was everything.

Collin sat there for hours on his solo stake-out. It was five-thirty and he was ready to give up. He'd been holding in a piss the whole time. Then he saw Siobhan escorting a stone-faced Orla out of the medical facility. His heart became a black hole.

He watched as they waded through the small gathering of daily protestors who made camp outside Planned Parenthood, and got to their car about fifty yards away from his. Orla's head was lowered to avoid the protestor's eyes.

Her stoic face and puffy eyes made it clear that everything Jesse told him was true.

Collin considered confronting them; getting out of the car and joining the jeering voices of the misguided protestors. But what would that accomplish? The writing was on the wall. She'd lied to him, she'd hidden this from him. She had, without words, made it clear that if she did love him, she didn't love him the way he deserved to be loved. She didn't love him fully. She didn't love him honestly. She didn't trust him with the truth.

He looked at the ring and tears filled his eyes. They were done. She didn't need to tell him, why should he tell her?

Collin pulled the ring out of its case and held the diamond in his hand. He threw it at his passenger side window. The diamond hit fast in the center. A large web-shaped crack formed in the glass. The cracks slowly expanded. His window, like his heart, was breaking more and more.

An anger he'd never felt before rose in him as he watched Orla and Siobhan drive off. He gripped the steering wheel and used all his might to try to rip it from the dash. When that attempt failed, he slammed his fists into the horn. The sound terrified the parking lot protestors. Fearing they'd be chased down by a car, the protestors ran for cover in a practiced, almost military, fashion. Collin couldn't care less. He was seething.

The anger was easier to understand than the despair and grief it was protecting.

C OLLIN FINISHED READING OVER the document for the fourth time, when he simply said '*Fuck it,*' to himself.

The sun was rising over the ocean. Collin enjoyed the view his room offered. He'd done all he could—this was what his studio asked for, *more* than they'd asked for. He wasn't going to do any better with more editing or polishing. He saved the document as a PDF, attached it to an email addressed to Lana with Gene copied, and sent it off.

He unceremoniously crashed onto his bed and was asleep before his head hit the pillow.

While Collin slept, the sun rose. The bright light was soon muddled and dimmed as storm clouds moved in from the southeast. Winds rose and rain fell.

The hurricane had arrived.

14
LANDFALL

RAIN DRIZZLED OUTSIDE NOAH'S window as he sat down at his desk to FaceTime his father. The sun had barely risen, but Noah couldn't sleep. He knew his father would be awake, so this seemed as good a time as any to tell him he would be a grandfather. The ringing ceased and Noah's computer screen was filled with the frantic scene in his father's wheelhouse.

Merchant marines were running in the background as lighting struck massive waves in the distance. Those nearby crashed the deck. The frame could not remain steady, it jolted to and fro with the unpredictable ocean's attacks.

"All hands to positions," Jesse ordered. "McConnell, starboard. Thirty degrees, now!"

He turned to face the screen, finally acknowledging Noah's call.

"Son, I'm going to have to call you back. We're getting smacked around by this storm."

"Dad, it's important!" Noah said. He watched his father and crew race to outmaneuver mother nature from the comfort of his bedroom.

"Whatever it is, I'm sure it can—" the frame crashed to the ground and immediately disconnected. Noah was left with the fear that his father was in mortal danger, but also the instinctual certitude that he would survive, find out about his son's present circumstance, and then simply return to sea without so much as a word.

Noah could feel the disappointment his father would have, and it crushed him worse than any wave ever could.

Noah paced back and forth, balled his fists until his nails dug into the flesh of his palms and he could take no more. He took books and threw them around the room to dispel his pent-up rage.

Orla, having been awoken by the sound of literature attacking dry wall, entered her nephew's room in a haze.

"What the hell is going on?" she said. Then she saw the tears in her nephew's eyes. "Oh . . ."

"He's never fucking here," Noah said. "Never! All I want to do is tell him what's going on."

Orla, not normally the one who consoled her nephew in fits of rage, impulsively hugged the boy. She held him close until the anger subsided and tears flowed freely.

"I know. I know," she assured him. She didn't, of course. How could she know what it was like to be a sixteen-year-old boy with a child on the way? Though she said it with such confidence that Noah believed her, and that was all that mattered.

After a few ghoulish sobs, Noah was finally able to breath in a steady rhythm again. The panic attack was nearing its end.

"I'm going to be there for my kid. Unlike him. I'll make sure of it."

"Hey! Your dad isn't here so that you can be," she made him look her in the eyes as she reminded him of the harsh reality of parenthood, "life ain't cheap. Everything you have here is because he goes away. He does it for you and your mother. Because that's what a father does. He sacrifices to provide for his family. Be glad you have your dad. Your mom and I would give anything to see ours again."

The chiding rang true to Noah, as much as he wished it didn't. He wanted to stay angry. Anger was simpler than understanding. Anger was simpler than dealing with the complexities of family dynamics. Anger was simple, and that's why it shouldn't be trusted.

"He's going to kill me when he finds out."

Orla laughed at her nephew, knowing how unfounded his fear was.

"He's not going to kill you. He'll just maim you," she said. "Come on. The storm's here and we don't have to work. Let's make your mom take us out for breakfast."

"WAIT—" JESSE WATCHED AS his phone flew off its mount on the command center. It smashed into shards. Noah would not be happy that he'd been disconnected so abruptly again. His wife would not be happy that he'd lost another phone. This was the third in a year.

He rolled his eyes and focused on the task at hand.

The angry sea was a lot like Siobhan, Jesse thought. He loved them both most when things were turbulent. This storm gave him the same butterflies as his impassioned wife. Only the sea didn't rant and rave about her friend's husband seeing a therapist behind her back.

"What's he hiding?! It'd almost be better if he was cheating. He's *emotionally* cheating!" he remembered her saying.

He missed the sound of her voice. Even when what she was saying was ridiculous or obnoxious. Siobhan told Jesse everything. Things she shouldn't tell him, things he wished she'd keep to herself. If anyone told Siobhan a secret, Jesse knew it within the hour, whether he wanted to or not. He was her mental vault. Without his phone, he'd be without her mundane stories.

Three months at sea never got easier, but it made the reunions all the more joyous. It was a miracle they'd only had one child. The three months at home were spent making the most of lost time: distance and hearts.

The sea and Siobhan were both a challenge. Jesse never backed down from a challenge. Challenges need only be navigated. After twenty years at sea and eighteen years of marriage, the maps were drawn in his subconscious.

Jesse didn't have time to worry about whatever it was that his son was so worked up about. It could wait until he was back ashore. It's not like he'd killed someone or gotten a girl pregnant.

Taking or creating life—those would make the cut.

Jesse laughed at the absurdity of his son trying to tell him something like that. Not a chance in hell. Probably just got into a college they wouldn't be able to afford.

Noah and those damn computers. Higher education was a scam. He was glad he had gone to the merchant marine academy when he did. Otherwise, he might have ended up like his sister-in-law.

Jesse tried to navigate outside the path of the hurricane, but mother nature had other plans. The winds had shifted, and he was in charge of getting his twenty-five-man crew back to shore safely. Something one-hundred-and-fifty-miles-per-hour winds and nine-ty-foot swells made quite difficult.

Jesse stood at the helm, watching as the bow of the ship pierced through a wave. A category-four hurricane was just another day at the floating office. He barked orders to his team. They executed with precision. A well-oiled machine. That was what leadership got you.

Commanding respect was far more important than issuing commands.

Jesse had built this crew over the better part of a decade. There were no other men he'd rather spend this time away from his wife and child with. Mikey, DeVonte, and Josè were all his bunkmates at the academy. Noah called each of them uncle. Everyone else was either from the same year or fresh meat straight from the academy, doing all the grunt work he'd so long left behind.

Chain of command made life simple: do what you're told and you'll survive. Everyone on his crew did what they were told. That's how they'd survived this long.

The storm was unrelenting, the waves were treacherous. All his electrical equipment had been knocked out. Jesse used his maneuvering board to figure out his next move. He took account of their heading, the wind direction, speed, and traced out a course. Judging by the sheer ferocity of the storm, Jesse assumed they were near the center. Buys-Ballot's law applied if he wanted to take avoiding action.

They needed to put the wind on their starboard bow and maximize speed. The ship didn't need to outrun the storm, just to get out of the worst part of it. Jesse gave the order to Mikey, who then gave an order to DeVonte, who then gave an order to Josè, who took off to give his orders to the first engineer.

Chain of command. It was like watching an intricate set of dominos. Soon enough, they were on the heading he had charted, and while the storm was heavy, they were on course to make it home.

Whether or not it was the right decision, he wouldn't know for some time. A lesson every leader learns is that you can't let fear stop you from acting. You can only hope to live with the consequences of those actions. All you can do, when you're in the middle of a storm, is decide what to do.

15
UNBELIEVABLE

COLLIN COULDN'T DECIDE WHAT to do. He stared at the caller I.D. as his phone rang. His heart raced. Lana was calling. No executive had ever called him the same day he'd turned in pages. Hell, no one had done it the same *week*. It often took a fortnight just to receive an email acknowledging receipt. Then there would be two to three weeks of radio silence before an email would come through to schedule a call that would then be rescheduled at least three or four times before the call would happen.

Lana, on her personal cell phone, was calling, and Collin couldn't wait any longer. He answered.

"I asked you for a story area and you sent me a full outline?!" she said.

"I know it's a little long," Collin said. "But—"

"It's fucking *perfect*," Lana said, and let that sit in the air for a moment before adding "We're sending you to script. One note."

Collin was aghast. This was not how things worked. There was never just one note. You never got sent to script off the first draft of an outline. Writing for television was a team sport. Or, at least, most executives thought it ought to be. Collin couldn't believe what he was hearing and knew better than to protest.

"Shoot," he said.

"The grandmother-in-law character. She's a little unbelievable. Maybe tone her down a bit."

As Lana was getting into her note for the character based on Beth, an altercation going on downstairs took Collin's attention away from his executive's notes. He heard someone yell "Go fuck yourself," but forced himself to ignore it and tune into the task at hand.

"Like, no one would actually call another mother a shitty mother to their face," Lana said.

"You've never been around my family," Collin said calmly into his phone. He moved to the hall and looked down the stairwell to find his sister chasing Orla's mother with a small cast iron skillet at the foot of the stairs. A crash came from downstairs. Something metal had been thrown and clanged on the floor.

"What was that?" Lana asked.

"The unbelievable," Collin said. "Hey, Lana, looks like I've got a situation here. Anything else?"

"Just get me a draft. Two weeks. No later. You're behind for this development season and I want this on the air before I croak."

"Consider it done. Gotta go," Collin hung up.

He took a moment to let himself enjoy this win before the sound of something expensive crashing to the floor shook him back to reality.

"Are you calling me a shitty mother?!" he heard Val say.

"If the boot fits, dear, shove it up your ass," Beth said.

Proud to have predicted this dialogue, even if Lana would never believe it, he raced out of the room.

C OLLIN CAME DOWNSTAIRS TO find a war going on in the dining room.

A breakfast spread was destroyed by shattered glass on the dinner table. Beth was in the midst of a heated argument with Kip and Valerie. Collin was followed down the stairs by Allan and Eliza, who had also heard the glass breaking.

"The whore apple doesn't fall far from the whore tree," Beth shouted at Valerie from the safety of the opposite end of the table. This filled Collin with righteous fury.

"What did you say?" he said.

"I said your sister and her daughter are whores. Though from the rags she wears, I doubt she makes a profit."

Valerie jumped onto the table and grabbed a butter knife.

"I will cut you, bitch," she said as she kicked over plates of eggs and bacon to make good on her threat.

Beth must have walked in and saw that the kitchen did, in fact, work, they had simply refused to keep cooking for her. Collin fireman-carried his sister off the table and held her back from buttering Beth's bread. He turned to Beth with a fire in his eyes while his sister writhed in his grasp.

"You need to get out of here."

"I'm not going anywhere," Beth said.

"Leave. It's what your best at, isn't it?"

This struck a nerve and Beth's stoic face gave way to the most emotion anyone had seen in days.

"Ohhhh," Valerie said, calming down, but still hanging off her brother's shoulder. "Is someone a shitty mother and projecting onto me?"

"You don't know the half of it," Collin said.

"And that's all you know. *Half* of it," Beth spat.

"Please, fill in the blanks I don't know."

Collin put Valerie down and began to make a list of the counts against Beth with his fingers.

"You divorced a man dying of brain cancer," One finger. "Shacked up with some French fuck in Florida," Two Fingers. "And left your daughters alone to watch their father slowly die," Three fingers.

"What part am I missing, exactly? Cause, you know, I actually went to the funeral."

"Yeah, well, I raised those daughters while he played hero to tourists and lived at that frat house of a fire department eighty hours a week. Their father no longer being alive didn't change much for me."

Nothing she could say would provide an adequate defense to the counts against her. They were all technically true, if a bit overstated. So she played the victim.

"But when shit hits the fan," Beth said, "everyone comes crawling back to Mommy."

"I could purposefully throw my pregnant daughter into a gorilla enclosure and still only be the second biggest cunt in the room."

She dropped the butter knife on the table and it clanked against shards of ceramic.

Eliza, recognizing the physical threats were over, grabbed Collin by the shoulder and dragged him into the kitchen. She held the door open for a moment.

"Beth, you're not going anywhere. I'll be right back and we'll all calm down."

She closed the door and spoke directly to her son in hushed tones.

"Go out and get supplies. The hurricane is supposed to get bad tonight, we need to board up the windows."

Collin couldn't believe his mother. Had she been listening to anything that was happening out there?

"She cannot stay here, Mom!"

"Honey," Eliza said with all the motherly warmth she could muster. "Just go. Calm down. Let me handle this."

"She called Audrey—"

"That's why she's staying right here."

"Mom!"

"And she'll be getting a bill in the mail for every day, as soon as she heads back home."

A jaunty smile snuck across Eliza's face. "Do you know the holiday rates we charge per night for the basement apartment?"

She held out the truck keys for Collin.

He took them and matched her grin with one of his own.

16
You Shouldn't Be Here

AUDREY LEFT THE HOUSE early that day with her aunt. She was feeling like a prisoner in Windward House, and Casey was the only adult who could conceivably be considered childish enough to relate to a teenager on a personal level.

They started with a quick stop at the beach, but with the hurricane warning in full effect there wasn't much they could do. Instead, they found their way to the Washington Street Mall. Audrey loved this mall. It was the kind of small town, mom-and-pop-owned shopping district that bigger cities tried to shamelessly replicate and capitalize on. When she was younger, her parents had taken her to visit her uncle Collin out in California and he had taken her to The Grove, which was almost an exact rip-off of the cobblestoned streets she and her aunt now carried a multitude of bags across.

The wind picked up and the skies grew grayer and more foreboding than they had been that morning. Casey was a smoker, and the wind blew a loosie out of her hand as she tried to light it.

"Fuck," Casey said.

She tried to save the smoke from the rivers running between the cobblestones, but quickly gave up her gallant attempt and replaced it with another from her Tory Burch clutch. She took a deep, almost orgasmic inhale as she lit the cigarette.

Audrey hated cigarette smoke regardless, but now that she was breathing for two she felt she had all the right in the world to passive aggressively cough in her aunt's direction.

"Just cause you're pregnant doesn't mean I can't slowly kill myself."

Casey took profound pleasure in each drag, as if Audrey's abhorrence of her habit made it all the more engaging.

"I'd complain," Audrey said, "but you bought me all these clothes I won't be able to wear again for a year."

"If you're lucky," Casey added with a cloud of cigarette smoke. "Bitches blow up when they start their brood."

Audrey stopped walking and leered at her aunt.

"I'm just saying," Casey continued, "cardio is key."

Audrey shook her head. Crass Casey can't be contained. Making a big deal out of what she said was never worth it. This was something Audrey had learned as a small child watching her mother and aunt get into verbal battles that would make Vikings blush. She started walking in step again.

"Real talk," Casey added, "I've wiped your ass. Which, you're finally going to know the joy of. So, I deserve to know: what do you want to do? With or without the baby in the picture."

Audrey smiled. While Casey had made it all about her, as was her way, she had done what only Collin—who only wanted to know so he could use it for character development—had seen fit to do. She asked Audrey what she wanted to do with her life.

"Plan is to skate and make content while Noah's in school," Audrey said.

"Won't you have a, I don't know, *baby* to take care of?" Casey asked.

"What do you think the content will be about? Skating and taking care of the baby. Then, when the baby is a little older, I can get a degree in business and either take over Dad's place and, you know, franchise it. Or Dyrdek it—start my own brand and try to expand. I've got the social following so marketing will be simple."

"Yeah? And how in the hell do you plan to maintain that following while you're playing house or on bedrest? The audience for rebellious, punk, skater girls doesn't have much overlap with the trad-wife momma bear demographic."

"I'll be the one to blend those demos," Audrey said with an arrogance only teenagers are capable of genuinely believing. "Dad put me on a skateboard as a baby and forced a camera down my throat my entire life. You think I don't know how to bring different demos together? L'Oréal and Nike sponsor me. I've been doing this since I was literally an infant."

"I don't know. Pregnant teens don't usually get lionized by society. You're going to get a lot of hate. Parents aren't going to want their kids following in your footsteps," Casey said.

There was no emotion in her words, just the cold calculation of a woman who crunched numbers and made a lot of money by being right about human behavior.

"As long as it isn't an obituary, it's good publicity," Audrey shrugged.

Casey had one hell of a poker face when it came to business. Audrey assumed this was a power she had perfected after years in boardroom battles.

"When you get to the point you want to expand your empire and need capital, call your favorite aunt," Casey said. "I'll want good percentages, though."

"That'll start once this one is in school," Audrey rubbed the nearly undetectable bump under her jeans.

"Waiting until the little one becomes the state's problem eight hours a day. You're smarter than you look," Casey said with a wink. "I'll introduce you to some of my friends in P.R. Let's see if we can make you into a household name."

Audrey couldn't contain her smile. Now she knew, despite how her parents might feel or how the world might see her, that she was making the right choices. Casey didn't make bad investments.

Audrey and Casey window-shopped for a few minutes before walking past a handsome police officer who doubled back when he recognized Casey. She didn't even notice him.

"Hey!" The officer said. He was young, even for Casey, Audrey thought. The mere fact that a cop was talking to them put Audrey on edge.

"You never got back to me about," he said, noticing Audrey, "You know . . ." he made a hole with his left index and thumb while passing his right index in and out of it. Audrey rolled her eyes. Did he think she was five years old?

"Eww," Casey said. "You're a cop?!"

"You fucked a cop?!" Audrey said.

"I didn't know he was a cop!"

"Dale," he said, and offered Audrey his hand to shake. She glared at him, incredulous.

"I left you on read for a reason," Casey said. But Audrey could tell there was a spark between her aunt and this unfortunately handsome man-boy who seemed too dull to be intimidating.

Audrey had learned from her father at a young age to be overly pleasant, but curt, when dealing with police. Most of them only had a high school education. Cops should have to have law degrees. Gutless guys with guns and badges who could kill with impunity should at least be forced to learn the law they espoused to enforce.

Unfortunately, as her father told her, being right wasn't worth your life. She said nothing as her aunt and the boy in blue continued to flirt.

"You wanna . . . take a ride? In the cruiser. I'm hoping to get off soon."

Audrey could not believe anyone would be dumb enough to think a line like that would work. She anticipated her fiery aunt's belittling retort.

"If I give you my credit card," Casey said to Audrey, "will you not tell anyone that I left with a cop who used that line?"

Audrey was torn. She could chastise her aunt for poor taste, or she could have a credit card with no spending limit at her favorite shopping center. How easily could her integrity be bought?

"Deal," she said, and Casey handed her the credit card along with her cigarette. Incredulous, Audrey threw the cancer stick to the ground and stomped it out.

"Let's go," Casey said to Dale.

"Cool," he said as he took her hand. They ran off like children sneaking out of school.

"Make sure you use protection!" Audrey called after them.

"I had my tubes tied at twenty-five," Casey yelled. "Plus, everyone has herpes. Live a little."

"You have herpes?" Dale asked, confused.

"Not right now," Casey said as a lightning strike made landfall in the distance.

THUNDER CRACKED AS COLLIN loaded the family truck with plywood. The parking lot of this mom-and-pop hardware store was packed with locals gathering last-minute supplies. The physical activity was helping him get his mind off the fight with Orla's mother. He took the final plywood piece off the dolly and hurled it into the truck bed. It landed with a crash that was overpowered by another clap of thunder.

Collin struggled to get the dolly back to the loading zone. The wind was dangerous. Every step forward was met with powerful resistance. While he wrestled with the wind, Dale's cruiser pulled into the parking lot. Collin could see there was a woman in the front seat and assumed that Orla was riding with her man to get supplies.

This was too good, he thought. Nothing seemed more apt than to ridicule Orla's boy toy while he regaled her with her mother's most recent melodrama.

Collin dropped the dolly off in its corral and followed the cruiser as it made its way into an alley behind the hardware store.

A newspaper flew into Collin's face. When he peeled it off, he saw the headline: YOU SHOULDN'T BE HERE—EVACUATIONS ORDERED. He rolled his eyes and tossed it aside.

Collin forced his way through the gales into the alley and found purchase behind a dumpster. The smell was rancid. The wind forced the grotesque mixture of rotting seafood, sawdust, and sewage into his nostrils. Collin gagged on the smell, forcing him to move away to see what was going on behind it.

Parked a few yards away, Dale and, who he assumed to be, Orla were together on the hood of the cruiser. This made Collin sicker than the essence of dumpster he was trying to escape. Orla's back was to him, but Dale noticed Collin attempting to escape the dumpster bouquet and stopped dead.

"Get out of here!" Dale said, doing his best authoritative impression. Collin was forced to think on his feet.

"Is that girl under arrest, officer?" he said with a sarcastic tone. That was when he learned the horrible truth. The woman on the car with her legs wrapped around Dale was not Orla. It was his sister.

Casey had turned around and was equally horrified to see her brother approaching.

"*Casey?*"

"Shit," Casey spat as she removed Dale from herself. She quickly pulled up her underwear.

"Hey, you're Orla's friend from the carnival, right?" Dale tucked in his shirt and zipped himself back up.

"Wait what?" Casey said as she hopped off the sedan.

Collin's mind shifted into an instinctual state, processing all the visual data that surrounded him. This asinine excuse for a lawman was not only fucking the former love of his life, but was cheating on her with Collin's own sister.

The badge on Dale's chest and the gun on his hip disappeared from Collin's mind. Too much else was happening for those to be a concern. Collin calmly walked up to Dale and swung a hard right at the officer's cheek. It knocked him down to the ground. Collin felt Dale's jaw dislocate, but he was still conscious. That would be a problem.

Collin remembered the badge now.

"Holy shit, dude!" Casey gasped. Collin looked to her and, in taking his eye off his opponent, gave Dale enough time to retract the collapsible baton from his utility belt, extend it, and slam it into Collin's ankle. The pain was excruciating.

In a fair fight, Collin was the better man, but cops don't fight fair, they don't know how to.

From his serial-killer-comedy research, Collin knew police were only required to do *four* hours of hand-to-hand combat training a year. They receive *one-hundred-sixty* hours of weapons and firearms training.

They shoot first and beat non-violent suspects with batons because they can't fight.

Collin fell to the ground and the force of impact knocked the wind out of him.

"Fuck," Collin let out as he gasped for air. Dale mounted him and was going to ground and pound Collin's face, before a sharp pain incapacitated him. Casey had kicked him in the balls from behind.

"Defund police!" Casey yelled as she tried to come up with a reason for helping her brother avoid a beating. Dale fell beside Collin and writhed with pain. Casey knelt down and whispered into Dale's ear.

"I do have herpes now," she got up and yelled "ACAB!"

Dale didn't know what to say, and he was too busy taking deep breaths to speak. Casey hightailed it out of there. "You're on your own now, bro."

"Thanks," Collin yelped. He tried to stand in order to follow suit and get out of dodge. His ankle, however, needed some time before running would be possible. He limped his way back to the dumpster before he heard the footsteps. Dale was rushing him at full speed and tackled him onto the concrete.

"You're under arrest," Dale said.

"For what?"

Dale punched Collin in face, looked him in the eye and reminded him who started this.

"For that."

"Oh," Collin spat some blood. "That."

Dale cuffed him and pulled him up to his feet. Dale opened the rear door of the cruiser and, for only the second time in his life, Collin was put in the back seat. He had preferred the time sans handcuffs. Dale landed himself in the driver's seat and adjusted the rear view mirror so he and Collin could make eye contact.

"You're lucky you're white," Dale said.

"Did you just say that out loud?"

17
WORTH IT

DALE AND SOME OF his officer buddies took turns battering Collin. He hit a cop, so Collin had prepared himself for this treatment upon being booked. Collin knew that cops were cowards, especially the ones in small towns without the burden of being visible on a national scale.

Small town cops can hide their crimes. Most departments can't afford body cameras in their budgets, and therefore still treat detainees the way they were taught by their small-minded, old-school fraternity. They threw all their strength into the attacks, which were all to the body. They couldn't leave any marks that might show up on the intake picture.

Collin got a little extra for being charged with assault of an officer. They really went hard when he refused to show them any pain. They wanted him to break, but years of using boxing as a prescription for anxiety had built up Collin's ability to take a beating. He was a hobbyist, but had taken harder body shots from training partners. Most of these officers looked like they spent more time in bowling leagues than boxing gyms.

He took breaths when he could and tried to imagine the fun he'd have if he ever got to testify against them in a civil suit. This got him through the booking beat-down.

The officers threw him into a holding cell. The only other occupant was someone Collin recognized: the man from the bar who was wearing an elephant costume. Collin recognized him as he wore the same costume now, only it was covered in vomit.

The Elephant Man swayed on his feet. Like a drunken ballerina, his movements were graceful but off balance. He slid down next to Collin and looked him over.

"Damn," said the Elephant Man, "they fucked you up. What'd ya do?" The man's breath was hot with bourbon and stomach acid.

"I punched a cop."

"Oh shit. I hope she was worth it."

"How'd you—"

"—The only thing worth potentially getting shot for is a woman. Or a man—if you swing that way. What I'm saying is, you only risk a bullet for some primo sex."

He hiccupped before going on, "Or a whole lot of land. But you don't look like the revolutionary type. Or, like, a lot of drugs. Or money. You know," he paused, contemplated. "You know, now that I think of it, there's a lot of things I'd be willing to get shot for . . ."

"I guess," Collin said. He took slow breaths to deal with his bruised ribs. Every inhale forced him to wince.

"So, was she worth it?"

Collin really took a moment to think about this. How *did* he feel about Orla? He thought he was doing all this to get some verisimilitude into his pilot, but you don't fight a cop for your craft. And he definitely didn't do it for Casey. Casey knew what she wanted and was far from being taken advantage of.

He did this for Orla. He cared about Orla, even after all these years. He wanted her to be treated well, to be respected. The idea that someone she trusted was betraying her . . . it drove him to rage. How could someone lucky enough to have her love betray it?

Shit. He still loved her.

It was a truth he'd repressed since he'd moved away. A truth he'd ignored because he knew that loving someone and being loved back were two very different things. Was this unrequited, long-ignored love worth the situation he found himself in? Was Orla worth the bruised ribs, ringing headache and busted knuckles?

"She used to be," Collin said.

The Elephant Man took that answer in, let it stew alongside the spirits in his bloodstream.

"Well," he said. "If it makes you feel any better, assaulting a police officer only carries . . ." he had to do the mental math. Collin assumed the elephant man was calculating what he knew from his former run-ins with boys in blue. " . . . Like, a five-to-ten-year sentence, max."

"I'm fucked. I'm fucked." The anxiety was kicking in. "I just snapped. God damn it."

For the first time since the alleyway, Collin considered the full ramifications of what he'd done. He was not going to get out of this. No more show. No more California winters. He was going to spend the next five-to-ten years learning inmate politics in the New Jersey prison system.

His mind immediately went to work. At least he would be able to turn this story into a movie when he got out. He'd be able to find a way to make the brutal reality of prison into something comedic. The moment he was out, Gene would be able to sell him as a dangerous entity. Executives ate that shit up. They're powerless against someone who's lived the experience. And going to jail for love sells.

That was that. Collin would do the time, learn how it all worked, and then repackage whatever traumas he might experience into a profitable pitch. He imagined the fights he'd get in, the moral conundrums necessary to survive.

How would he deal with being forced to join a prison gang?

He thought of it like another master's degree. He could learn how fencing stolen goods worked, maybe get the down-low on what one needed to do in order to crack a modern-day safe. He would thrive in the mandated routines. Lights up, breakfast, time outside the cell could be spent reading in order to avoid prison drama that could get him killed, lights out. Wash, rinse, repeat. Just as Collin was coming to terms with his new future as a felon, a uniformed officer approached the cell.

"Collin Cassidy, you're free to go."

"I am?" Collin was shocked. He had lived a whole prison life in his mind. He was going to miss the routine.

"You're lucky your friend came by." The officer spat through gritted teeth. "If it were up to me, you'd be in the hospital awaiting trial."

"Friend?" Collin was confused.

"Maybe she was worth it," The Elephant Man put a hand on Collin's shoulder and sized him up.

Was he worthy of her, given the circumstances? Collin knew the costumed lush was right.

He thanked him with a nod and tried to stand up. The drunken elephant compressed his grip on Collin's shoulder. There was more he needed to say. He spat on the cell floor. He scrutinized Collin, unsure if he was ready to hear what he might impart.

"You got twenty bucks I could borrow?"

RAIN FELL FROM THE sky, thick and heavy. Orla stomped out of the small police station and into the pool of a parking lot. Her sneakers were soaked, her socks soggy, and it was all Collin's fault.

Noah helped Collin, who was still dealing with the ramifications of his sister fucking the police. He limped after Orla like puppy who just had its nose rubbed in its own shit. He winced going down the stairs. His ribs were giving him the most trouble.

Collin whispered to Noah. "How did you guys know I was here?"

"Casey told Audrey when she met up with her at the mall. Audrey called my aunt."

"Why didn't *they* come get me?"

"The storm's getting bad. You had the truck and the keys to your rental." Collin checked his jacket pocket where he felt the keys and made them jingle.

"Son of a cock," he rolled his eyes and sighed.

When Collin and Noah got to the car, Orla was already inside white-knuckling the steering wheel.

"You can have shotgun," Noah said, while he stole the back seat for himself and left Collin in the rain.

"Thanks . . ."

Collin took a deep breath, opened the door, and let out a whelp as he sat in the passenger seat. Every movement he made caused excruciating pain. Orla stared straight ahead just like when they were at the bar. She couldn't stand to look at him. His left eye had bruised over—Orla noticed it and felt the tinge of compassion she was otherwise trying to suppress.

"I got Dale to drop the charges," she said through gritted teeth.

"You didn't have to do that."

"I know," she said. Collin took in her anger and spat back some of his own.

"Why are you mad at me? I didn't cheat on you with my sister."

"You may want to rephrase that," Noah said.

"Who the fuck do you think you are?" Orla said.

"I'm not the guy that cheated on you, that's for sure."

"Did you think you were defending my honor or some other archaic masculine bullshit? Do you honestly think that justifies what you did?"

Collin turned and looked at Noah in the back seat.

"Do you see now why you're crazy to want to get married? I caught her boyfriend cheating and she's mad at *me*!" He turned back to Orla and continued. "Also, let's not forget, Miss This-is-all-about-me, that he was fucking my sister in an *alley*! Do you think that, maybe, just *maybe*, that's why I hit him? And that, perhaps, it had absolutely nothing to do with you?"

Orla considered this for, perhaps, half a second before making sure Collin knew his defense was bullshit.

"Why did you follow them into the alley in the first place?"

"I was . . . He . . ." Collin had nothing. "*Fuck*!"

Orla started the engine, victorious. She floored it and the wheels hydroplaned. As the wheels found purchase in the puddle of a parking lot, they left the police station, a wake forming in the rear view.

T HE STORM WAS GEORGE Clooney on a boat with Mark Wahlberg level dangerous. Almost perfect.

Storm surges flooded the roads to a level where driving was technically possible, though not advisable. The engine might not flood, but the tires might not hold their grip on the road. Orla had driven in storms like this before. She kept her speed to a crawl, but even at a low speed, the car left a wake behind as it crept forward.

No one had spoken since they left the police station, and this was no time for a podcast or music. The rain pelted the windshield. This and the wiper's high tempo metronome were the only score to the daunting drive.

"I was going to tell you about how much of a bitch your mom was being," Collin said, breaking the awkward silence.

"What?" Orla said.

"Why I followed Dale into the alley, when I . . . thought you were there. I thought you might want to know your mom was in top form this afternoon."

"Oh, no." Orla shook her head. Her mother could always be counted on to embarrass her. "What did she say?"

"She called Audrey a whore. And Val, technically."

"She *what*?!" Noah said, leaning forward.

"That's Mom," Orla said and shrugged it off. She was not surprised.

"How are you two not more upset?" Noah said.

"Your grandmother sucks," Collin said, turning to acknowledge Noah. "Nothing crazy, just normal *came of age in the Reagan era* racism. So she's at least self-aware enough to try and hide it, but not as well as she thinks."

"Don't get her started on rap music," Orla said, as she started to laugh.

"That's not fair," Collin said, "she hated Eminem too. He had all those songs about killing his mother."

"And she wondered why I listened to him so much," Orla said.

Collin chuckled.

She and Collin used to shit-talk her mom together all the time while they were at the hospital with her dad. This slow car ride through flooded streets started to feel like old times.

"But yeah, Noah," Orla said, "your grandmother does not want you to have a baby with Audrey for vastly different reasons than your mom."

"Is anyone going to say anything to her?" Noah said.

"You can't fix old people," Collin said. "You can only wait for them to die off. Then the next generation thinks you're the worst. It's a cycle. We all suck in different ways. We'll all continue to suck."

Orla couldn't take her eyes off the road, but began to steal glances at Collin. She was feeling bad for blowing up at him, despite him deserving it. She decided it was time to change the subject.

"Boyfriend may have been a bit of an exaggeration," Orla said.

"What?" Collin was confused.

"It wasn't serious," she said, "Dale and I." She glanced over at him just long enough for him to see, before turning back to the road. "I haven't really done . . . serious, since . . . you know."

Collin used all the tact left in his battered and bruised body to not make a joke about how that information would have been more useful a few hours earlier. He summoned all the courage he had to respond in earnest. She was finally letting him in. He had to match her honesty with a bit of his own.

"There hasn't really been anyone in a while that's made me want to stick around," he said.

"Well, we have that in common," she said.

Collin reached over and placed a hand on Orla's knee. He did it on instinct. It was something he used to do back when they were together. Recognizing the muscle memory, she let him.

They both remembered that feeling; that comfortable place where things just made sense and they didn't have to call attention to it. They could just exist. Together.

"Are you two bonding over being emotionally stunted?" Noah said.

Collin and Orla both snapped their necks back at him.

"Not the time, Noah!" Orla said.

"Can you not?!" Collin said.

The tires hydroplaned and Orla lost control of the car. It skidded between lanes and spun out on the watery street. Orla turned into the skid and got the car back on the road just as quickly as it went off. Luckily, they had the streets to themselves.

"Fuck!" Orla said.

Recognizing just how close that was, she placed her non-driving hand on the hand Collin was now gripping her knee with. Her touch made him relax. They took a deep breath in sync, calming each other down. They said no more.

They stared straight ahead into the storm, smiling but terrified.

18
SHARING IS CARING

S OAKED TO THE BONE, Collin, Orla and Noah dashed into Windward House.

They found Beth sitting on the couch reading a book about serial killers. Collin thought it was a shame that most of the people who loved serial killers so much never got to meet one. He recognized Beth's book as he had read it for research during a staffing gig.

Hearing the door slam shut, Eliza ran in from the kitchen. The sight of her son's bruised face frightened her more than the storm raging outside. She gave him a once over before slapping him herself.

"What kind of a dumb motherfucker hits a cop?!"

"Motherfucker? Mom, really?" Collin said.

"Shut up and give me a hug," Eliza commanded. Collin embraced his mother despite his injuries. While they hugged she added, "You're lucky you're white."

"Mom! You can't say shit like that," Collin said. Kip entered the room, having overheard.

"She's right though," Kip said. "If I hit a cop? Dead. Wouldn't even get a protest." Eliza let her son out of her clutches and moved to her son-in-law.

"It's what everyone is thinking. Might as well 'keep it real.'"

"You always do," Kip said. He extended his fist for a dap that Eliza bumped. Collin watched this with a confused grimace.

"Don't encourage her," Collin said.

"You two," Eliza said, turning her attention to Orla and Noah, "are staying here. No one should be out in that storm. Come on. Let's get you dry clothes."

Orla forgot how much she loved Collin's mother. It had been some time since they'd really been together, but she always remembered Eliza as the most compassionate woman she'd ever met. Compared to her own mother, the woman was a saint.

The years Collin and Orla dated, Eliza was always there to give advice or shit-talk her son behind his back. She was the life of parties and made sure everyone felt welcome in her home. Eliza was everything Orla wished Beth would have been. There may have been a part of her that dated

Collin simply to stay close to his family. He was lucky and acknowledged it time and time again.

Orla could barely stand to be in the same room, as she was now, with her mother. Orla met her mother's gaze and felt the need to acknowledge her existence out of courtesy more than desire.

"Mom," she said "nice to see you again. We almost forgot you were in town."

"Well," said Beth, "someone's got to take care of things."

"What have you actually done?" Orla said.

"A mother does a lot of things she never gets credit for. Wouldn't you agree, Mrs. Cassidy?"

Orla wanted to castigate her mother. She wanted to go over every excruciating detail about how she'll never be forgiven for the way she treated Orla's father, how she hasn't been there for anyone in far too long and expects everyone to kowtow to her every whim when she deigns to appear. Instead, Orla took a breath and turned her attention back to Eliza.

"We really should get out of these clothes."

Beth, seeing that she was not going to get the reaction out of her daughter that she wanted, left. She made her way down to her basement suite.

"Come on," Eliza said, cooling the tension, "you look like you're about Casey's size. She won't mind sharing."

Collin snorted, held back his laughter. Orla punched him in the arm as they followed Eliza up the stairs.

"Shut up," she ordered. Collin raised his hands in surrender. He was shutting up. As they reached the top of the stairs, he couldn't help himself.

"Sharing is caring."

Orla turned to face Collin, her lips curled into a seductive grin, and brought her hand up to his chest sensually. Collin was taken aback. He didn't know where this affection was coming from. Orla then flicked his ribs with her middle finger. She held her finger in Collin's face as he doubled over on the stairs in pain. She smiled and made her way into the hall while he whimpered in a ball.

"I told you to shut up," she called from the hallway.

AFTER THEY CHANGED CLOTHES and got dry, Collin and Orla were immediately put to work.

Collin's father was able to retrieve his truck from the hardware store parking lot before the wind and rain picked up. He and Kip hadn't had the time, or the help, to board up the second story windows before it became too dangerous to be on a ladder in the storm. It was too late to cover the windows with plywood from the outside, as one should, so Collin and Orla had to help cover the windows from within.

In Audrey's room, they hammered from opposite sides, working their way together. Audrey and Noah were huddled around her ancient iMac, attempting to FaceTime Jesse, this time together. Just as it seemed the call was about to connect, the screen went black, and all the lights in the building followed suit. Collin was mid-swing when the blackout occurred and hammered his thumb instead of a nail. He yelped like a pup whose paw had been stepped on.

"Motherfucking shit!" he swore, trying to curtail the sharp pain of yet another injury today.

It was pitch black and no one could see anything.

"Power's out," Orla said.

"No shit. Fuck!" Collin illuminated himself when he flicked a lighter on with his hammered thumb. He bit his tongue to stop the onslaught of expletives he wanted to express.

"Good thing Grandma makes us keep a million candles in every room," Audrey said, bringing a lavender-scented candle to her uncle for a light.

Audrey used her candle to gather more, and soon she, Noah, Collin, and Orla all had their own. After a few more were lit and placed on the dresser, the room was a menagerie of floral and sweet scents battling each other for olfactory hegemony.

Gathered around a circle of candles, the room resembled a teenager's attempt at a séance. Each of the teens and their adult counterparts held candles of their own. If they hadn't been forced into this situation, one might think they had gathered to tell ghost stories in their pajamas.

Noah, underlit by the candle he held, worried about his father.

"What if he doesn't make it back?" he said.

Audrey pulled him close and rested her head on his shoulder. This was her way of letting him know everything would be OK, despite her having no idea whether it would.

"He's gonna be fine," she said.

"But that storm . . . He's out there."

"Listen," Collin said, "I know your father. And I can tell you with certainty, a little hurricane won't stop him from coming home."

Collin pulled out his cell phone and scrolled past more than a decade of photos in his cloud. This hurt his thumb more, but he acted like it was fine.

Collin pulled up a picture of him holding a small baby. He held his phone out for Noah to look at.

"That's you."

"You still have that?" Orla was shocked. She remembered taking that picture.

"Of course," he smiled. Collin and Orla gazed at one another for no more than a moment. In that moment, they were both reminded that they had far more good than bad times together. Just that one really bad time.

"You were there when I was born?"

"We drove your mother to the hospital," Orla said.

"When your mom was in labor," Collin said, "I called Jesse. He was already at sea. And do you know what they crazy son of a bitch did? He turned the tanker around and beat us to the hospital."

"He almost got fired for it," said Orla, "but he told his bosses seeing his son's birth was more important than shipping electronics to India."

"Aww. That's sweet," Audrey said.

"Then, when they tried to fire him, he threatened to leak the fact that they were overworking employees in violation of the Longshore and Harbor Workers Compensation Act," Collin said.

"Significantly less sweet, but way cool," Audrey said.

"If there's anyone bad-ass enough to navigate through this storm and back home, it's your dad," Collin said.

Noah wasn't fully sold on this pep talk, Collin could tell, but he seemed less anxious.

Audrey let go of him and gave her uncle a tight hug. She appreciated how much he seemed to care about her love. Collin was surprised by his niece's affection—he loved that he was receiving it, but it was killing him.

"Sorry, I forgot!" She let him go, realizing he was in pain.

Collin took a moment to calm himself and breathe through the pain. "I love everyone here, OK?" Collin said. "Just please don't touch me!"

He took deep breaths holding his bruised ribs.

Orla caught his eye as he hugged Audrey, and the two seemed to come to a silent détente. She always thought he'd left and never looked back. The fact that he had the picture of him holding Noah after all these years so easily accessible, and remembered that day so clearly, forced Orla to acknowledge that their time together had truly meant something to him; that it had been as hard for him to leave as it was for her to make the decision she made.

This understanding also brought forth a unique sadness. Orla had to concede, once and for all, that Collin hadn't left of his own accord. She had pushed him away.

19
Storms and Surges

The streets of Cape May were flooded. Storm surges made the town and the ocean one in the same. Fish swam along city streets, following the cars being swept from their parking spots, allowing the machines to lead their schools.

A dolphin that had been swept along with the surge found the mall to be most interesting. Swimming along cobblestone corridors, the cetacean window-shopped the same stores Audrey and Casey had plundered earlier that morning. The jewelry store held the marine mammal's attention most: the gold, silver, and diamonds sparkled every time lightning struck. This mesmerized the newest mammal in Cape May. The old mammals—the humans, the prisoners of the zoo, and the forest dwelling predators and prey—had all fled or were held up in their homes.

Beth, already fed up with her treatment in Cape May, was furious when the electricity went out. She was trapped alone in the basement apartment. It was pitch black in her windowless, subterranean cave.

"Where is it?" she said to herself, searching for her cell phone. "Wait . . . a-ha!"

She found the phone on the coffee table she had been feeling the top of and turned on its flashlight feature to get her bearings. Turning to her left, she saw a basket filled with beach toys and inflatables in their boxes. There was a massive inflatable pizza box. Looking at it made her hungry.

The water outside was rising and putting more and more pressure on the bulkhead, which sat at the top of the far set of stairs and lead to the backyard exit of the basement. The creaking of the bulkhead was getting louder and more consistent.

This startled Beth. She frantically moved her flashlight around the apartment until she found herself face to face with the breaker box.

Water seeped through the bulkhead and slowly made its way down the stairs, unbeknownst to Beth. A loud groan emanated from the bulkhead as it began to bend under the mounting pressure of the flood.

Beth ignored this and focused on the breaker box. She found the tripped breaker and switched it back. Nothing. She flipped the breakers back and forth in a desperate attempt to play God and let there be light. While she tried in vain to bring back the electricity, the bulkhead finally gave way to the enormous pressure of the storm surge.

Water began to rush into the basement with a crash Beth could not ignore. She watched as the keys she left on the coffee table were washed away by the raging rapid pouring into her cold-water-flat.

Beth ran up the opposing stairs, which lead to the main house, but the door was locked and only the keys she lost in the rapids could open it. While normally it would be a fire hazard—or in this case a water hazard—for a home to have doors that did not unlock from the inside, the Cape May Historical Society had been firm with Allan on this point when he was renovating. The doors must be fashioned in the style of the time at which the home was built, and that included skeleton keys as the only accessible means of locking and unlocking. Allan told Beth this the first night she took up residence in the apartment. At the time, she thought it was a quaint—albeit annoying—gimmick for their business. Now, like Allan, she decided all historians deserved the death penalty.

Beth rushed down the stairs, hoping she could find the keys with her phone light. She slipped, sprained her ankle, and lost her phone in one poor step.

She screamed out in pain. At least the freezing cold waters, which were rising more every minute, would keep it from swelling up. She tried to put weight on the injured foot in an attempt to go up the stairs where the water was coming in, but the pain was too much. She was forced to plead for her least favorite thing in the world.

"*Help*!" she screamed.

***

ALLAN WAS WORKING BY candlelight barricading the front doors with a two-by-four. He could have sworn he heard something, but brushed it off as the sounds of a storm raging around him. He was glad to still be there. Evacuations tended to be unnecessary for hurricanes in the north-east. The notices were mostly ignored by longtime residents, the storms never as bad as the meteorologists expected them to be. Allan preferred to stay with his property so he could manage whatever damage needed to be repaired himself.

He hammered away at the last few nails wondering how many permits the historical society would force him to purchase before he could repair the door he was barricading. Between hammer strikes, he swore he could hear someone knocking. He stopped, his ears perked up again.

"Help!! It's flooding!"

He heard the voice coming from down below. He was sure of it this time. He made his way over to the basement door and jiggled the handle. Locked.

"Open the door!" he yelled through the oak barrier.

"I can't find the keys!" Allan's eyes rolled so far into the back of his head he could see himself thinking *this fucking cunt . . .* He took a deep, calming breath.

Beth had been standoffish, rude, and downright hateful to his family these past few days, and now she had the gall to put herself in mortal danger. He was over it. Collin, Orla, and Audrey bounded down the stairs and found Allan in a deep existential battle with the basement door.

"Dad, what's up?" Collin said.

"She locked herself in the basement."

Allan was matter of fact, no hint of emotion in his voice. It wasn't clear if he thought she would be fine or if he simply did not care whether or not she was. Eliza entered from the kitchen carrying a candlestick.

"It's just a little water," she said to her husband.

He pulled her close to share an intimate, *schaden-freude*-laden laugh and kiss with his partner of over forty years.

"I know my mother is an unrepentant cunt—" Orla said.

"I was just thinking that myself," Allan said.

"I *heard* that!" Beth screamed from the watery depths.

"But she's still my mom . . . Can we just break down the door?" Orla asked.

"Not a chance in hell," Allan said. "That door was hand-milled and designed by some fancy Edwardian architect when the property was originally built. The historical society will charge my ass with treason if we break it down."

People argue all the time over what a human life is worth, but Allan was certain Beth's life wasn't worth what it would cost him in time or treasure to knock down that door. He would rather Beth perish in a watery grave and potentially fight involuntary manslaughter charges, than face the wrath of the Cape May Historical Society. Hell, if she died, he might be able to sue the society and get normal locks. Allan smiled at the thought.

"Dad, is there anywhere you haven't barricaded yet?"

Allan had to think about that for a moment. He was meticulous about storm prep. Too many seasons of water damage and dealing with the damn historians. Then it clicked.

"Casey wouldn't let me into her room."

CASEY SAT ON HER bed, laptop open, wearing only a bra and thong. She was showing off the goods to Dale via FaceTime.

"I thought you deserved a treat for letting my brother go," she said. From what she could see in the background, Dale was in a hunting cabin full of taxidermized deer heads.

"I love treats!" he said, and Casey started to undo the clasps on her bra. She held the cups on with one arm while she gave Dale a slow strip tease.

Collin opened her door and pushed his way to her balcony window without so much as looking at her. Casey never locked her door, especially at Windward House. She didn't even know where the key to this room was.

"Dude, what the fuck?" Casey said, holding her bra in place. Orla followed him. Then Allan entered, saw what was going on in the room, turned on his heel, and left.

"Eliza! Your daughter's doing one o' them Only-Fangs things! Get your ass up here! I need to go wash my eyes with acid," Allan screamed down the stairs.

Casey quickly covered up with a blanket, spinning her laptop as she pulled the sheet. Orla saw that Dale was watching Casey's attempt at seduction. Orla glared at Casey with annoyance and pity in equal parts.

"Are you fucking kidding me?" Orla sighed.

"Is that Orla?" came the laptop speakers. "Hey, babe! Why don't you join us?"

"Don't kill me," Casey said. "I didn't know he was your beau until today. And, I mean, at this point, why stop?"

"Actually, you two deserve each other," Orla said.

"Hey!" Casey said, offended.

"Aww, thanks, babe!" Dale said at the same time.

Audrey entered the room.

"How do you even have an internet connection?" she asked her aunt.

Casey held up her cell phone. "Mobile hot spot. Duh!"

"Tell Dad to get the front door open," Collin said as he opened the French doors and allowed wind and rain to spew into the room. Collin went headlong into the gales to the balcony. Things were crashing all around and water raged below.

"I'm coming with you," Orla said, still in the bedroom. Noah, who had been caught up on the happenings by

Audrey, entered the room and pushed his way through the wind to meet his aunt.

"Me too."

"No," Orla scolded him, "you stay inside."

"But . . ."

"I said stay! Jesus," she said, "Just stay here and try not to impregnate anyone else!"

She glared at Casey as she exited to the balcony to meet Collin. Casey and Noah shared an awkward glance.

"You wish," Casey said.

OUTSIDE ON THE VERANDA, Collin took in the view below. The streets were flowing like a river. Debris floated on the water and flew through the air. Orla was close behind him. Collin shimmied down the gutter, but lost his grip. He fell on his back and splashed into the water. He sunk below the surface long enough for Orla to get nervous. Just as she was about to scream his name, Collin stood up in the waist-deep water.

"Fuck, that's cold," he said.

"Be careful!" Orla yelled. She was stealthier and more precise in her climb down.

Once in the water, the two of them trudged around the back of the house before hearing a high-pitched squeak. They looked around confused before spotting two dolphins swimming past. Collin and Orla stared at the magnificent sight for a moment. When the Dolphins were no longer in their plane of vision, they continued to the basement bulkhead.

Collin took slow, careful steps through the damaged bulkhead and down the basement stairs. Orla held on to his shoulder and followed. Beth was sitting at the bottom of the stairs, keeping herself above water.

"Took you long enough," Beth barked.

"You make it really hard to want to save you," Orla said, before taking her mother in her arms and lifting her up. Beth used Orla as a crutch while they made their way up the stairs. Beth's shoes, soaked for some time, failed to find purchase on a step. She slipped from her daughter's grasp, fell, and hit her head on the stone staircase.

Collin rushed to check her—she was unconscious. Orla tried to lift her.

"She's too heavy. I can't get her alone," she said.

"I am *so* telling her you said that."

He and Orla both took a side and lifted Beth's dead weight together. They struggled just to move her.

Collin's body was still in shambles from his booking beatdown, and every movement was excruciating. It was going to take them a long time to get her out of the basement and then back inside the house.

"Damn," Collin said. "She is heavy."

Lightning struck and thunder cracked simultaneously. The strike was nearby. They needed to get out of the water as fast as possible.

"I have an idea," Orla said. She left her mother on the stairs in Collin's capable hands and went back into the basement. She pulled a box with a giant inflatable pool float shaped like a pizza. Orla took charge of her mother and tossed Collin the box. He took her meaning and removed the inflatable from the box and began to inflate it. This would take forever as well.

"*Worst.*" Blow. "*Plan.*" Blow. "*Ever.*"

A LLAN FINISHED UNDOING ALL the work he had put in barricading the front door and opened it to the storm. Luckily, the porch was built high enough that the water wasn't anywhere near breaching the main home.

Collin and Orla were nowhere to be found. Noah looked around and could not spot them either.

"It's been a half-hour, I'm going after them," Noah said.

As he bounded down the porch stairs and assumed lifeguard mode, Collin rounded the corner. He pulled the unconscious Beth on a giant piece of pizza. A rope tied to Collin's wrist anchored him to the raft. Orla pushed the pizza from behind.

"Little help?" Collin shouted. Allan and Noah descended the porch into the water and helped pull Beth to safety. Noah took his grandmother's feet while Allan grabbed her arms. They carried her into the house.

Collin sat on the porch and tried to catch his breath. Orla let go of the inflatable pizza raft and the wind sent it flying into the air. Collin's arm was pulled by the rope still tied to his wrist. He was jerked across the porch and his face smashed into the railing.

Collin was used to pain at this point. The fight with Dale, the intake beating, the electricity going out while he was hammering, and now this inflatable cheesy bastard all conspired to inflict maximum damage to every part of Collin's body today.

"*Et tu*, pizza?" he said.

He struggled to get his arm free, but he had tied a slipknot and it only got tighter. Orla pulled her father's pocketknife out and cut the line sending the pizza flying off into the great beyond. Collin thanked her with a dazed nod, the railing to the face had rung his bell. She helped him back to his feet.

"Look at that . . ." Collin said.

They both stared out into the flooded streets where the two dolphins they saw earlier struggled to swim against the current, unable to go back to the sea, trapped in this new normal mother nature's whim had forced upon them.

Orla held Collin at the waist to steady him. He reached around her shoulder and they eased into an old rhythm neither had felt in over a decade as they turned to the raging storm they had just waded through. Tempestuous winds hammered down while they watched the storm in awe, holding one another close. A few yards away, lightning struck the same spot twice.

Orla was about to rest her head on Collin's when Allan roared from the threshold.

"Get the fuck inside! You can get nostalgic when you're safe and dry."

With the potential for a jubilant tête-à-tête to turn into anything more destroyed, Orla helped Collin back inside.

20
WHAT THE FUCK ELSE DO YOU NEED?

C ASEY STOOD OVER BETH'S unconscious body, trying to figure out if she was still alive, when her eyes began to open.

Beth was confused for a moment, seeing only Casey Cassidy's head hovering over her like a beheaded ghoul. She was disoriented and heard a rhythmic slamming she assumed to be her headache. She cursed under her breath. She heard slam after slam, over and over, until she was able to acknowledge that the sound was coming, not from an internal pain, but an external stimulus.

Hammering.

Beth turned to find her daughter, Mr. Cassidy and Collin as they hammered nails into plywood over the main entrance. She laid on the floor, no idea how she got there.

"Ugh. My head," she said, sitting up.

Upon hearing Beth return to the world of the waking, the rest of the Cassidy and Monteiro family gathered
around. Eliza and Valerie each took a shoulder and hoisted
her up to her feet. It was then that Beth saw her only
grandson holding the girl he had gotten pregnant on the
couch in a loving embrace. This enraged her scrambled
brains.

She could no longer stand for this. She could no longer
watch as more of her family made the same bad decisions
she did. Children shouldn't have children.

"Noah, get away from that girl!" she screeched.

"Mom, calm down," Orla said, making her way to
her mother. Beth's head was still ringing with pain, every
sound was a new trauma that incensed her further to her
breaking point. She thrashed, pushing Eliza and Valerie
away. Without their support, she stumbled to her knees.
They tried to help her again, but she shooed them away.
She wanted to stand on her own. She took a moment and
got herself upright.

"No! If she had any sense at all, she would do what you
did and take care of this situation once and for all."

Everyone in the room shifted their gaze from Beth to
Orla.

Her mother had just outed her. This HIPPA violation
was not surprising—her mother was never very good at

keeping secrets. That was how she lost custody in the first place.

Beth had never felt a sense of shame, so why would she protect her daughter's? This was neither the time nor the place for her mother to start discussing her past medical choices with a room full of the people that choice deprived of a grandchild, niece or nephew, and cousin.

Orla could see the disappointment in Eliza's eyes. That hurt far more than her mother's recklessness.

She respected Collin's mother. Losing Eliza's affection was a cross she could not bear.

If there was one part of their failed relationship that gave Orla a semblance of relief, it was that she knew Collin would never speak poorly about her behind her back. He may have hated her for what she did—may have been so mad that he ran three thousand miles away from her without so much as a word—but he would never have done what her mother just did.

She could see Beth processing how her words had just been interpreted by the room. Her mother could never let a bad deed go undefended.

So she went on the offensive.

"Oh, don't look at her like that," Beth continued. "She had to."

Beth turned her ire to Collin, literally pointing the finger his way.

"*He* was moving three thousand miles away. They were never going to work. Her life would have been ruined if she hadn't listened to her mother."

"I never even told you I was pregnant," Orla said, exasperated. Somehow, her mother had found a way to make herself the center of attention. She was rewriting history, once again, and giving herself a starring role. Only this time, she wasn't totally wrong. Orla knew Siobhan had told their mother about her pregnancy. Siobhan told their mother everything. Siobhan told *everyone* everything. Beth had redesigned the situation to seem like she was a part of it. This was an unconscious process. Siobhan told her, Orla is sure she suggested terminating the pregnancy, and Beth took that as her having played a part in Orla's life. The truth, however, was very different.

"You want the truth, Mom?" Orla asked. "You are the reason I decided to get the abortion. Not because you gave me any motherly advice, or whatever fairytale you've concocted in your head. I was afraid that, if I became a mother, I'd be just like you."

"Orla, stop grandstanding, it isn't cute, and this isn't about you," Beth said, fully ignoring her daughter's admission. Her rant was still not finished. Beth turned to

Audrey and, with a stern, forceful, voice she continued. "Your life will be ruined too, if you do this. You're a child, you can't *have* a child."

She looked into her grandson's tear-filled eyes. Noah's fist was clenched, every muscle in his body tensed. He did his best to bite his tongue. He must taste copper.

"And you . . . You should not waste your time with . . ." Kip forced his way between Beth and his daughter. He put a hand on Noah's shoulder and calmed the boy. He knew his rage well, but had many more years of practice controlling it.

Kip was sick of playing the model minority and if anyone was going to fuck shit up, it would be him. Audrey was *his* daughter. No one talked to his daughter that way.

"With what?" he prodded. "Go on. Say it."

He bore a hole through Beth's head with his eyes. He wanted her to give him a reason. Maybe he would go to prison today too.

"With *trash*," Beth said.

Before she could get another word in, she felt a sharp pain and the light flittered in front of her eyes as her body fell back to the hardwood floors.

Eliza had hit her with a right-cross Mike Tyson would have been jealous of.

Beth was out cold. Again.

"**I** LIKED HER BETTER unconscious," Eliza said, shaking her now sprained wrist. Audrey, with tears in her eyes, snuck her way back upstairs while the confrontation was happening. Noah tried to follow her, but she shook her tear-stained head at him. She wanted to be alone so he let her go. Noah would have to swallow his anger alone in a house full of strangers.

With Beth no longer rambling, the group returned their gaze to her daughter.

"Did you ever tell him you were pregnant?" Valerie asked, genuinely curious. There was no judgement in her question. It was bred from curiosity, not animus.

Valerie couldn't comprehend not telling her partner about the inner workings of her uterus. Kip would say she told him too much.

Orla lowered her head in shame, unable to meet Valerie's gaze. She was not ashamed of her decision—that she had made soberly and with great thought. The way she dealt with it, however, was what she was ashamed of. Not talking about it with the only other person who had taken part in creating the situation.

She'd wanted to curse the birth control brand she was on at that time; wanted to blame the Irish car bombs they'd drunk the night she'd assumed the insemination happened. She'd wanted to blame anyone or any*thing* else.

She looked back at Collin who was on the verge of tears himself.

"No," she said.

"How could you—" Valerie said.

"Stop," Collin said. He knew where this was going and needed to stop it.

"She never told you before—"

"I said stop! OK?" Valerie was taken aback by the force in his voice. This was not a conversation anymore.

"Orla did what she thought was right for her at the time. I, obviously, was upset when I found out. I'm still upset. But the only one who gets to make that call is her. Not you, not me, not the unconscious twat on the floor. Only her."

He was solid in his conviction on this matter.

That conviction gave him the courage to say what needed to be said to his sister on his niece's behalf.

"And the only ones who get to decide whether Audrey and Noah get married are Audrey and Noah. Not you, not me, not Orla."

Collin put his arm around Noah's shoulder. He wanted to make sure the boy knew he believed what he was about to say.

"He loves her, she loves him." He looked at Orla, who was thankful for his intervention and quick change of subject. "What the fuck else do you need?"

Thunder cracked as Valerie and Kip were forced to consider these words.

Eliza pulled her son's head to her forehead and smiled. She was proud of the man she had raised, especially in that moment, and let him know without a word. She let him go and turned to her daughter and son-in-law.

"I should go check on Audrey," she said.

"Mom," Collin said, "Let me."

Eliza felt like she might understand the emotions of being young, pregnant, and unwanted better than her son, but she also knew how much Audrey looked up to her uncle. She would let him be the one to talk to her.

Eliza nodded her assent and patted him gently on the cheek.

Collin went up the stairs, looking back at Orla as he did. He wanted to stay there with her; knew she needed him. She mimicked the nod his mother had just given him. She knew that the pregnant teen needed his comfort more than she did in that moment. She was a big girl. She could handle his family.

Beth moaned in pain. She was waking up and nobody felt her input was necessary any longer.

"Anybody have anything that will keep her quiet?" Eliza said, her natural sarcasm peaking through.

Casey, taking her mother at her word, rummaged through her purse. She pulled out an old Altoid container filled with pills.

"Vicodin or Percocet?"

21
Almost Had You

A UDREY SAT WITH HER back up against the boarded-up bay windows in her bedroom and tried not to cry. The tears came, despite her best attempt. She was mad at herself for letting Noah's grandmother get to her. She knew the old bitch was bat shit, but her words still rang in Audrey's head.

Maybe she was right. Maybe all of this was childish nonsense. Maybe she was just a dumb kid.

For the first time, Audrey wondered whether she was making the right decision. Was she in love with Noah? Does she even know what love is?

The revelation that Noah's aunt had been in a similar situation with her uncle, who'd she'd known for years, who she'd *lived* with . . . Orla didn't even blink at the notion that she should terminate her pregnancy, and she had the benefit of being in her twenties with a college degree.

Audrey wondered if she was being naïve. Beth wasn't wrong, she was still a child. What the fuck did she know?

It was a light knock on her door that broke her out of that self-destructive meditation. Collin slunk his way into the threshold.

"Leave me alone!" Audrey demanded.

"You mean like I have your whole life?" Collin spotted the horse-head plushy that was sitting on Audrey's bed. He picked it up and smiled. He remembered finding it at the mall a few weeks before Audrey was born. She still had it. That made him smile.

"Just go write your stupid show. You don't know me."

Collin kept his eyes on the stuffed horse head. Mostly, because Audrey's words cut too deep. He didn't know his niece. Not in the way he ought to; not in the way he wished he did. He wasn't around for her while she was growing up. The mysterious uncle bit was no longer cute. He was a stranger to this girl, no matter how many Christmas or birthday gifts UPS brought bearing his name.

"There's a reason for that," he said and sat on the bed.

O RLA DECIDED TO HIDE upstairs. She wanted to get out of the firing line her mother had set up for her *down*stairs. Eliza tried to be nice, but Orla could tell that the idea there had been a potential grandchild she wasn't aware of wasn't leaving her mind any time soon. She would never say anything—Eliza was too decent—but her eyes betrayed her dismay, and Orla couldn't stand to disappoint her.

Orla heard Collin and stopped just short of the door. She could tell by the timbre of his voice that he needed to confess something to his niece. Orla wrestled with whether she should leave the two of them to talk in private or give in to her curiosity. She put her back to the wall and listened just outside the threshold. If she were a cat, she'd be dead.

Collin held the horse-head plushy in his hands. He squeezed it. Tossed it from hand to hand.

"You were born just before I left for LA . . ." he took a moment to find the right tone—wistful was what his voice landed on; whether that was intentional or instinctual was unclear.

"Just after I had found out about . . . what Orla did. I didn't care about the abortion. What hurt was that she didn't tell me what was going on with her. She didn't trust me. She didn't care about how I felt, and that made me feel worthless."

A pang of guilt rang through her heart. This was what she had been avoiding all these years. As much as she'd blame Collin for leaving, she was glad he had. He had left for California before she'd even known he knew.

———

O RLA WOKE UP IN her childhood home, her eyes burning, her cheeks seasoned with salt.

A groan escaped her. Too many emotions all at once erupted in a frustrated wail. Holding her head in her hands, she willed herself to get out of bed and grab her cell phone from its charging spot on the bureau. She'd texted Collin the night before, but hadn't heard back.

> **Had to help Siobhan with some stuff, be back tomorrow.**

Still no response. Weird. Collin always texted back immediately. She typed a follow-up.

> **Did you get this?**

> **Still at Siobhan's. Will head back to Philly later this afternoon.**

No three dots. Nothing. Where was he?

She got out of bed and changed her underwear, noticing some spotting. The doctor had said that might happen. She decided the T-shirt of Collin's that she slept in was enough to head down to the kitchen in to make coffee.

Siobhan was in the kitchen, looking sleep-deprived while she put Cheerios on the high chair for six-month-old Noah. Most of the Cheerios ended up on the tile floor. Orla stared at Noah playing with his food. She froze.

"Coffee?" Jesse said.

He was fully dressed and standing by the coffee maker. Orla hadn't even known he was home. Jesse had a calming effect on everyone around him. Orla began to defrost.

"I thought you were working?" Orla said.

"I got back a few nights ago."

"How do you think I was able to come up to Philly without this little guy?" Siobhan said. "Right, Noah? Did you miss Mommy?" Noah smiled a single tooth and clapped his hands, crushing Cheerios.

"Right," Orla said.

"Have you talked to Collin?" Jesse said.

"He's not answering my texts."

Orla could swear Jesse looked concerned. Like he knew something he wasn't saying. His face contorted in a pained expression. He wanted to say something, but Orla could tell he was biting his tongue.

"I'm sure he's just sleeping," Jesse said, unconvincing.

"Yeah," Orla pretended to agree. "And yeah, coffee, please."

Jesse poured and handed her a mug of Dunkin' Original Blend. The smell helped Orla relax. The grounds grounded her.

"Thanks," Orla said, and took her coffee back to her room.

She was not in the mood for conversation. At least not with Jesse and Siobhan—they knew too much already. She needed to talk to Collin. Probably already should have, but that Rubicon had been crossed. She put her bag together and put on her bra and jeans, but kept wearing the shirt she'd slept in. She tied back her hair in a bun and looked herself in the mirror.

No more wallowing in self-pity.

Orla said her goodbyes to Jesse and Siobhan. She tickled baby Noah to see that new tooth one last time, then she got in her car and made the lonely drive from Cape May to Philadelphia.

The ride was uneventful and gave her the time to practice what it was she was going to say to Collin when she got back.

After parking the car and making her way into the apartment, Orla was not ready for what she found. She put her key in the lock and opened the door.

"Collin! I'm back."

No response.

"Collin?"

Orla put her bag down in the living room and could feel that something was off. She checked the bedroom.

All of Collin's drawers were open and emptied. At first, she thought they had been robbed, but all of her stuff was in its rightful place. She checked the closet. All her clothes where she left them, all his gone. The fear started to settle in.

"Collin!" she screamed. "Where are you?"

In the kitchen, she saw a note scribbled in sharpie on Collin's USC acceptance letter. It read:

**You should have told me. Don't call me.
I'm not coming back.**

As much as Orla would have loved to play the victim and act like she was hurt, she understood. Upon reading that note, she realized she wasn't upset. She was relieved.

Now, she would never have to hear how he felt about the situation; she'd never have to listen to his side of the conversation; never have to consider how he felt.

She had long-before admitted to herself that they would have to break up when they went to graduate school. He'd saved her from two difficult conversations.

Despite all her relief, she fell to the floor and wept.

B ACK AGAINST THE WALL, with tears in her eyes, Orla continued to eavesdrop on Collin and Audrey's conversation.

"So when you see me—" Audrey said.

"You remind me of what I almost had," Collin said. "It's not that I necessarily wanted to be a dad then. But, you know, the idea that Orla and I could have had a family together—that was what I always wanted. Sure, it might have been too soon. But like you said, what's the point in waiting to share the love you have?"

Outside the room, Orla's heart rose into her throat as she bit her tongue. She wanted to scream out, but choked her circulatory system back to where it belonged.

"You almost had a cousin you could have grown up with. I almost had you. Or someone like you. Or someone completely different. Truth is, I'll never know what I almost had. That's what hurt the most. The not knowing what could have been. 'Almost' is the worst word in the world. Almost is the lack of a thing. I wouldn't wish almost on my worst enemy."

Collin tossed Audrey the horse head. She caught and cradled it, like she had every night for sixteen years.

"I gave this to you before I left for Los Angeles. It was supposed to be a *Godfather* joke."

Orla slid her back down the wall and fell into a squat. It felt like she'd had the wind knocked out of her. She struggled to breathe; felt like her heart was going to explode. She thought she was dying. She recognized the symptoms.

Her first panic attack since finding out she was pregnant.

She laughed through the frantic gasps for air. This was exactly what it felt like. She had calmed Collin so many times that she knew exactly what to tell herself.

Deep breaths. In. Out. In. Out.

She allowed herself to feel the anxiety. She immersed herself in it. Wallowed in it. Felt like she deserved it.

It passed almost as soon as it came. She steadied her breath and wiped the tears from her eyes. She exhaled in long ten-counts, trying to stay as silent as possible.

"And now I'm just the joke you're using for your dumb show," Audrey said.

"That dumb show gave me a reason to get to know my niece. Something I should have done a long time ago," Collin said.

"Until you go back to LA for another ten years."

Collin took a deep breath. He wasn't used to talking to teens, just writing outdated dialogue for twenty-something actors playing them.

"Can I give you some honest advice?" he said.

Audrey remained silent.

"Don't give up on love. 'Cause I did and I'm miserable. People get cynical about how things never go the way they planned. Maybe they don't go the way we planned because we're too busy planning what life should be when we should just be living. We worry so much about what love *should* look like instead of just loving."

The tears flew down Audrey's face. Collin reached over to wipe them away before adding, "If something feels real, then it *is* real. Fuck what the world wants you to be. Orla and I . . . We gave up on each other because we thought that's what we were supposed to do. We were young and we thought moving on was what was right."

He knelt in front of his niece, penitent.

Orla felt the long pause in her bones. Collin was unaware the subject of his confession was listening.

Guilt filled her chest.

She decided she should leave.

She did not move a muscle.

"But I haven't felt right in a long time," he said.

22
THE WRONG CHOIR

ALLAN, ELIZA, AND KIP slammed a shot of whiskey in the kitchen. All three glasses hit the candle-covered table simultaneously. Valerie sipped her glass of wine, contemplative.

"We're not like her. Are we?" she said, pointing her glass at the unconscious woman on the couch they were all overseeing. Beth's chest was still rising and falling.

Casey had administered the correct dosage. Beth had been in pain—they'd helped kill that pain. It had nothing to do with the fact she was, herself, a giant pain in the ass.

Eliza shifted in her seat, uncomfortable with what she knew she was going to say, despite every fiber of her being telling her not to tell her children what to do. That always backfired. She had learned that a more Socratic method yielded much better results.

"Do you know how old your father and I were when we got married?" Eliza said, and stared her daughter down with a poker face. It was time to put all her cards on the table for the good of her granddaughter.

"Twenty-three!" Kip yelled, assuming it was part of their drinking game.

"I was nineteen, your mother was eighteen," Allan said. "And we were only that old because we had to wait until you mother turned eighteen."

"I was eighteen for three whole days before the ceremony," Eliza added.

"What?" Valerie had never heard this before. Her parents never regaled her or her siblings with the details of their courtship. She just knew they had been high school sweethearts.

"Why would you get married so young?" Kip said

"Because we loved each other," Allan said, matter of fact.

"And he knocked me up," Eliza admitted.

"That too. But it was mostly the love part." He looked to his wife, knowing her response before he said, "Right?"

"Sure . . ." she said and patted his knee.

Valerie did some mental math. It didn't add up. "But you didn't have Collin until you were . . ." she double checked the math, it all added up to "twenty-five?"

Valerie watched as her parents shared a look they seemed to have perfected over many years dealing with their children. She assumed they were communicating telepathically. Allan put his hand in Eliza's hand. Eliza choked as she said, "It turned out to be a false positive."

"But I still loved her," Allan said.

"And I still loved him."

"So, we got married."

"Despite both our parent's objections."

"Hold on. Rewind," Kip said. "You gotta give us the whole story."

Eliza and Allan shared another telepathic look. They had a whole conversation without speaking a word. The micro-adjustments of their facial muscles allowed them to intuit exactly what the other was thinking.

Where should we start? Eliza thought.

At the beginning, probably, Allan thought.

No need to be a smart-ass, dear.

Allan grimaced and sat up in his chair. He poured himself a top off. His eyes shifted to the boarded-up windows. He could see the flashes of lightning through the thin area where the plywood sheets met.

"Oddly enough, it started a lot like this. Except it was fucking freezing," he said.

*P*ITTSBURGH, *PENNSYLVANIA. JANUARY 1978.*

Flurries so thick, Allan could barely see five feet in front of him as he drove. Joe DeNardo's voice was on the radio telling the city about a snowstorm that would eventually dump a massive twenty-seven inches on steel town. 102.5 WDVE was playing a clip from his forecast on the eight o'clock news.

Allan was quite aware of the storm. He was battling it in his '67 Chevrolet C20 pick-up. The normally teal paint job was covered by a thick layer of snow. Allan cursed himself for not picking up new windshield wipers last week. His were struggling to do any damage to the constant onslaught the blizzard threw at him.

Allan, a seventeen-year-old high school dropout, cursed himself again for staying late to help with the framing job. He needed the money. His father had kicked him out of the house when he announced he was leaving academia behind, which was exactly what he'd hoped for. He'd been trying to leave the old drunk behind since he grew big enough for the lush to think twice before raising a hand to him.

Allan took after his mother's father, a massive Swede who's Viking lineage was well documented. He was taller than his father by a good seven inches. When Allan turned fourteen, the power dynamic in the home shifted. Puberty had taken what little advantage his father had. It showed up too late to stop Allan's mother from leaving, but early enough to help him save himself.

Belts, as his father found out one night, were for keeping pants up and nothing more. If used for any other purpose, they'd be quickly turned on the perpetrator, leaving him a broken man covered in welts. Lessons were given from son to father, instead of the usual manner.

For the last year and a half, Allan worked as a carpenter's apprentice. The big difference between apprenticeship and college—you get paid to learn instead of the other way around.

He built homes. It was good, honest work. He liked working with his hands. He liked creating things.

He did not like how bad the roads were.

There was a twenty-four-hour diner not too far up the road. The girl who worked the counter was cute. Allan stopped there for dinner at least three days a week, but still hadn't mustered the courage to say more than, "Turkey meatloaf," to her.

If he could make it to the diner, he could wait out the storm somewhere warm with food. Much more enjoyable than the shoebox he called an apartment.

The chevy crawled along the black ice covered by sleet and topped with fresh powder. After what seemed like forever, the parking lot lights and neon signage for Warden's Diner came into view. Allan always wondered where the name had come from. He took the turn into the parking lot in what seemed like slow motion. He wasn't taking any chances.

The diner had been built in the fifties and hadn't been updated since. White tile floor and faux marble tables were punctuated with blood red chairs and booths. Any other night, this place would be filled with customers.

Tonight, no one else was dumb or desperate enough to be on the roads. He was the lone patron. Allan preferred to sit at the counter near the kitchen. He told himself it was because the food got to him quicker. Really it was her.

The girl wore a form-fitting white and red waitress uniform. Her name tag read ELIZA. She was sixteen and stuck taking orders at her family's diner. Her dark hair was pulled back in a tight ponytail. Allan made his way to his usual seat and was relieved when Eliza smiled.

Most of the staff had called off. Despite this, Eliza's father had decided the family would stay the night and work. So much for catching Carson tonight. She watched as the tall teen with the weathered face walked in.

He was a mystery to her. She thought she remembered him from school, but one day he just stopped showing up. Then, a few weeks ago, he'd started showing up again at her diner. She knew exactly what he wanted and when he sat down, she told him.

"Turkey meatloaf. Right?" she added the 'right' out of politeness. Customer service. Her father was around here somewhere. Allan, having his only words taken away from him, was forced to come up with new ones. The best he could muster . . .

"How'd you know?"

"You're here every Monday, Wednesday, and Friday. Order never changes."

"I like what I like," he grimaced. He liked her. She knew he liked turkey meatloaf. That was a start.

"We aim to serve. Let me get that in for you."

She disappeared into the kitchen to drop the ticket.

Allan's heart raced. He was alone in this diner with the diner girl. Eliza. Holy shit. He was going to have dinner and she was the only one around to have a conversation with. This was the closest he'd come to a date in his life.

He needed to steel himself, have more to say when she got back. Oh, God. What was he going to talk about? Crown molding?

She came back through the swing-doors and put her elbows on the counter and her head into her hands. She looked at Allan, studied him, and decided talking to him was better than being with her family in the kitchen. She could say she was doing her job. Customer service.

"I put an order in for myself, too. I don't think we'll be getting much more company." She motioned to the nearly whited-out windows.

She was eating too. One step closer to a real date.

"Everyone's gotta eat," Allan said.

"And they do it under the watchful eye of the warden."

"Why do they call it Warden's?"

"The original owner of the diner was a warden at the state correctional institution. After a few years dealing with murderers and rapists, he thought he could handle customers."

Eliza paused and gave Allan a look that indicated he couldn't.

"After a few years, he missed the murderers," she said.

"You love what you love," Allan said. It got a small smile out of Eliza. Was this going well?

"He got his prison job back and sold the place to my dad."

"Sentencing you to have dinner with me. The bastard."

Eliza sensed a kinship in this young man. They were on the same frequency. She didn't believe in coincidences, but his presence made her feel oddly safe. She didn't know this kid—and he *was* a kid, a boy. A boy with sad eyes and strong arms. Just the way she liked them.

"I usually have it with Johnny Carson."

"So, I have no chance at asking you out then? Famous boyfriend and all."

He said the words, but hadn't even realized it. Once the conversation started, it was like he was on autopilot. He saw the opening and took it. He'd come a long way from *turkey meatloaf*. He braced himself for the fallout.

"Johnny doesn't believe in labels," Eliza's nose scrunched up as she tried not to smile. She hadn't expected to get a date tonight. She decided they were on one now. If they had another—and she hadn't decided that they would—it would be their second.

"What do you believe in?" Allan asked.

Eliza thought about that for a moment. She wanted to really consider the question. What did she believe in?

"I don't know," she said, laughing. "But I can tell you what I don't believe in."

"What?" Allan asked, hopeful.

"I don't believe in coincidence." She looked into his eyes. Like she was trying to see if they were feeling the same things. Trying to read his mind.

"Everything happens for a reason?" Allan said with an unintended sharpness. It was a sentiment he'd never really agreed with. He couldn't see *why* he was born into a family like his.

"Everything happens. It's up to us to find a reason," she said.

"Order up!" was shouted through from the kitchen.

"Let me go find our food."

She moved back through the swing door and into the kitchen, leaving Allan alone with his thoughts.

It's up to us to find a reason.

Eliza returned with the turkey meatloaf for Allan and a bacon cheeseburger, fries, and a chocolate milkshake for her. She dipped her fries in her milkshake as they continued to flirt with one another.

Allan told her about how he'd emancipated himself and Eliza learned why his eyes were so sad. She was lucky enough to have a family that cared. Or at least cared that she was fed and housed.

She told Allan how she felt like her parents cared more about the diner than they did about her. He understood that all too well. They talked for hours, but it seemed like minutes.

Eliza's father checked every hour or so on the dining room. He came out in his grease-stained apron and kept a close eye on the sole customer who was keeping his teen daughter so occupied. Allan would order a small plate when it felt like he needed a reason to stay. By three a.m. Allan had ordered onion rings, two milkshakes, and waffles. He and Eliza shared them while they caught each other up on the sixteen or seventeen years they had spent not knowing each other.

When the sun rose, Allan felt compelled to finally call it a night. It was literally the next morning.

They said their goodbyes and Allan used all the power he had to stop himself from kissing her.

She wished that he would. But she understood that a boy whose mother left him might not know what it was a girl wanted. Instead, he asked if he could have her number. That would hold her over at least. She wrote it on a check and handed it to him, still hoping for him to kiss her. She felt a pang of fear run down her chest as he walked away.

When he tried to open the doors, they were blocked by the snow. No one was getting in or out until the twenty-seven inches of packed snow was removed. Allan turned around and walked back towards the counter.

"Guess I'm stuck here," he said.

"Thank god."

She jumped the counter into his arms and did what he was too proper to do. Eliza wrapped her legs around his waist and kissed him hard. They were now on their second date. It was a new day, after all.

He held her by the hips and allowed himself to embrace her. She felt him get hard and pressed into him. He was embarrassed, while she was deciding if she really believed what she said earlier.

"Bathroom," she commanded. Not a question. Not an offer. An order.

"Are you sure?" he said.

"This is the reason," she said, before grabbing his face, and kissing him with all her might.

Allan, still holding Eliza in his arms, threw open the bathroom door. She hopped down from his arms and unbuckled his belt. She pulled him out of his pants and held him until he moaned softly.

"I've never . . ." he said.

"Me either," she said.

She wanted him. She slid her underwear out from under her skirt, jumped back into his arms, and they became one. They writhed together as he moved up against a wall for additional support. She bit his neck as she moved through the pain into pleasure.

This is the reason, she thought. His sinewy arms tensed as they held her up against the wall. She dug her nails into them as they climaxed together.

That was when her father threw open the bathroom door.

"**I** DID NOT NEED that level of detail," Kip said.

"You said you wanted the whole story," Allan said, sipping his whiskey.

"We fuck. How do you think you came to be?" Eliza said, looking at Valerie.

"I got it, Mom." Valerie wanted to throw up.

"When I got pregnant, my parents wanted to send me away. So, I went away. With Allan."

"You ran away?" Valerie was shocked.

"I did," Eliza said, looking at her daughter. "But I did it for love, not to follow some shitty band."

"I didn't know it at the time, but it was technically kidnapping," Allan added.

"They'll never catch you, dear."

"Kidnapping?" Kip said. "Jesus fucking Christ."

"*Technically*," Eliza clarified. "I went willingly."

"And now," Allan continued, "instead of making *mucho dinero* renting this place out to MERTs, we host our family vacation on fourth of July weekend. Celebrating our independence from our parents with the family we created."

Allan and Eliza shared a deep kiss. All these years and none of their passion has waned.

"So, when you try to tell us you can't let Audrey marry that boy, who she clearly loves, because they're too young. You're preaching to the wrong choir, honey," Eliza said, finally telling her daughter how she felt.

"Didn't you ever wonder why you never see your grandparents?" Allan said.

"I thought it was because they lived on the other side of the state, not because you two ran away together as teenagers."

"I mean, Pittsburgh does suck, that's true," Allan laughed before Eliza swatted him playfully.

"You never wondered why we don't go back?" Eliza let her daughter have a moment to digest that before she went on.

"We can't tell you what to do, but those kids are going to do what they want regardless. Just like we did. So, the question you have to ask is: do you want to be a part of their lives, or not? Because either way, that baby is coming."

A buzz could be heard as electrons were slowed by ancient wiring. Lights flickered and then light flooded the room. Kip and Valerie both eyed the unconscious woman on the couch. They had the same thought in that moment.

Shit...

23
FAMILY TRAITS

T HE SUN ROSE OVER the sea, illuminating the damage that had been done overnight. The formerly pristine streets were strewn with debris. Power lines were downed, homes waterlogged and flooded.

Fish flopped in the front yard of Windward House, desperate in their attempt to take in what little water was left after the surges receded into the sea. They writhed in the orange glow of morning, nautical vampires trapped in the sun's dry embrace.

Collin, Audrey and Noah wanted to clean up, but the damage was beyond their abilities. They mostly marveled, open-mouthed, at the mass of sea life struggling to survive on land. Collin gave a subtle gesture to Orla that she recognized from their years together. It was a look that said, *let's get away from the kids.*

"Let's go check out the basement," he said.

Kip and Valerie came outside with coffee so Orla felt OK leaving the teens to collect lobsters in the front yard. At least they'd eat well tonight. She and Collin went around back, leaving Audrey and Noah with the coffee-toting adults.

"Hey, little man," Kip called out from the porch. "I'm gonna ask you this once, and I want the truth." He put his arm around Audrey. "This girl right here, I will kill to protect her. Am I gonna have to kill you?"

"Never," Noah said, steadfast in that conviction. Kip and Valerie shared a knowing look, and took deep breaths.

"OK," Kip said, with resignation.

"OK?" Audrey was bewildered.

"OK." Kip repeated.

"We give you our permission," Valerie clarified.

"Mom, really?!" Audrey's face lit up at the possibility. She still didn't believe it. There was no way. What had changed their minds? When her mother nodded her assent, Audrey hugged her tighter than she ever had.

"But you have to promise you both go to college at Temple, so it's free. You can both stay with us while Noah's in school to keep expenses low. We can help watch the baby. Well, your father can. I have a real job."

"I run one of the most popular skate parks in the city!" Kip reminded her.

"You babysit teens and do occasional ramp repair," Valerie said.

"Grandpa Allan does the repairs," Audrey added.

"I'm having a moment with my future son-in-law. Can ya'll not put me on blast right now? Shit . . ."

Audrey and Valerie shared a laugh. The first one they'd had together since coming to Cape May. Kip and Noah nodded at one another. Two men, who want what's best for that girl hugging her mother with tears of joy in her eyes. They shared a silent understanding.

"So you're pitching us the plan we had all along?" Audrey said, the sarcasm passed down from her grandmother coating her words.

"We wrote you off as dumb kids," Kip said.

"You're our kid, so we kind of assumed, you know?" Valerie said. They embraced one another and seemed happy. One might even confuse them for a family.

"You can get back on the circuit after the baby is born," Kip said, ruffling up his daughter's hair.

"And I'm gonna tear shit up."

C OLLIN AND ORLA MADE their way down the stairs that led into the basement apartment. Collin's body wailed in pain with every movement. The acetaminophen and ibuprofen cocktail Valerie had suggested for him last night had begun to wear off. Collin wanted to feel the pain for as long as it would stay. The absurd order of events that had led to bruises covering most of his midsection were also what led to him spending this time with Orla.

Worth it, was all he thought as he held his ribs in place.

Within two steps, they hit water and saw that the whole basement was a lagoon. There would be no fixing that.

"Hey," Orla said. "Can we hang out tonight? I want to take you somewhere."

"You're not sick of me?"

"Not yet."

Water splashed them both in the face.

"The fuck?" Collin said, wiping water from his eyes.

High-pitched squeaks rang in their ears. They realized they weren't alone in this basement tank. Two dolphins swam where Beth had slept nights before. Their tails rhythmically jerked, splashing the humans. It seemed they were making the best of the forced proximity in their vacation rental.

"Are they?" Orla said. Collin cocked his head, unsure of what he was seeing.

"I think I have a new addition to the Kama Sutra," he said.

"Oh, we've done that one before. Or was that with Dale?"

"Nope, it was me. I remember your blowhole well."

"You've never been in my blowhole. And you never will." Orla took a beat to watch the unholy act the dolphins were engaged in.

"Unless I've had wine," she corrected.

"You used to drink a lot of wine." Collin's check bones rose as he cracked a smile. This was the Orla from his memory. This was the woman he'd fallen in love with.

"Still do," Orla winked.

"Who do we call for dolphin removal?" Collin said.

The high-pitched squeaks came to a climax, as did the dolphins.

"He knows what he's doing," Orla said, impressed.

"How can you tell which is which?"

L ATER THAT AFTERNOON, AFTER emergency responders had cleared most of the roads for travel, Siobhan arrived at Windward House. Her car slowed to a crawl and crushed the corpses of fish as she made her way to the parking lot. She was in no mood for words and made her son get in the car before he could explain what happened. Beth limped out of the house sans suitcases. All her belongings were in the flooded basement being guarded by randy dolphins.

Beth hobbled toward her daughter, sporting a black eye.

"Mom, what happened?"

Beth said nothing and joined her grandson in the car. Kip and Valerie approached Siobhan.

"Long story short," Valerie said, "my mom kicked your mom's ass."

Siobhan couldn't stop herself from laughing. This whole situation had got so out of hand it was all she could do.

"That makes sense. She's the worst, isn't she?" Siobhan said.

"She really is. I almost respect it."

"Listen," Kip said, "we know you're in a hurry, but we wanted to tell you face to face. These two have our blessing to get married."

"We're not trying to make you the bad guys," Valerie said, "but the ball is in your court now."

"Great. Just wonderful."

Siobhan didn't have the emotional stamina to put up any kind of fight right now. She was tired from riding out a hurricane on her own—her son and sister had abandoned her—and she'd spent the night raiding the wine cellar before it flooded. Now she was paying the price.

Beth rolled down her window, stuck her bruised face out and yelled, "Siobhan, let's go. I need a doctor so that I can call a lawyer."

Siobhan rolled her eyes in apology to Kip and Valerie. Her look let them know she understood how ridiculous her mother was.

"I can't really think right now," she said. "I need to talk to my husband. He's due home in the next day or so."

"No need to explain to us. Do what you need to," Kip said.

"Thanks. And thank you for taking care of him and Orla last night."

Siobhan moved back to her car and got into the driver's seat. She refused to meet her mother's gaze while she backed out and drove her family home.

"Your dad's going to make me help clean this yard if we go back inside," Kip asked, "isn't he?"

"You and me both."

"Let's go get brunch somewhere far, far away," Kip said.

Valerie surveyed the damage. The roads were covered in debris and at least two rival schools of fish. They weren't driving anywhere.

"You got a pilot's license I don't know about?" she said.

"We can walk and pretend we're helping people."

"This is why I love you."

Val grabbed her husband's hand. They walked away from Windward House, fingers intertwined.

S IOBHAN PULLED UP TO her water-damaged—but still standing—home. There was a car in her spot. It was the cerulean Dakota four-by-four she knew so well. A smile spread across her face.

"Mom, is that—"

"Jesse!" Siobhan slammed the car into park. Noah and Siobhan threw their doors open and ran to the tall, bearded man who was exiting the truck in their driveway.

"Hey, beautiful," he said as Siobhan ran into his arms. He kissed her with all the pomp and circumstance necessary after spending a quarter of a year at sea. After performing part of his marital duty, Jesse turned his attention to his son.

"So, buddy, what have you been trying to tell me?"

Siobhan put a hand on her son's shoulder and they both took a deep breath.

"What?" Their looks startled him. "You didn't kill anyone, did you?"

"Worse," Siobhan said.

Jesse was quite confused, but knew it was serious after he investigated his wife's car. He was far more afraid of what he saw in there than navigating through a hurricane.

"Why is your mother here?"

24
FINE

THE SILENCE WOULD HAVE been unbearable if wasn't for the crashing waves and cawing gulls who delighted in the scraps left behind by the hurricane. Noah watched as two gulls fought over a fish, while he sat next to his father on a sand dune they had shared many times before.

The beach was where they went to get away from Siobhan. It was the place where Jesse had taught Noah how to box, how to use a pocketknife, and where he gave him the talk he now wished he had been more specific about.

Jesse, despite finding out he would soon be a grandfather, was calm and contemplative. As a leader, he tried to lack judgement. He simply took in the information and let it marinate in his mind. As a father, he wanted to shake his son silly and scream.

He calmed himself before speaking.

"I want you to tell me something, son."

Noah looked his father in the eye, the same way Jesse had taught him to on this very same beach. He looked at him the way Jesse thought a man should look at another man with whom you had a disagreement. He was firm, but open. Jesse had taught him well. That gave him comfort as he asked his son the question he had to ask.

"Would we still be having this conversation if she weren't pregnant?"

It was a fair question. It was also one Noah was more than prepared for. He wouldn't go so far as to spill his guts like he had at the bar with Collin and Casey. But he was going to tell his father the truth.

"I've wanted to marry her since we learned to swim together, sir."

"Just because a girl lets you pee on her does not mean she's the one," Jesse jested. He wanted to lighten the mood.

"Dad, I'm serious."

Jesse couldn't stop the pride from escaping his stoic face. His son's determination was admirable. Maybe he had taught him too well.

"I know," he said, "but I don't think you understand how serious this is. You're not ready for this kind of responsibility."

"With all due respect, sir," Noah said, gaining confidence, "is anyone ever ready for the responsibility?"

The poise and confidence in his son's statement hit Jesse like a punch to the gut.

"No. They are not," he had to admit. "I sure as hell wasn't. But you're my son. And I have to do what I think is best. I cannot give you permission to do something so reckless."

There was more to marriage than love. This was something Jesse had learned over the years. He doubted his son would understand. Marriage wasn't just about caring for another person, being there for them, or making love to them. That was the easy part. Marriage was a business. A business run by co-CEOs who never really knew what it was the other one wanted the business to do. There were financial considerations, social obligations, and, worst of all, tax implications. Marriage, at the end of the day, was a contract. And children weren't allowed to enter into contracts for good reason.

Jesse watched as his son took in that information, stood up, and shook the sand off his shorts. Noah looked at his father, not happy, but with a distinct resolve.

"Fine," Noah said.

Fine, Jesse thought. *Shit*. He might have underestimated his boy here: he wasn't getting angry, he wasn't throwing a temper tantrum. He was gazing at Jesse with the calm of a hostage negotiator.

"Are you OK?" Jesse asked.

"Nothing I say is going to change your mind, is it?"

Jesse shook his head. Despite the resolve in his son's eyes, every fiber of Jesse's being told him this was a bad idea. They were going to be parents together, regardless. They were going to spend every day together when that happened. That wasn't something Jesse could, or even wanted to, stop from happening.

The legal consequences of marriage, however, those could wait. Better to see how the relationship looked after two years of changing diapers in a constant state of exhaustion. He was as determined as his son. They were at an impasse.

"Then I did what I had to," Noah said. He stood up, wiped the sand off his jeans, and began to walk away from the dune his father still sat upon. He stopped and turned to face him. Noah was at eye level with his father, despite lacking the high ground.

"Just know that, the moment it's no longer up to you, I'm going to do what I think is right. Whether you agree or not."

Jesse stood in an attempt to take even more of the high ground his son had seized. He understood the honesty and bravery Noah was trying to display.

"Is that so?" he said.

"It is," Noah said. "And nothing you say is going to change my mind."

Jesse put his hand on his son's shoulder. If he were a different kind of man, he might tell Noah how proud he was of him right now, or how much he loved him, or how worried he was for him.

Instead, he just nodded.

He understood his son's words: they'd be married in a few months, when Noah turned eighteen. They already had the girl's parents' permission.

All Jesse was doing was buying time. His son might resent him for it, but he was OK with that. The more time he had to see how this all played out, the more likely it was that his son could make an informed decision. Jesse wanted to buy as much time as he could. He wanted his little man to remain a boy as long as possible.

Noah understood his father's nod. He understood all his unspoken reservations. His father would have to be the one to admit he was wrong. It would take years, but Noah knew it would happen.

A few years from now, he'd be working for a tech company, Audrey would be running her business, and they would be an amazing team raising an amazing kid and his father would have to admit that all he had done was postpone the inevitable.

Noah wouldn't tell him '*I told you so*'. He'd simply do the same thing he was about to do. His father would know.

Noah extended his hand. Jesse took it and gave it a firm shake.

Father and son understood one another—it was Jesse who pulled Noah into a hug.

Noah felt this meant he won. Jesse had taught him in any negotiation there was a winner and a loser.

Noah didn't feel like a loser. Nor did his father.

25
BAD BLOOD

COLLIN FOUND THAT IF he took deep, slow breaths he could curb the pain in his ribs that rose and fell with every breath. His face was black and blue around the jaw and right eye socket. It looked worse than it was.

The locals at the C-View Inn did not give him a second look. Brawls happened, and small towns talked. No one cared if you got your ass kicked. Most of them had punched a cop in the face before. A few of the old timers raised their beers to Collin in solidarity as he made his way to the bar. They knew how it went.

It was karaoke night. A ninety-year-old man with tubes in his nose connecting him to an oxygen tank, crooned Sinatra's 'I've Got You Under My Skin'. Collin listened and thought that the oxygen should be considered a performance enhancing drug. USAADA would put an asterisk next to the old man's performance.

The regulars were decked out in red, white, and blue. One of those old timers paid for Collin's beer. He wore a Vietnam veteran's cap and yelled across the bar.

"Dale's a dip shit!" The vet said.

Collin raised his glass to the old vet and looked around the bar. He hadn't seen Orla, and she'd told him to meet her there. The karaoke host came over. He gave Collin his card.

The host was a moonlighting lawyer.

"I heard about your incident with the CMPD. If you want a nice little pay day, give me a call," the host said.

"Appreciate it. Let me think it over," Collin said, while he examined the host's card.

"Sue the fuck out of 'em," the vet said. "Cops are fascist fucks." He showed Collin his beach patrol tattoo. "We save lives, they just fuck them up."

"Don't wait too long," the host said. He took a picture of Collin's face, blinding him with flash. "Want to make sure those bruises are visible for evidence."

"Do me a favor: add me to the top of the karaoke list and I'll give you a call tomorrow." Collin lied.

"Deal." The ambulance chaser really wanted this case.

After a few sips of beer, Collin spotted Orla at a table.

"Gotta go, gents. Thanks for the beer." He patted the vet on the back in thanks, shook hands with the host, and moved to her.

"I thought you had something to show me?" Collin said.

"Don't you remember," she said. "Karaoke night?"

Karaoke night was when Collin and Orla had met for the first time.

ALL THOSE YEARS AGO, Orla watched as the handsome MERT with the beard and shaggy hair walked into the bar. He still looked surprised that no one had even tried to card him. Orla didn't like that he wasn't from town and was trying to roll into their bar. But it was the off season.

Maybe he was new in town.

Jesse was singing 'Going Away to College' by Blink-182. Orla hated how good her sister's husband was at everything he did. It was annoying. The MERT sat down at a table across from Orla and the friends from high school she was meeting up with. She noticed that they needed one more seat. There was one right next to them, but Orla decided she wanted the excuse. Orla looked over at the MERT, sitting alone in the locals bar.

Jesse sang about how the world was an ugly place as Orla made her way to the MERT's table.

"Can I borrow this chair, sir?" she said, going up an octave on the *sir*.

She could tell she had startled him, but before she could follow up with the ice-breaker she had planned, he quipped right back.

"No, you can keep it," he said, and raised an eyebrow.

"JUST NEVER CALL ME sir."

Collin and Orla finished his line together at the same table years later. They shared a laugh at the simple way years together had begun.

"I still can't believe you got me to invite you over to our table," she said, looking at him the way she did all those years ago.

"Just a MERT, right?"

"You were . . . You *are*," she said with a smirk. Collin smiled, it hurt his jaw.

"We had some good times here," he said.

"We did . . ."

Silence filled the air. Collin couldn't help himself. He needed to know.

"Why didn't you tell me?"

Orla didn't know what to say.

"I'd have given up everything for you," he said.

Orla knew he meant it. She struggled to find words.

"I even . . . Never mind."

He wanted to tell her about the ring, but that might be too much. She didn't need to know that. It wouldn't change anything now. They were getting along—why ruin it?

"What?" Orla said. She needed more time to think.

"Nothing. I just . . . I don't know. I've been thinking a lot about what could have been. And I feel like I prefer that timeline to the current one."

"Things happen for a reason." Orla could only muster platitudes.

"Things happen," Collin said. "It's up to us to find the reason."

That was something his mother told him all the time while growing up.

"That's why I'm here now. To find the reason."

Collin and Orla both took a long sip of their beers. They shared a meaningful glance while the carbonation tickled their tongues. The alcohol could help to loosen them up, but they needed a lot more.

Orla didn't know what to say. There was no 'right' thing *to* say.

"Collin Cassidy, you're up!" the karaoke host called out through the sound system.

"You signed up?" Orla asked.

"Needed to get a little something off my chest."

Collin made his way over to the karaoke stage. He took the mic and nodded to the host.

A copyright-infringement-free arrangement of 'Bad Blood' by Taylor Swift began.

Collin sang like a tone-deaf elk directly to Orla. What he lacked in vocal ability he made up for in showmanship. He moved about the bar, engaging other patrons to sing along with him. He spotted the Elephant Man downing a shot at the bar, grabbed him, and the two of them scream-sang at Orla together about how sad it was to think about good times.

Collin hammed it up for the chorus.

Confidence is what matters most in life—and karaoke.

Collin had learned this in Los Angeles, where karaoke nights were frequented by quasi-professional singers.

They might be able to carry a tune, but Collin could carry a room.

There were no winners in life or karaoke, just those who did their best and those too scared to try. Collin was trying. He hoped Orla could see that.

Orla couldn't stop herself from smiling. The song choice was so on the nose and so poorly performed that it was absurd. Which she knew was exactly what Collin was going for. He always knew how to make her laugh, even in the most uncomfortable of times. He had the innate ability to turn even the most serious occasion into farce. Something she wished she could do.

When the song ended, the entire bar cheered. Orla rolled her eyes. She knew what he was doing. She *liked* what he was doing. She knew he knew she liked it. The coy grimace he made as he returned to their table told her so.

"Thank you, thank you. Thanks . . ." he high-fived his new fans and sat back down.

"Well? How'd I do?" he said, and took a sip of beer to quench his dry throat.

"Taylor Swift? Hollywood has changed you."

"She is the voice of our doomed generation."

Orla stood up and grabbed her purse. "Come with me," she commanded and walked out of the bar without so much as a look back at Collin.

Collin knew full well what that meant. She had used that line and intonation many times in the past when she was ready to go.

He jumped out of his chair and followed, leaving a half-full beer that was then stolen and drunk by the Elephant Man.

O RLA DRAGGED COLLIN INTO the empty headquarters of Cape May Beach Patrol. She threw him up against a wall and kissed him hard.

She pressed into him. He winced.

"Fuck!" he screamed. "Ribs . . . ribs."

"Don't be a little bitch," she challenged him.

Stared him down.

Kissed him harder.

Forced him use the pain.

He let it add to the pleasure and lifted her in his arms, the way he used to do it all those years ago. It was excruciating, but he wouldn't let a little pain get in their way. Not this time.

He took a deep breath and forced her to the wall. Her legs wrapped around him. Their hips pressed into one another. Collin let the pain pass through his body in deep inhalations as their lips met. He pressed his lips into Orla's and bit her bottom lip to give a little of what he was getting. Her eyes rolled in the back of her head as she let his teeth press into her flesh.

Orla remembered all the times when they were younger that they'd snuck into the lifeguard shack to hook up. Those memories fueled the passion in this moment and filled her with warmth she wanted to share with Collin.

She'd fantasized her current reality; remembered their younger bodies doing this same dance. They were dancing with their own ghosts. Collin pulled off her shirt, but held her hands at the wrists, trapping her with the fabric while he slowly kissed from the nape of her neck down to her breast.

"Captain Ruane?" A pitchy voice rang out from the entrance. Collin and Orla's attention snapped in that direction.

A teenage lifeguard stood at the door with their headquarters keys in hand and a date on their arm. It would seem great minds thought alike. The teens stared at the adults for a long moment.

"If you leave now," Orla said, "I won't rat you out."

"If you leave, I won't rat you out," the teen replied.

A sexual Mexican standoff. Who would be the first to draw?

"Who do you think they'll believe?" Orla fired.

"Damn it."

The teen had been hit. They huffed and left with their date.

"And lock the door," Orla yelled before Collin took her face in his hand and picked up where they had left off.

O UTSIDE, FIREWORKS LIT UP the night sky. The fourth of July display was reflected on the surface of the ocean, doubling the majesty. Bomb's bursting gave proof that love was still in the air. Just like the explosions in the sky, Collin and Orla crescendoed multiple times throughout the night. When they thought the fireworks might be done, more came. And they came more.

As sunlight began to peak through headquarters' windows, Collin and Orla were naked under a blanket on the floor, in desperate need of hydration and nutrition. She rested her head on his hairy, toned, chest. She ran her fingers through the hair absentmindedly.

"Fuck," she said.

"That is what we did," he said.

"May be a new record," she said.

The sun shone in their eyes as they laughed, too exhausted to do anything more. Collin pulled the blanket over both their faces, trying to hide from the light of day. They kissed in their small blanket fort.

"I read your plays," Collin said, "They're amazing. I like the one about the couple who got into different schools."

"That's sweet," Orla said. She closed her eyes and tried to fight having to get up anytime soon. She was flattered for a moment, but remembered that she had never shared her plays with Collin.

She pulled away from his embrace. The blanket flew off and the two of them were bathed in morning light while the ocean crashed in the distance.

"How the fuck did you read that?" she said.

"I just . . . I saw them on your computer and I—"

"You stole my plays?"

"Steal is a strong word. I pirated them."

He was trying to be cheeky. He hoped the charisma would get him out of this one.

"Pirating is stealing!" she said.

"No one actually believes that," he said.

"You don't get to unilaterally decide to steal someone's work."

"I don't think you get to lecture me on unilateral decisions."

The jab landed. Orla's eyes widened. This again.

"Really? I thought we were past this," she said.

"Past it? How could I be past it when you won't talk about it with me? You told everyone else about it: your sister, Jesse."

"I did *not* tell Jesse."

"You told Siobhan, that's the same as telling Jesse and you know it," he said. Orla hated that he knew her family so well.

"Orla, you told your mom, but you didn't tell me. Your *mom*!"

Orla knew her mother's revelation would come back to bite her in the ass. She was at a loss for words. She knew he was right, but did not want to admit that.

"I did not tell my mom! That was Siobhan, too."

"We don't have to worry about this right now. Come to LA! I can help you develop any of your plays into shows. This could be huge for you!"

He meant it. He really thought Orla was going to pick up her life and move across the country to follow *his* dream instead of her own. Even after all these years, he still wanted her to come to him. To live life on his terms. She scoffed while she scrambled to put her clothes back on.

"Oh, so I'm just a cash cow to you now, huh? You want to take my plays and pimp them out to your friends in Hollywood?"

"I thought you'd want—"

"You thought I'd what? Give up my entire life? Follow you across the country? Well, guess what: I don't want what you want. I don't give a fuck if my plays get produced. I write them for fun! I like teaching. I am a teacher. Even if the abortion never happened, I was never going to move there with you. I'm never moving to Los Angeles. That's *your* home. It's *your* dream! My home is here. I want to stay close to my sister and nephew. I want my family to be a family!"

"Bull-fucking-shit," Collin said. "You're leaving your family the moment you get that job at NYU, aren't you?" He saw the look of horror on her face, "Yeah, I know about that too. Don't give me the I'm-here-for-my-family schtick. You're here because you have to be, not because you want to be."

"And you're so noble? I'm surprised you're still here. Usually, by now, I'd have come home to an empty apartment."

"You know why I left."

This was a challenge. He wanted her to do what she never did. He wanted her to tell him what she was feeling all those years ago.

Orla said nothing. She continued to search for and put on her clothes. Collin waited for a reply while she put on her bra. She gave him nothing.

Having dressed fully after dressing Collin down, Orla moved to the door. Collin scoffed.

"Are you serious right now?" Collin said. He was stunned, he didn't know what else to say. Who got this worked up over someone liking their writing?

"Yes. Because I thought maybe, just maybe, you had changed. That what *you* wanted wasn't the most important thing in the world. That you might give a shit about the people around you. But you're still the same selfish asshole who moved three-thousand miles away and didn't give a shit about who he was leaving behind."

"Are you fucked in the head?" Collin tried to find his clothes, but was too angry to get dressed. He was sick of being blamed for what she did.

"You think I was just going to leave you behind? Fuck all the way off. I was going to ask you to marry me!" he said.

He was seething. Insulted by the insinuation. Did she really think he was not thinking about his and Orla's future when he made the decision to go to film school? Did she really not understand that he just wanted to be a man worthy of being with her? That he wanted to provide for her while doing what he loved?

Orla processed this during a long silence. She did not believe it for one second.

"Bullshit," she said.

"I have the ring in my desk drawer in Los Angeles. Come with me. I'll prove it to you."

Orla had no idea Collin was ever considering marriage. She doesn't know if *she* ever considered it.

His admission took her aback. Tears welled up. How could this be what he wanted?

"Why didn't you say anything sooner?" she said.

"Because the day I bought the ring you had a fucking abortion before you even told me you were pregnant! That's why! Because I wanted to spend the rest of my life with you, and you didn't even have the decency to let me in on a potentially life-changing decision."

"It was my body—"

"And it was *our* child inside of it," he said.

"I didn't need your permission!"

He stood up, stark naked, covered in bruises, and bared his soul.

"Yeah. It was your decision. No one is saying it wasn't. I don't give a fuck about the abortion. But fuck you for not telling me. Fuck you for not thinking I even deserved to know. Did the years we were together mean nothing to you?"

Tears welled up in Orla's eyes and, hard as she tried, she couldn't stop the flow.

"We were kids," was all she could come up with before a sob leapt out of her.

"That's not an answer."

Collin wasn't going to let her off the hook this time. He wasn't going to give in to the emotional terrorism of tears.

"Well? Did they? Because if they did, forget all the *down with the patriarchy – my body, my choice* bullshit."

He marched right up to where she was perched at the door, and looked her right in the eyes when he said, "You were well within your rights to do what you did, I'm not arguing that. I would have understood. Hell, I would have taken you to the clinic and held your hand; been there for you." Collin started to bawl.

They were both terrorists now. He needed a moment before he could continue. After a deep breath . . .

"Tell me, right now, why you didn't think I should know that the woman I loved was pregnant?"

Orla said nothing. She wiped tears from her cheek and hyperventilated. The truth was she didn't have an answer other than the fact that she was scared.

"Huh? I'm waiting . . ." Collin prodded.

"Fuck you."

It was all she could say between sobs. She didn't know what else to say. How do you tell someone who wants a clear and simple answer that you don't have one. That you never had one.

"A well-reasoned and articulate response. Bravo. No wonder you're the top academic at Cape County Community College."

The low blow landed, and Collin immediately felt guilty. He saw the hurt cut across Orla's face. He hit her with her own biggest insecurity: the thought that she wasn't good enough. That she really was only here because she had no other choice.

He cursed himself, but it was too late for remorse. She was gone.

Orla slammed the door behind her. That door was shut for good now.

A moment later, the door opened. It was the Elephant Man, his suit torn, looking like he'd been in a bad bar fight.

"This is what happens when you stop ignoring the elephant. Happy birthday, America," he slurred. He stumbled into the room and gave Collin's naked body the once over.

"You look like shit," the Elephant Man said. "Nice dick," then fell face-first onto the floor and passed out.

Collin wasn't sure who'd fucked up worse.

26
IF YOU CALL

COLLIN THREW HIS LUGGAGE in to the rental car's trunk. He slammed the trunk shut, done with this trip. This would be the last time he ever listened to his agent.

His parents, sister and brother-in-law were all in what used to be the front yard, watching as a crane dangled a dolphin in a harness. The dolphin squeaked angrily at its rescuers. All it knew was that it had been separated from the mate it had booked the basement apartment with. Its mate was just as frenzied and turned the basement into a whirlpool while animal control worked to subdue it.

One of the animal control guys fell into the pool and found himself going for a ride in the current. It was looking like they were going to have to use the tranquilizer gun.

Collin hugged his mother goodbye.

"Have you tried—"

"*Mom*," he said, "I've called her a hundred times. She doesn't want to talk to me. And, honestly, I don't have much more to say to her."

Eliza and Allan shared a knowing glace, the old married couple knew that sometimes they had to step back and let their children make their own mistakes. It had taken them a long time to learn this lesson, and they were not going to give in to bad habits now.

Eliza wanted nothing more than to yell at her son to drop everything and go beg Orla for forgiveness. She didn't actually know what had happened, but she assumed it was her son's fault. He was too much like her, it *had* to be his fault. Instead, she just hugged him and braced herself for a long communication drought. Collin forgot how phones worked when he was in California.

Audrey ran out of the house, knowing her uncle was about to leave. She had not yet learned this hard-fought lesson her grandparents were holding tight on.

"Don't give up," she said, reminding her uncle of his own advice. This was why Collin didn't give advice. It always came back to bite you in the ass.

He hugged his niece and smiled at her sadly. Now wasn't the time to tell her that, sometimes, things just don't work out the way you want them to. Sometimes, happy endings are just for the stories we tell to distract ourselves from the bleak reality.

He was part of the problem. Collin was a happy-ending peddler. He contributed directly to Hollywood's immoral massage parlor pedigree.

"I'll visit you guys in Philly for Halloween. I promise."

He put his arm on her shoulder as his lips curled into a mournful smile. They both knew it was a lie. He couldn't afford more than one flight back east a year. Los Angeles real estate was a leash to the city itself.

Audrey hugged him for a long moment before letting him leave. He peeled her off and kissed her forehead.

"I'll call you," he said. Then whispered, "For research."

With a wink gave her another quick hug goodbye. Audrey couldn't hide her grimace.

Collin waved his goodbyes to the rest of his family, got in his car and drove away. He looked in the rear-view mirror and saw the screaming dolphin get shot with a tranquilizer dart. It writhed in the air trying to get back to its mate.

Sometimes it's better to be put out of your misery than to fight an unwinnable battle.

C OLLIN DROVE THROUGH CAPE May, awed by the speed at which the community clean-up had happened. There was still a lot of work to be done, but the roads were clear, the electrical grid was up and running, and businesses were open. People can bounce back from anything. Tourists spent their money where they could, mostly because they were hungry and hadn't had power for a long stretch of time.

The MERTs were at the mercy of the locals. Collin saw that the C-View Inn was open and hopping. With the beaches closed, he was sure that if Orla was anywhere in town, she'd be there. His niece's words, *his* words, rang in his head.

Don't give up.

Kids listen. That was their big problem. They learn from adults and adults don't know what the fuck they're doing. The cycle continues that way forever.

Fuck it.

He made a sharp, last moment turn into the bar's parking lot.

Collin entered the bar and, for the first time in a long while, it was filled with tourists. Normally, they'd be eyeballed out of there, but with the hurricane and the holiday they were welcomed with open wallets.

He spotted Orla downing a shot at the bar. It clearly wasn't her first.

She chased it with a big swig from her beer, then she turned, saw him, and immediately flipped him the bird. Collin marched in her direction before Jesse's broad body blocked his path.

"Not a good time, Col," Jesse said.

"I just want to apologize."

Orla heard this and turned towards her brother-in-law and Collin.

"Tell him to fuck off and die," she slurred, and slung back another shot.

"I don't think she'll remember it," Jesse said pointedly. Collin took a beat, collected himself, and grabbed a napkin off a nearby table. He scribbled a note and handed it over to Jesse.

"Do you always have a pen on you?" Jesse asked, as he hovered trying to read what Collin was scribbling.

"Hazard of the profession."

"A true writer is prepared for any situation," Jesse joked.

"I wish you'd never told me."

Collin said it in a cold, matter-of-fact tone. Not like he was angry. Like he was picking up a conversation that had been paused a long time ago.

"No, you don't," Jesse assured him.

Collin remembered when he and Jesse were close. Jesse was such a good friend that, at one time, he'd told Collin something that meant he wouldn't hear from Collin again until this very moment.

Jesse had done the right thing when it was the hard thing. Jesse might have been the best friend Collin had ever had.

Collin hated him for it. He hated that, if it hadn't been for Jesse telling him something he deserved to know, his life might have been more than making up dead dick jokes for Netflix. Because he hated him, he knew he could trust Jesse to get his message to Orla.

"Make sure she gets this. When she's not—"

"I will. You heading out?" Jesse said, wistful. He hoped Collin could stay and not make a mess of his sister-in-law. At least less of a mess than she was making of herself.

Collin nodded the affirmative. He wanted to stay there. Have a beer and catch up with Jesse. It had been a decade and Collin hadn't said a word to him since the day he got the call. He told himself he was setting boundaries.

He was just building walls.

"Hope we see you again." Jesse put his massive hand on Collin's shoulder. Collin felt his strength reverberate through all the bruises on his body.

Jesse meant what he said. He wanted Collin and Orla together probably more than Collin. Jesse spent years with Orla after she and Collin broke up. He saw, firsthand, that no one ever made her laugh the way she did when she was with Collin. He missed Collin as his backstop in arguments with the girls. If he had to hear one more thing about this guy seeing a therapist from Siobhan, he was going to need one himself. He missed the dynamic of having what was essentially a brother-in-law. Someone he could have a beer and sit in silence with while their significant others gossiped in the other room.

Jesse was an only child and always wanted a brother. His parents never gave him one, but he had his brothers on the ship. He needed one on the home front. He had given up hope that Collin would ever come back. Just seeing him renewed that hope.

And if the pace at which Orla was drinking was any indication, she still cared. She only drank when she wanted to dull the part of her that cared too much.

"Tell her I'm sorry," Collin said. He was pleading with Jesse, desperate to fix this.

"She'll know," Jesse said, extending his hand for a shake.

Collin pulled his old friend into a hug. They didn't need to talk about their past. Collin knew that, right now, Jesse was just protecting his family, and Jesse knew that Collin was protecting himself.

Jesse understood why they couldn't have a relationship like they used to. That was life. People changed and it didn't mean that anyone was wrong. People just do what they need to do. They go on living their lives. A good hug was more than enough for the both of them.

When they came apart, Jesse held up the napkin and read it.

"You mean it?" he asked.

"Absolutely," Collin assured him.

The silence became awkward. Jesse folded the napkin and put in in his pocket. A MERT stumbled into him and spilled beer on Jesse's pants. Jesse quickly pulled the napkin from the pocket and waved it to dry any liquid that might have been absorbed.

"Sorry, man," the MERT slurred.

"Just go," Jesse ordered, mean-mugging the drunk MERT while putting the napkin in the breast pocket of his tank top.

"That's why we don't let MERTs in here," Jesse said. Collin got him a few more napkins to dry off his shorts. Jesse patted his crotch and wiped down his legs.

"Make sure she gets that," Collin said again.

"You know I will."

Jesse was always calm. It was unnerving. Collin was willing to bet that if you placed Jesse in the middle of a house on fire, he would simply walk out of it. He imagined a local news stooge interviewing him afterward. He'd just shrug and stoically tell the cameras: *I just put one foot in front of the other.*

Collin took a calming breath. He was stalling. There was nothing more he could do here. He watched as Orla downed another shot and waved Siobhan over indicating she wanted more. A pang of guilt ran though his heart.

She was right to be upset with him. He was just as right to be upset with her. Two rights made a wrong.

"I ought to get outta here. Plane to catch. There are enough MERTS here anyway."

"You're no MERT," Jesse said. "You're one of us." He patted Collin on the back. That meant a lot. Collin took it in, but didn't respond.

"See you soon," Jesse winked, indicating the note that now sat safely in his breast pocket. "I'll guard it with my life." He put his hand over his heart to protect it and took a sip of his beer.

"Just get it to the lifeguard," Collin said grinning.

He turned to leave, but couldn't make himself move. Every atom in his body told him he should just walk to the bar and talk to Orla. He ignored the subatomic universe.

Just put one foot in front of the other.

27
WHAT GOES UP

ORLA'S CELL PHONE ALARM was going off and she could not for the life of her find it. The incessant blaring was crushing her skull. This hangover was worse than any of the others had been the past month. There were only a few more weeks of freedom until the fall semester prep would have to start. Late August was the beginning of the end.

She was enjoying summer. At least that's what she told herself when the Auntie Em's took hold. She could barely deal with the light in her room and patted her dresser like a blind woman looking for a lost object. After some searching, she felt the phone stuck to a napkin. She turned the alarm off and stared at the napkin. Her brother-in-law had given it to her back in July. It read simply:

If you call me, I'll come back.

Orla contemplated the contents of the napkin, considered calling, but the pain in her head had transferred to her stomach. It turned and growled.

"Oh, god." She was going to be sick and forced herself to the bathroom.

She left the napkin on her bed while she retched.

C OLLIN AND GENE EXITED the CBS building, this time stone sober, but giddier than they had ever been stoned.

"Straight to series!" Gene grabbed Collin by the shoulders and shook him. "You did it, you son of a bitch! You'll be running your own show."

Collin was still sifting through the shock and awe of the meeting with Lana. They had loved his script. That hadn't stopped them from giving him a ton of notes on the first draft, but Collin had addressed them all, while still being able to tell the story he wanted.

Now the studio wanted to pay him an absurd amount of money to cast it, produce it, and hopefully make more than one season of it. They were investing in him. He wasn't sure if he was worth the valuation.

"Yeah," was all he could mutter.

"I'll get into all the deal stuff in the morning, should be pretty simple."

It would be anything but. Collin had an idea. "I want the writer's room and set in New York," he said.

"Are you fucking kidding me?" Gene lost any semblance of patience he had with his client. "You just got a series order and you want me to tell them they need to set up shop in New-fucking-York? Do you know how expensive that'll be for the network? The taxes alone!"

"Just do it."

Collin had made up his mind. He was done with LA; he was done being thousands of miles away from his family.

"The studio wanted me to write a family comedy, I did," he said. "But only because I spent time *with* my family. I need to be closer to them. I need to see them regularly if this show is ever going to work long term."

But not too regularly, he thought, which was why he chose New York instead of Philadelphia. He still wanted his space.

"They could pull the order over something like this," Gene warned.

While they spoke, Dolph Lundgren sat down across from them and checked his cell phone. Collin glanced over and felt relieved, he knew it had been him last time. He turned to Gene, and in a bad Russian accent said: "If it dies, it dies."

Dolph overhead, shook his head, and sighed.

"I have a masters in chemical engineering, you know," the actor chimed in, "I'm more than just *Rocky IV*."

Collin simply walked away without another word. Gene apologized to Dolph with his eyes.

"Can you believe that guy?" Dolph said.

"I should have been an insurance adjuster," Gene said.

O RLA SAT ON THE toilet scrolling mindlessly on her cell phone. Out of nowhere, her face contorted in pain as her stomach turned. Having no other recourse, she vomited between her legs and into the toilet.

The heaving was over quickly, but it got Orla thinking. She was definitely not hungover this time. She looked down again.

Oh, fuck! How long had it been?

She opened her ovulation tracking app.

"Oh shit . . . Fuck. Shit, fuck. FUCK!"

C ASEY CAME DOWN TO Cape May. She wanted to stay in the city, but her sister and niece needed to do some baby shower planning with her mother. She felt obligated to join in on the girls' weekend.

They had figured out the date, the venue, and the guest list. Then they drank the rest of the weekend while Audrey spent most of her days at Noah's house.

Valerie and Kip had left to go grab lunch. They started to take more and more day-dates together. They said they were getting as much time in as they could get before the baby came. They knew that the moment they became grandparents it would mean no more sleep, no more peace and quiet, as they would be helping Audrey with the baby. This meant they were going to lose a lot of time for themselves.

Allan and Eliza were out running errands—there was still a lot of work to be done refinishing the basement. Luckily, Allan listened to Casey when it came to the flood insurance. The policy kicked in and they were going to be able to fully renovate the former Dolphin tank, Historical Society be damned.

The sales team at the local hardware store had become best friends with Allan over the years and they were helping him stretch every penny of the payout.

Casey kept hooking up with Dale. It was nice that she didn't have to force him to jump out the window in the morning. That didn't stop her from making him do it. She liked watching him climb down from her balcony. She wondered if this was a new kink. She'd have to ask the shrink.

It was a perfect situation: Dale was conveniently located just far enough from her primary residence that there was no chance anything serious might be possible, but close enough that last minute weekend booty calls were always on the table.

Casey preferred women in the city anyway. Dale's complete lack of ability to stimulate her intellectually stood in stark contrast to his prowess in the physical realm. No one can have it all. He was the perfect boy toy and that was enough for Casey, who treated men and women and everyone in between like objects regardless.

The weekend was over, and Casey was packing her bag when she heard the scream.

No one else was around to hear the ghastly sound. It shook the normally stoic Casey to her core. Something was wrong.

While Casey could negotiate with real-estate developers, media moguls, and bad boy billionaires with ease, she was not apt at dealing with what sounded like physical—or worse, emotional—pain.

She was frozen. She hoped someone had left the TV on and some horror movie was playing on cable. She heard a thud, and the scream assaulted her ears again. This time she recognized the voice.

It was Audrey.

Casey ran out of her room and down the hall to Audrey's. She opened the door to find a terrifying amount of fresh blood staining her niece's sheets. Casey ran over to the opposite side of the bed and found Audrey curled up on the ground, clutching her stomach in pain, blood staining her pajamas from the crotch down.

Audrey wailed like a banshee.

"You're gonna be OK, just hold on," Casey said, not knowing if that was true. Audrey let loose a gnarly, heart-wrenching, shriek. That was when Casey saw a bulge appear in Audrey's pajamas, soaking them in even more blood and viscera.

"Oh, my god . . ." Casey pulled out her cell phone and immediately dialed 9-1-1.

"Valerie?! Where the fuck are you?!" she screamed as she waited for the call to connect.

C ASEY SAT NEXT TO her mother and father in the cold, sterile hospital waiting room. There were people with minor injuries, some fingers in bags of ice sat in the laps of disgruntled teens wearing chef's coats, and a few sick children clinging to their mothers for comfort.

The doctor pushed into the room with an indifferent glaze in his eyes. This was just another day dealing with the depth of desperation that is humanity. He'd stitched up his fair share of morons today. He'd seen so many missing thumbs and burns the past few months that the Monteiro girl's case felt like a reprieve—a chance to practice medicine and not simply work as a limb mechanic.

He scanned the room looking for the Cassidy family. Kip and Valerie returned to the waiting room with coffees in hand. They rushed to the doctor.

"How is she? How's—" Kip said.

"She's had a miscarriage," the doctor said. "She lost the baby. I'm so sorry."

He said this because he knew it was the right thing to say. While the case felt novel today, in comparison to all the firework fed amputations and reattachments, this was the eighth infant mortality he had dealt with this quarter. He was numb to these matters.

The doctor adeptly stepped back and to the right when Kip dropped his coffee, and avoided it spilling all over his lab coat. A few splashes still made their way onto his scrubs. At least it wasn't blood. Blood was much harder to get out.

The family were all stunned silent. Even Casey felt what she could only describe as *sads*.

Allan and Eliza took it the hardest. Allan pulled his wife of over forty-five years close and held her. They put their foreheads together and looked into each other's eyes the way only couples who have made it through the toughest of times together can. They spoke telepathically again, not wanting to interrupt their children with their thoughts.

She's going to need you, he thought.

I know. But what can I do? she thought.

You can tell her about Jack.

"I need to run to the house," Eliza said, "I'll be right back."

She pulled her daughter into a tight squeeze and grabbed Kip in along with her. She wasn't going to let them go without knowing this was an important errand that needed to be attended to. After hugs were completed and tears were shed, Eliza left the hospital on a mission.

C OLLIN AND GENE ONCE again found themselves in the waiting area of CBS television studios.

"I can't believe you," Gene said. He felt like he'd just caught Collin with his wife in flagrante delicto. Gene didn't have a wife. Or a girlfriend. He didn't even like women. Collin had angered him so much that his own fantasies were being whitewashed like a series developed for prime-time.

This was the fifth meeting with the studio in as many weeks to hammer out the details of Collin's series being shot and produced in New York.

The studio was not happy about this choice. It would add millions to the budget and the entire point of producing four-camera sitcoms was that they were supposed to be cheap.

There had been meetings about locations, meetings about labor cost, meetings about meetings, and meetings to discuss what would be discussed in other meetings.

While all this was going on, Collin had to start working on a series bible to be handed out to his staff, if the production ever got the official go ahead. He'd been reading so many garbage scripts sent to him by agents that he wondered how in the hell anyone got work in this god forsaken industry.

"Do you see the shitstorm you've caused?" Gene said. "When we get in there, let me do all the talking."

He was exasperated. Gene had used about every favor he had in this town to keep the conversation going and not simply have what was a green light for a series order fall apart because his client had decided he wanted to be a family man. A family man who didn't even have a girlfriend.

This was the last time he would ever give a client advice. Advice always came back to bite you in the ass. He'd told Collin to reconnect with his family and now he wished he had suggested going to therapy. Therapy always drove people away from their families.

"I got it. I got it," Collin said. His phone began to vibrate in his pocket. He took it out with the intent to silence it, but saw that his mother was calling.

"Gimme one sec. I gotta take this."

He put the phone to his ear.

"Hey, Mom, I'm about to go into—what?" Collin said.

Gene could tell something was up.

"What? Mom . . . Mom . . . It's OK. I'm on my way." Collin hung up the phone.

"I have to go," he said.

"*Go*? What could possibly be more important than this?" Gene said.

"The family it's about. You said you were gonna do all the talking anyway."

The skittish receptionist approached Collin and Gene.

"Lana's ready for you, Mr. Cassidy . . ." Collin rushed past her without a word. "If that's OK, sir . . ."

He was gone. Gene was left alone to pick up the pieces.

"Family emergency," Gene said.

"He'll pay for his insolence," the receptionist said, under her breath, before returning to her desk.

"What?" Gene only heard mumbles.

U RINE FELL IN A stream onto the absorbent pad of a pregnancy test. Orla was back on the toilet, hands between her legs, attempting to mark her territory on the test thoroughly.

She shook it out and placed it on the sink to let it set. Waiting two and a half minutes for a result was going to kill her.

Her cell phone rang. It was Siobhan. She ignored it and stared dead ahead, dreading what she would learn in the next few minutes. She ran her hands through her hair, then remembered where one of those hands had recently been. She took it out and looked at it, disgusted with herself.

Her phone rang again. Siobhan. Frustrated and looking for a distraction, she answered this time.

"What?!" she listened to her sister and her eyes grew wide.

"Wait . . . what? Oh, my god. OK. OK. I'll be there as soon as I can."

Orla hung up the phone. She couldn't go anywhere yet. She sat there and stared at the pregnancy test mocking her from its perch on the sink.

ELIZA DROVE HOME AT a speed that would have made that Vin Diesel fella from those car movies Kip made her watch proud.

She rushed up to her room at Windward House. In the back of her closet, behind all the holiday decorations she needed to change with the seasons, she found the box she was looking for.

She pulled the picture she was targeting and examined it in wistful admiration. She brought the picture to her heart and held it there for a moment before placing it in her purse. Tears welled, but there was no time to reminisce. She needed to drive faster back to the hospital.

———————————————

C OLLIN SAT IN AN economy seat on a red eye flight to Philadelphia. Philly was the cheapest and easiest airport to fly into. He could rent a car and be in Cape May in forty-five minutes if traffic wasn't bad.

They had taken off moments ago. The woman sitting next to him was trying to soothe her infant child while they dealt with the changing pressure in the cabin for the first time. The child's ears hurt and all they could do was cry.

Collin couldn't look away from the crying baby. He wished he could do something to help, but all he could do was watch the child scream in pain.

A UDREY WAS NUMB. NOT from the drugs—and there were plenty in her system at this point—from the experience. The ordeal that had been the last few days.

Noah laid in bed spooning her in the tiny twin hospital bed. He was doing his best. He ran his hand through her hair. He held her close. He didn't say a word, and this is what Audrey appreciated most. She didn't want to hear words right now. She wanted to feel. She felt numb and empty. Empty most of all.

A few hours earlier, she had been full of life, literally. A home to another soul. Now she felt like a haunted house.

She wanted vengeance for the crimes that nature had wrought inside of her. But that would have to wait. She felt nothing now, only emptiness; only the lack of what had once been and almost was.

Almost had you.

Her uncle's words made more sense now.

Eliza entered the room, cautious and slow, like a researcher in the wild trying not to spook their animal subject. She knew that this situation would require a delicate touch.

She glanced at her granddaughter who stared right through her. Audrey couldn't even process that someone new had entered her room. Eliza pulled a chair up to the bed and sat directly in front of her mourning granddaughter.

"Noah, honey. Could I have a moment with my granddaughter?"

"I don't want to leave," Noah said.

Eliza knew he was hurting too, but she needed time alone with her granddaughter. She cast a clandestine look she had been using since Audrey was an infant. Audrey recognized it immediately. The look meant grandma wanted to discuss something privately. Just the two of them.

"Just go," Audrey said, barely audible.

"Are you sure?" Noah did not want to leave.

Audrey closed her eyes hard, asking him to leave was physically excruciating to her. She needed him there. Regardless, she nodded and sent him away holding her tears back.

"OK. I'll be right outside."

He kissed her forehead, nodded to Eliza, and headed to the waiting room.

There was a long silence between Audrey and Eliza after Noah left the room. Eliza reached her hand out to her granddaughter. Audrey took it and held on for dear life. Eliza took a deep breath before telling her granddaughter a story.

"I was seventeen when this happened to me," she said, "so I'm not going to tell you you'll feel better soon. You won't."

The honesty brought light back into Audrey's eyes. She met her grandmother's gaze and loosened her grip on her arthritic hand.

"Your grandfather and I, we don't really talk about it. At least, not with our kids. They don't need to know. But I was much further along than you." Eliza reached into her purse and pulled out the picture she had retrieved from Windward House.

It was an ultrasound. She handed it to Audrey, who studied it like a long-lost relic.

"This is your uncle Jack," Eliza said.

"You knew the sex?" Audrey asked, realizing she'd never know if she had a boy or a girl or anything in between. The words felt awkward in her mouth. She hadn't planned on speaking. Those words also brought tears to her grandmother's eyes. Whether they were because of her uncle or herself was not entirely clear.

Eliza nodded her head frantically, the tears welled up and fell in a constant stream. She took a deep breath and continued her story.

"You're never going to forget. But I can promise you, the pain will subside. It won't happen fast or all at once. But gradually you'll start to find your way again."

Eliza dabbed her wet eyes with the tissues on Audrey's bedside table.

"And then, if you want, when you're ready, you'll have children . . ." Eliza started to sob, but forced herself to stay strong for her granddaughter.

"Just know they'll remind you every day of the sibling they'll never meet. But you'll watch them grow and laugh and play and cry and fight and fuck and have children of their own, who will have children of their own. And it makes it a little easier."

Eliza let a little laugh slip through. She was thinking about all she'd been through. How she wouldn't trade it for the world.

"Mainly because they'll drive you insane and you'll want to kill them all for one second of peace and quiet."

This got Audrey to laugh, which sounded angelic to Eliza. If she could get Audrey to laugh through the darkness, then she was doing her job. A skill she felt she had passed down to her only son. A son too far away to use the gifts she gave him when his family needed him most.

"And they'll be giant assholes from time to time," she laughed again. "But they'll get that from you, so you can't really blame them, and you'll love them anyway."

Eliza firmed up her grasp on Audrey's hand. She really wanted to drive this last part home. "But you won't forget. So . . . Just know that I'm here if you need anything. Ever."

Audrey's cheeks were soaked with tears. But this was a good cry. A cathartic cry. She was hyperventilating and needed to slow down her breathing.

She sat up for the first time in what felt like days. In and out, Audrey took deep, calming breaths. She stepped off the bed and hugged her grandmother while letting out hard sobs. Eliza soothed her and let her cry it out, the way she wished someone had let her.

"I know, honey. I know. It's OK."

28
MUST COME DOWN

C OLLIN HAD FOUND HIMSELF in waiting rooms a lot recently. It felt like he had spent his whole life in waiting rooms. Waiting for good news, waiting for bad news. If you were waiting for your life to start, every room was a waiting room.

The Cassidys and the Comstocks sat together, waiting for any updates on Audrey's status. Collin and Jesse offered each other a quick nod, neither knowing what to say to the other. Siobhan FaceTimed with Beth, who was safely back in Florida outside Eliza's right-hook range.

Orla was the only one who hadn't shown up.

Collin moved over to his mother and father. Eliza looked like she had been through the ringer.

"How is she?" he said.

"About as good as can be expected," Allan said.

Collin nodded. There wasn't much else to be said.

Valerie and Kip embraced him. Valerie rarely hugged her brother outside of cordial goodbyes after family events. It took him aback, but he let her squeeze him.

"Thanks for coming back," Valerie said.

"Of course."

She let him go and Kip pulled him into an even tighter, harder hug. Kip was the softy. Collin patted him on the back in hopes of getting air back into his lungs. Kip squeezed him tight. He had been crying for what seemed like days.

"I kinda got used to the idea of being a Poppy, you know?" Kip said.

Kip sobbed and Allan put a hand on his shoulder. Allan had been comforting Kip like this for some time now, and the reaction was automatic.

Noah came out of the room and into the waiting area. He was exhausted, emotionally and physically. The two families all intercepted him on his path.

"They're going to release her today," he said, "she's still obviously upset, but otherwise she's gonna be OK."

"Well, this is a blessing in disguise," Beth said.

"Mom," Siobhan angrily whispered, "you're on speaker!"

"I will hit her again. I'll fly there. I'll do it," Eliza whispered to Allan.

Everyone was taken aback at Beth's words. She seemed not to have learned the lesson of keeping her mouth shut. It was Noah who had been through too much too soon in his young life to put up with his grandmother's bullshit anymore. He ripped the phone out of his mother's hand.

"Stay out of my life," the teenager ordered his estranged grandmother.

"*Excuse* me?" she said with faux shock.

"I didn't want to marry Audrey because she was pregnant. I wanted to marry her because I love her and never want to be with anyone else. I know that's hard for you to understand, Grandma, because the only person you've ever loved is yourself."

He let his words sink into his grandmother's black heart for a moment.

"Here's the deal," he continued. "Either you accept that this is my life . . ." He looked to his mother for approval. Siobhan was stunned and proud of her son. He was standing up to her mother in a way she wished she could. She nodded her assent for him to go on.

" . . . That these are *our* lives, and you don't get to dictate anything about them. Or stay in that swamp you crawled out of."

Noah hung up on her. He was not going to give her the opportunity to play the victim.

He gave the phone back to his mother and his father squeezed his shoulders and looked him in the eye.

"I've wanted to say something like that to your grandmother for twenty years."

Jesse pulled Noah into a hug.

He was proud.

J ESSE, SIOBHAN, VALERIE AND Kip all entered Audrey's hospital room. Noah followed in tow. Jesse stopped at the entrance to the room and let his wife and Audrey's parents continue on to her bed. Jesse needed a moment alone with his son.

He reached into his jacket pocket and pulled out a diamond ring.

"This was the ring my father gave to my mother."

He held it out for Noah, who took it and inspected it, confused.

"How'd you get Grandma's ring? Isn't she in a state prison?"

"Your grandfather gave it to me and said, 'Your mother is a crazy bitch, but I got this off her finger before she robbed that liquor store.' So . . . I got your mom a different ring."

"Crazy runs in the family, huh?" Noah said.

"Every family. Take it," Jesse said, holding out the box to his son.

"You . . . you mean it?"

Jesse nodded. Tears welled up in Noah's eyes. He hugged his father.

"Now go ask that girl to marry you. The right way." Jesse released his hold on Noah, patted him on the shoulder, and watched as he walked towards his mother and future wife.

Siobhan caught his eye and nodded back to him. They were in alignment.

Noah knelt by Audrey's bedside. He held up the ring.

"Will you still marry me?"

Audrey looked at her parents, then at Noah's. Everyone seemed to have changed their minds. She held back tears—she was pretty sure she had cried out any she might have had left in her body—but then more came.

She couldn't get the words out and so she nodded emphatically '*Yes. Of course*'. They embraced and held each other in that hospital bed where they had shared the worst moment of their short lives thus far.

They were happy in this moment. Their parents were happy for them.

"I'm worried about Orla," Siobhan whispered to Jesse, "She never showed up."

"Let's get home," Jesse said, and everyone was ready to do just that.

A UDREY WASHED HER FACE in Noah's bathroom. He shared the bathroom with his aunt and Audrey wondered where she had been. The thought came and went. She was still coming to terms with the reality that she was no longer pregnant. She had planned so far into a future that was no longer relevant.

She wasn't sure what to do now.

Skating seemed so unimportant, but it felt like the next logical step, getting back on the circuit. She stared at herself in the mirror. She tried to shake herself back to reality, but when her arms flailed, they knocked something off the bathroom sink.

She picked the big stick up off the ground and saw that it was a positive pregnancy test. That was when Audrey realized someone was crying nearby.

It all registered in an instant.

Audrey dashed out of the bathroom down the hall to Orla's bedroom.

Inside, she found Orla sobbing on her bed. Audrey knew that feeling well. She walked over and slid herself under the covers with her soon to be aunt-in-law. She spooned Orla the same way Noah held her in the hospital bed.

"History really does repeat itself, huh?" Audrey said. A laugh made its way in-between Orla's sobs.

"Is it my uncle's?"

Orla nodded, tried to wipe the tears from her eyes.

"Are you sure? Couldn't it be—"

"No," Orla interrupted. "There's no way it could be Dale's. He was sterilized in a hunting accident."

"Probably for the best."

Audrey let that hang in the air for a moment before adding, "You have to tell him."

"Would you stop being the mature one here? I'm the adult," Orla said, laugh-crying.

"There's no such thing as an adult. We're all just kids pretending like we know what we're doing."

"Seriously, stop it," Orla said.

"He just sold a show," Audrey paused for dramatic effect. "Trap his ass."

They laughed, cried, and held each other. Both going through opposite ends of a similar traumatic experience.

29
YES, YOU ASSHOLE

T HE WEDDING WAS PLANNED to coincide with the end of tourist season. Late August was still warm enough for a beachside wedding, but had the added bonus of being mostly clear of MERTs. The ceremony would be a simple affair: gather everyone on the beach, have a lifeguard captain officiate.

Noah slid the wedding band onto Audrey's finger where his father's diamond already rested. Dave, the ancient lifeguard captain who was brought in to officiate, was in his sixties and an old friend of Orla and Siobhan's father. Dave was well known as the main supplier of marijuana in Cape May County before legalization. He was kept safe from prosecution by his friends, Orla and Siobhan's father in particular, in the CMBP. Now, he owned a dispensary. A legitimate businessman. If only Rian could see him now.

Dave smoked a rather large blunt with Noah's groomsmen before the start of the ceremony. Ordained in the Church of the Flying Spaghetti Monster, he was a pastafarian priest. He even wore a spaghetti strainer on his head in his driver's license. He got ordained to avoid paying as many taxes, as a man of a flapping fettuccine God could when his business was less legitimate. He was, after all, always an entrepreneur.

"With this ring, I thee wed," Dave said. His strainer tilted and he readjusted it.

"With this ring, I thee wed," Noah repeated.

Noah was decked out in a goodwill tuxedo. It took all the tact he had to not rip off Audrey's punk wedding dress right then and there. She'd found a lace dress from the eighties at Goodwill. After she'd ripped it in all the right places, Audrey had perfectly tailored it to her body by stitching the rips together with safety pins. It was the all-white converse sneakers that really pulled the ensemble together.

The honeymoon was at the forefront of his mind.

His groomsmen, Rob and Tom, were stoned out of their minds on Dave's weed. Noah still hadn't told them he planned on leaving the band. He might not be a father anytime soon, but he was still dead set on growing up at least a little bit. Save his family, all of Noah's guests were teenage lifeguards he had grown up with on the cape. They were all dressed in their uniforms as they were technically on the clock.

His mother and father sat on the benches that had been brought out from lifeguard headquarters. His grandmother wore a scowl that Noah now assumed was just how her face perpetually looked. Noah and Audrey repeated their vows as Dave struggled to remember his ditalini dogma.

Allan and Eliza were both holding back tears next to Kip and Valerie. They did their best to remain stoic. Kip was not successful. Valerie held out tissues for him to dry his eyes. His little girl was growing up and there was nothing he could do about it.

Audrey's skater friends had their parents make the drive down from Philadelphia. There were a mix of Audrey's friends, their impatient and perturbed parents, and Kip's students in attendance.

Collin thought the juxtaposition of Audrey's skater friends and Noah's lifeguard friends made the aisles look like warring factions from an eighties beach movie. Punks v. Surfers. He took out his phone and wrote that idea down. Just in case.

Collin sat next to Casey, who had brought along Dale as her date. The two of them maintained their posture and refused to look at one another. Collin badly wanted to punch him in the face again, but his ribs had only just begun to heal from their last encounter. He would have sued if not for the fact that he had very much started it, though he could always call the karaoke host.

"I now pronounce you man and wife. You may kiss the bride."

Noah laid one on Audrey and the whole crowd burst into raucous applause.

WHILE THE CEREMONY WAS simple, the reception was lavish. Collin had put up a pretty penny to book out Congress Hall for Audrey and Noah. This was his wedding present to them.

Waiters and waitresses wore tuxedos and handed out hors d'oeuvres. The management bit their tongues at the mix of skate rats and local beach bums. They were used to dealing with rich MERTs.

Collin stood at the bar, happy to watch the teens go crazy on the dance floor and take advantage of the open bar. The bartenders were under strict orders not to card anyone. A toddler ordered an old fashioned for her grand-father and Collin watched as the bartender made and garnished the drink appropriately before handing it to the child.

Audrey snuck up on Collin while he watched the child waddle over to her laughing grandparent. She surprise attack-hugged her uncle. He spilled his drink all over the bar.

"Jesus!" he said, startled.

"Have you talked to her yet?" she said.

Orla was across the hall with her sister and brother-in-law. She looked stunning, and that intimidated Collin even more than the fact that he had fucked things up so royally the last time they spoke.

"She doesn't want to talk to me."

"I think she has a lot to say to you."

Noah made his way over to his parents and aunt. He asked Orla if he could talk to her alone for a moment. She rolled her eyes and followed him to a corner of the dance floor where some skaters were sneaking beers. They didn't realize that this was New Jersey and no one cared.

A toddler in a tuxedo walked by the teens, he sipped on a scotch neat.

"You have to talk to him," Noah said.

"I know. I know. I just . . . What am I supposed to say? 'S'up, I'm pregnant.'"

"That is, verbatim, how Audrey told me."

T EENS CHOREOGRAPHED AWKWARD TikTok dances while others filmed them on the dance floor. The skaters and the lifeguards came together to create content rather than live in the moment.

The adult guests looked at the children with a mix of disgust and confusion as they awkwardly sipped their beers. Audrey and Noah, however, danced together as if they were the only ones in the room. They swayed in each other's arms, in time with the music, and the rest of the reception seemed to fade away.

That was until their friends started to insert themselves into the moment. The teens—mostly Audrey's skate friends looking for clout—forced the happy couple to play host. Noah and Audrey were swept up by the multiple factions of friends they'd invited. They were required to take selfies, send shout-outs to friends whose parents wouldn't let them come down to the beach. This was their first taste of adulthood. Of obligation. They didn't enjoy it as much as they thought. They just wanted to dance.

A large projection of a video confessional space played a live feed on the wall above the DJ booth. While no one was actively inside, images of past participants' well wishes to the happy couple played silently as the DJ mixed beats on the fly.

This was a part of the package Casey had chosen when she hired the DJ, though she had not paid much attention to it. The DJ took this aspect of his services very seriously. He kept a close eye on the live feed from the booth on his tabletop set up so that he could bring up family confessionals at any moment.

Collin watched as Orla chugged a mixed drink at her table. If he didn't say something soon it would be like the C-View all over again. Every part of him wanted to make the first move and go over to her. His muscles tried to override his nervous system and force him to make his way over to her. He stopped himself with every start. His brain kept his legs in check.

The ball was in her court now and he was not going to risk an off-sides penalty. That was how it worked right? Collin was never much of a sports fan. He simply knew that he couldn't be the one to chase after her. If she wanted anything to do with him, she was going to have to make that indisputably clear.

ORLA HAD THE BARTENDER put lime in all her soda waters to give the illusion that she was drinking. She didn't want questions from her family, friends, or co-workers.

Not drinking was an immediate red flag at a wedding. With this crew, you were either sober or pregnant. Both were considered a bummer, but everyone knew she was no teetotaler. No one needed to know what was going on in her body. Well, one person did.

She saw Collin across the dance floor. He looked frozen, as if he was stuck in that spot. She considered going over to him, but then the DJ abruptly stopped the music. Some kid slammed into the floor with a loud thud as others filmed him. The kid directing looked pissed, the music ruined his shot.

"Back to one," he shouted. And the kids found their marks.

On the projection, a live feed of Allan and Eliza appeared.

"Let's hear what the grandparents of the bride have to say."

Allan looked confused as he stared directly down the barrel of the camera. Eliza entreated him to sit up straight.

"Is this thing on?" Allan said. The whole wedding party turned their gaze to the projection and listened in. "I think the recording light is broken." He tapped the camera causing the frame to shake. "Definitely busted."

"It's recording. I think? You know I'm terrible with this stuff," she leaned into the camera lens as if it was a microphone, filling the screen with her mouth, "Hello?"

"These things are idiotic, what fucktard invented—"

The DJ cut them off there with a swipe on his iPad and returned the projection to slide show mode.

"Let's wait for some more technology-savvy family members. Back to the beats!"

He jumped right back where the music had left off and Fatboy Slim's 'Rockafeller Skank' blared through the speakers once again.

The teens went back to one on their dance floor content shoot.

"Action!" that same director teen shouted.

The director got the cell phone camera rolling and stood on top of a table as his crew performed an exact, and well-choreographed, homage to the prom dance scene from *She's All That*. The dancers surrounded Audrey and Noah, forced them to learn the choreography on the fly.

Audrey picked it up immediately—*She's All That* was her favorite movie. She talked about it all the time on her Instagram stories. Her friends planned this the moment she called to invite them all to the last-minute wedding. They were going to send her the video as a wedding gift.

Noah tried desperately, but could not get even the hand movements to seem fluid. Audrey kissed him hard to help alleviate his embarrassment. They laughed as Audrey's friends danced around them professionally.

C OLLIN REACHED INTO HIS pocket and pulled out the ring box that used to live in his office desk. He rolled the box in his hands, contemplating, before putting it securely back into his pocket.

Orla hadn't been able to gather the courage she needed from six soda waters with lime. She just had to pee. She walked over to the bar, grabbed a shot from some lifeguard kid, and shot it back before thinking about it. She immediately spit it out, all over the bar. Teens eyeballed her.

"Shit . . ." she rubbed her uterus and whispered, "That was a close one. Almost ruined your shot at Harvard."

She took a deep breath and marched her way across the dance floor, through the choreography, and over to Collin.

He watched her approach like a deer mesmerized by headlights. He was ready to be slaughtered.

"Hey," Orla said.

"Hey," Collin said.

"Can we talk? In private."

Collin nodded. Private was good. Private meant she wasn't going to kill him at his niece's wedding. Or was she? Private meant no witnesses . . .

They moved into a curtained-off area towards the back of the venue. It housed a soundproof booth in one of the smaller ballrooms. When they got inside, they recognized the space as the video confessional booth. They checked and there was no red light on the camera, they were clear. Or so they thought.

Unbeknownst to Collin or Orla, the camera was motion activated.

Casey had paid for the full package.

When they sat down to talk, the DJ was notified that the space was occupied and saw that they had entered. The music stopped again.

"You're killing me, man!" The director screamed at the DJ.

The DJ took his microphone in hand, and Collin and Orla sitting down in the booth loaded up on the projection. Orla seemed overwhelmed with emotion and Collin was doing his best to comfort her.

"It looks like the uncle of the bride and the aunt of the groom have something to say to our new married couple. Let's take a listen."

The speakers carried Collin and Orla's voices to the masses.

"Listen, Collin. There's something I have to tell you."

"I'm sorry I blew up at you like that. You didn't deserve it. Sixteen years of repressed bullshit came vomiting out. I—" Collin said.

"You were right," Orla said.

"I was what?"

"I should have told you. I'm not saying I would have made a different decision. But you were already set to move to LA . . . I just . . . I didn't want you to stay because I was . . . you know. And I already knew you were leaving, so I just . . . didn't. It was fucked up and I'm sorry."

The wedding guests all awed in unison. Audrey and Noah ran to the DJ booth and both yelled "cut the feed!" The DJ tried to swipe off the video as he did before but something was wrong. He swiped again. Nothing.

"It's frozen," he said, "Shit."

Audrey and Noah looked at one another then back at their aunt and uncle on the projection screen. What else could they do?

"What was that?" Collin asked.

"What?" Orla said.

"Did you hear people 'awing' when you said that?"

"Someone probably just clinked glass and made Audrey and Noah kiss ," Orla hated that bit. It was worse than the flower toss.

Orla hated weddings. She hated the concept of marriage. There was no reason to bring God or the government into your bedroom. She was here out of familial obligation, but still thought it was a mistake. People don't stay together because they sign a piece of paper promising to. They stay together because they choose to.

"Collin, just listen—" she said.

"No. My turn," he said. His eyes opened wide and bored into her soul.

"I want to be with you. I always have."

He stopped—swore he heard those *awws* again, but ignored it. "And I do want to be near my family. I asked the studio to set up my show in New York. They might kill it. I don't really care either way. I want to help you produce those plays. On Broadway, off Broadway, in a backyard. I don't care. As long as I'm with you. We're family. Whether we like it or not, we always were. So . . ."

Collin pulled the ring box out of his pocket. Orla's face dropped. God damn it. She was not expecting to have to deal with this.

"Collin . . . stop. Don't—"

He knelt down and opened the ring box.

"I do not want to marry you!" Orla yelled, panicked.

Collin just smiled and pulled the ring out of the box. He held it between his index finger and thumb. It had been a while since he'd looked at it. The ring was a one carat princess cut set in a fourteen-carat gold band. Collin thought he had done well with it for a young college kid.

Outside the booth, the reception was rapt with anticipation. Eliza hugged Allan, excited at the possibility of her family growing by more than just Noah. Casey and Dale stopped making out long enough to pay attention. She realized that because Noah and Audrey were married, something was off about Orla and Collin getting together.

"Pretty sure that is technically incest now anyway," Casey said.

"Keeping it in the family. Hot," Dale said.

"You're lucky you're pretty," Casey said while grabbing his face and shutting him up with more tonsil hockey. *And sterile*, she thought.

Collin was almost certain he heard the crowd outside gasp the same moment he had opened the ring box.

"I wasn't asking you to marry me," he said. "I just wanted to prove that I was going to back then."

"You're not?" Orla asked

"What kind of loser would try to get engaged at someone else's wedding? We barely know each other now. I love you. But we kind of need to start over."

"Did you have to get on one knee?" Orla laughed, her adrenaline still pumping.

"I thought it'd be funny. I was right. You should see the look on your face."

They both thought they heard the crowd outside booing. There was no mistaking it.

Orla, however, was relieved. So relieved she wanted to kiss Collin for not proposing to her. Instead, she grabbed his face, gazed into his eyes and said what she needed to say.

"I'm pregnant."

There was definitely a gasp that time. Collin was sure of it. So was Orla.

"Are you serious?" Collin asked.

She nodded yes.

"And it's mine?"

She nodded again.

"And you're keeping it?" He wanted to make sure.

"Yes, you asshole!"

"Hell of a way to start over," he said, and hugged her with all his might. She squeezed him back. This was way better than getting married. They were stuck with each other. They were going to be parents.

"Holy shit! I'm gonna be a dad?!"

Orla nodded the affirmative, tears dripping down her cheeks. They embraced one another and could hear literal applause from out in the reception. That was definitely applause.

"Wait . . ." Collin said. "Are you only letting me stay because you're pregnant or because you want me to?"

An impish smile crawled across Orla's face.

"I guess you'll never know."

She kissed him hard. They made out, unaware the whole wedding party was watching. Eliza finally entered and interrupted them with a hug.

"Mom? What're you doing here?"

Eliza pointed to the camera and flipped the digital screen to show it had been recording the whole time.

"Oh, fuck," Orla said.

"Another grandchild! About damn time," Eliza winked.

"What about the whole 'I'm coming back home' stuff?" Collin said.

"Yeah, whatever," Eliza grabbed Orla by the arm and dragged her away from Collin.

"OK. We have to get you started with prenatal care. Your hair is going to look amazing. Your boobs are going to get huge . . ."

Collin stood there alone, his new, old love taken away again.

Typical, he thought.

30
CANNABIS AND
COFFEE

TWO WEEKS AFTER FINDING out he was going to be a father, Collin's union called for a vote to strike against the Alliance of Motion Picture and Television Producers. They weren't actual producers. Producers developed projects, connected people, and, well, produced television and films. The AMPTP were suits. This was the official name a cabal of studio executives gave themselves during those brief moments they decided to work together, instead of competing against one another, so they could pay as little as possible for the talent, crew, and writers they needed to make their products.

The email came in while Collin was in the middle of packing up his Los Angeles apartment. The vote for a strike was overwhelming. Ninety-nine percent in favor. Picketing would officially start at eight a.m. the next morning. Today, the union representatives, and their counterparts at the AMPTP, would begin the public relations war.

The reasons for the strike were many and necessary. They mostly revolved around the studio's attempts to integrate artificial intelligence and remove as many human beings as they could from the creative process. Collin himself voted in favor of the strike, knowing full well that, if it happened, his show would certainly die. Though asking to move production to New York may have done that regardless. Union membership requires self-sacrifice. Especially in the face of plagiarism robots.

"Fuck," Collin said to himself, surrounded by half-packed cardboard boxes and the remnants of a life he was leaving behind. Moments after he read the email, a call came in from Gene.

"Fuck . . ." Collin said into the phone.

"Fuck is right," Gene said. "I got the official call. Studios are terminating all projects in development. *Daddy Issues* is dead."

"Fuck!" Despair made him monosyllabic. Collin sat down on his floor and hit himself in the head with his free hand, hoping that the repetitive motion would somehow reset his brain and change his reality. He cursed himself for already putting his couch into storage.

"I do have some good news. Lana wants to see you. To-day. You have less than twenty-four hours before meeting with executives means you're violating union rules."

"What time do I need to get to the studio?" Collin said, looking at his iWatch. He was ready to do whatever he had to in order to potentially save his show. His career. He had a new mouth to feed coming in less than nine months.

"She's not at the studio," Gene said.

"Where is she?"

LANA LAID IN AN oncology hospital bed, prepped for surgery. News cameras focused on her forehead, where dots marked in sharpie told the surgeons where to saw open her skull so they could remove the tumor in her brain.

Collin entered the room. Upon seeing the chaos, how-ever, he was about to turn heel and run. Lana caught his eye and nodded for him to come in. Her look said *just give me a minute.* Even at death's door, Lana was in full control.

Collin took a seat near the bathroom, away from all the publicity. Every Southern California news outlet was there. A small, young, feisty reporter from an ABC affiliate asked the first question.

"Ms. Radler, the Writers Guild of America, West has said the strike will begin tomorrow. Their main contention is the studio's use of artificial intelligence. Care to comment?"

"They should strike, for as long as they need to," Lana said. The press corps gasped in surprise. Many began taking notes, preparing their write ups for the evening editions.

"Are you saying the writer's demands are warranted?" a CBS affiliated reporter in a cheap suit asked. He wanted to remind Lana they both had the same corporate overlords.

"Of course they're warranted, are you people blind?"

None of the reporters reacted. They all held their microphones in Lana's direction. She continued.

"My counterparts in the streaming world want to do away with the entire system that allowed creatives to have sustainable careers in this town. I don't think Ted Sarandos can spell the word *residual,* so why would he think they're necessary for the people who create his company's success? Why hire young, up and coming writers at scale in writers' rooms, when you can just give Ryan Murphy and Shonda Rhimes three hundred million dollars each to make shittier versions of their network successes?" Lana looked over at Collin. He saw her resolve. She was determined to get her point across to the masses.

"There is so much untapped talent in this town," she said, tears forming in her eyes. "And what do these fucks, sorry, *my colleagues* at the AMPTP, want to do? Invest in artificial intelligence because paying some shitty start-up a licensing fee for their tech is cheaper than developing quality material with artists. These are the same people rebooting every piece of IP in their libraries. God forbid they have the foresight to find something new and original. Artists, crafts persons, deserve to make a living doing their work. The writers, and every other craft that has a contract negotiation coming up, should strike until they have protections for the future of their professions. My job is to find talented people and create projects that affect audiences emotionally. That way, I can force advertisers to fight tooth and nail to get their products in front of those audiences. I don't give a fuck if shareholders make an extra five percent return. I don't work for them, I work for the audiences. And I work *with* writers, not against them. Now get the fuck out of my room, I'm having surgery in an hour."

The reporters and their camera crews stood there speechless.

"Did I stutter?" Lana asked, "Get the fuck out!"

Slowly, the press filtered out of the room until Lana and Collin were all that remained. Collin moved to the chair at her bedside.

"Hell of a speech," Collin said.

"I got nothing to lose," Lana said, "Except this tumor. You, unfortunately, are going to lose a lot."

"Gene already told me. We lost the projects we had set up at Twentieth, too."

"Once the strikes hit, the studios hit back. Business is war. At least you're on the right side."

"So, when do you go in?" Collin asked indicating the marks on Lana's forehead.

"A few hours. Apparently, glioblastomas don't fuck around. It's rude that my cancer got my work ethic. My husband's a wreck. They won't let him join in the surgery. Fucking ethics rules."

Lana rubbed her bald head. Collin thought she was trying to feel where the invader in her brain might be.

"You're gonna be fine," Collin lied.

Lana reached out and grabbed Collin's hand. "What I got is incurable," she said. "Even if this surgery is a success, chances are it'll come back. It's a matter of when, not if. My brain and the industry are in the same boat. We might be able to fix some things for a little while, cut out the bad, but eventually, it's all gonna go to shit. Everything goes to shit."

"But we keep trying, right?" Collin said, tears filling his eyes. This was the first executive who truly believed in him. Who gave him a real shot in this industry. Now she, and it, were dying.

"We never stop. If I'm not fired after that interview—or dead—I'm gonna find a way to get you a show on the air. It might not be this one. Especially since your dumb ass pulled that last minute New York bullshit on us."

Collin couldn't help but laugh.

"If I'm alive and have a job, you have a job. But chances are . . ." Lana let the reality that she might not make it through this settle in Collin's mind. "That said, we gotta make sure that baby you have on the way has a roof over its head," she said and squeezed Collin's hand.

"How did you . . . We've only told . . ."

"Assistants in this industry can find out anything. And I mean *anything*. Wanna know where Jimmy Hoffa's body is?" she winked.

"Can I do anything?" Collin said. He felt helpless here. He hated feeling helpless.

"Don't fuck it up," Lana said. He knew she didn't mean his career. "Now," she said reaching into the purse on her bedside table. "Let's try to forget how fucked everything is."

Lana pulled her cancer-grade vape pen out of the purse and took a long drag before offering it to Collin.

"You're not contagious, right?" he said, hesitating.

"Stop being funny for free, it's bad business," Lana said. "Smoke, I could be dead in a few hours. This is my last wish."

Collin took a deep hit. It was, after all, an order. He was a good soldier.

ORLA'S INTERVIEW AT NYU felt like a dream. She expected to be anxious the whole drive into the city, but she was calm, collected, and confident. She was an excellent teacher, and she'd published multiple papers in the last three years that had been well reviewed. Orla subconsciously decided before she even stepped into the building that if they didn't hire her, they were idiots.

There were three professors in the white conference room lined with lime green trim. It felt like she was interviewing for a job at a tech start-up rather than for a distinguished academic institution. She had imagined wood paneling, stained dark and lined with first edition books. The sleek lines and glass walls gave Orla a surreal feeling. It felt anti-climactic, like most things we think we want do when we get them.

The director of undergraduate studies was a nebbish man who looked like he wanted to be Andy Warhol, but didn't have the talent to create anything himself. He was seated next to the director of graduate studies, a middle-eastern woman in her mid-forties who wore loud colors and a dour expression. At the head of the table was the chair of the English department, a woman about the same age as Orla with blonde hair and a bubbly demeanor more characteristic of a student athlete than a professor of early modern English.

They asked all the standard questions—and, Orla gave all the right answers. She knew they were the right answers when the female professors smiled and the Warhol wannabe rolled his eyes. The whole thing felt like it went by in a flash. Before she could even comprehend that she was in an interview, it had ended.

By the end, even Andy was smiling and engaged. She shook hands with all her interviewers. Orla thanked them for their time. The chair placed a hand on Orla's shoulder and with all sincerity said, "No, thank you for considering our department. You should already be running your own."

That gave Orla hope. Hope was dangerous. Hope, in Orla's experience, led to disillusionment or disappointment.

After the interview, Orla decided to go get a coffee and a bagel. She was in the city and may as well take advantage. That was when Collin called.

"How'd it go?" he asked, no hello.

"I think I nailed it? But who knows, I'm so bad at reading people," she said.

"Books are much easier."

"You finish packing yet?"

"Almost. I had to go meet with Lana today. The strike starts tomorrow."

"So that means . . ."

"No show," Collin sounded calm, despite the bad news.

"What about the other projects you had at Fox?"

"Dead or, at least, in a coma until the strike ends."

Orla could tell from the timbre of Collin's voice he wasn't the least bit anxious about the fact that he was now unemployed and, after giving up his Los Angeles apartment, technically homeless.

"What are you gonna do?" she said, while trying to avoid foot traffic on the packed sidewalks of Greenwich Village.

"Fuck if I know," he said. "I'll figure something out. I should be back on the East Coast by Friday, depending on how fast this U-Haul can go."

Orla placed a hand on her still flat stomach. She took a deep breath.

"We'll figure it out," she said. The plural helped calm the tension rising in her chest.

"Hey, before I go," Collin said, "Will you marry me?"

"We'll figure it out," Orla said, smiling to herself. Him asking and her not answering was a wonderful game they played now. Collin liked reminding her of her assumption at Noah and Audrey's wedding. He asked her to marry him every day, and she ignored, sidestepped, or joked about the answer being no. They both knew the love was there. It had never left. It was just on a long pause. The legal requirements could wait even longer.

Orla hung up the phone and exhaled the combined anxiety of having a now-unemployed baby daddy and not knowing the future of her own career ambitions, and decided to carry on with her plans. She needed coffee and a bagel. Maybe more. She was eating for two now.

As she walked into Murray's, her phone rang again. This time it was Becca. Orla rushed to answer.

"Hey!" Orla shouted, startling the other customers in line. She mimed an apology.

"I wanted to call to congratulate you," an excited Becca squealed through the receiver.

"I haven't gotten the job yet," Orla said.

"Actually . . . I just got out of the hiring meeting . . . and you did."

"I *did*?" Orla inched closer to the front of the line, disbelief covering her expression.

"You did."

"Holy shit."

"Welcome to the NYU department of English, Dr. Ruane," Becca said, proudly.

"I don't even know what to say."

"Back of the line," the large man at the counter said. Orla pulled the phone away from her ear.

"Sorry, what?" Orla said.

"Back of the line," he repeated, this time pointing to a sign that said:

Phone call in line, you do not dine.

"Shit, Becca I gotta call you back," Orla said.

"Sounds like you're at Murray's. It's worth the wait. Just get back in line," Orla mouthed *Sorry* again to the cashier. She moved to the back of the line.

"I ate there like four times a day when I was pregnant with number three," Becca continued, "Get some food in you and find a good real estate agent. Expect a call from the department chair in a few hours. I told you nothing!"

Orla hung up the phone. The interview felt like a dream, now her dream job was a reality. She was still worried about Collin not having work, but she decided it was a blessing. He could be on stay-at-home dad duty while she worked. She wondered how he'd take that news, but there was no time to think too deeply on it.

Back at the front of the line, bagels and coffee took priority. Collin could wait.

31
ROMANTIC LITERATURE

ORLA WAS NEVER COMFORTABLE at extravagant parties. She was, and always would be, a whiskey and beer by a beach fire kind of girl. The End of Summer Gala at NYU was not a scene she was used to, but it was, unfortunately, the best way to meet her new colleagues.

Collin, however, seemed more at home here than he had since coming to the east coast full time. Orla stood awkwardly at a table while Collin shot the shit with complete strangers as if they had been old friends. She grabbed a martini from the servers' tray, sipped it, and nearly gagged.

She spit what little hit her tongue right back into the glass.

Olives, why in the fuck do people like olives, she thought. Orla didn't even know how to hold a martini glass, her fingers kept going back and forth between the stem and the conical V. Collin dismounted from a conversation like a pro, he got a handshake from one and a pat on the back from the other. Finally, he returned to the table he abandoned Orla at.

"Martini? You hate olives," he said.

"It was all they had on the trays."

She placed the martini back on a server's tray as they passed by.

"Come on, let's get you a real drink."

He took her by the hand and lead the way to the bar. Orla liked this version of Collin. He was taking charge. He was in his element. It was all the more tantalizing seeing him in a suit. The boy cleaned up well. The wool jacket hugged his biceps in all the right places. She might even let him try to put another baby in her tonight.

Shit, she thought. Thank God she hated olives.

"Wait," she said and stopped Collin in his determined march toward the bar.

"What's up?" He must have seen the concern on her face.

She rubbed her stomach and looked up at him with puppy dog eyes.

"Damn it. I'm still getting used to pregnancy rules."

"We could relax and accept having a non-ivy-leaguer. Honestly, a few drinks will save us hundreds of thousands in tuition," Orla deadpanned.

"Never. It's not a real childhood if we don't inflict unrelenting pressure for perfection," Collin said and beamed when he made Orla cackle.

"Damn it," she said. "I kind of love you."

"Will you marry me?"

"Maybe we should get that drink," she said and Collin grinned.

"Who is this, Dr. Ruane?" Becca said, squeezing Collin's triceps. She was still handsy, but no longer pregnant. The newest edition of the Cohen clan was strapped to her chest. The babe slept so well Orla wondered whether or not they were breathing.

"This is Collin, he put a baby in me cause I got used to sleeping with a guy who was sterile, and condoms didn't even cross my mind," Orla said.

"I was raised Catholic so my mother would disown me if I ever used one," Collin said and extended his hand for a shake. Becca took it lightly and curtsied.

"I get it. Clearly." She nodded to the infant on her chest. "So, what do you do, baby daddy?"

"Now I see why Noah hated that name," he whispered to Orla before responding. "I'm a television writer. Or I was. We're on strike. I guess I'm a striking writer."

"Oh. Let me introduce you to the Dean of Tisch!" Becca said, and in her overexcitement the infant stirred. Orla breathed a sigh of relief. "She's one of my B-F-F's."

"Will you be able to stay sober on your own?" he said to Orla.

"Go, go. I should do my own mingling," Orla said.

"She hates mingling," Collin said to Becca.

"Oh, I know," Becca said. "You should have seen her at the BU faculty mixers, you'd have thought it was a full-on hostage situation."

"OK, get out of here, both of you," Orla said, pushing them away from her. She watched Collin's ass in his tailored pants and thought more about how she wanted to take them off right then and there.

Pregnancy was really fucking with her hormones. She'd always had a high sex drive, but never in her life had she been this horny this often. That she was not expecting. She should probably read *What to Expect When You're Expecting,* but it just seemed so cliché that she was avoiding it. Just like she was avoiding conversation at this party.

Orla walked over to the bar and ordered a Diet Coke with lime to create the illusion that she was imbibing.

"You hate these things too, huh?" A voice said from behind Orla. She turned to find the chair of the department she had met with during her interview.

"I'm no good at fancy. I always feel out of place," Orla said, sidling up next to her new boss.

"Same. If it isn't a bonfire in the woods with kegs and half-drunk hillbillies driving attendees in and out on ATVs, I can't relax," the chair said and sipped her neat whiskey.

"Change woods for the beach and we're on the same page. Doctor . . ."

"Mann. You can call me Juliet," Juliet said and extended her hand. Orla shook it.

"Nice to meet you, informally," Orla said.

"The way I prefer it. How you feeling about your class load for this semester?"

"Good. I'm excited, just . . ."

"Just what?"

"Just, kind of like this party, I wonder if I really belong here," Orla said, unable to maintain eye contact with Juliet

"You do. I hired you, and I'm a very good judge of character," Juliet said and raised her glass to Orla before taking a sip.

"It's just," Orla tried to gather her thoughts, "I feel like I've been at the community college level for so long . . ."

"Sometimes I almost miss teaching community college," Juliet said.

"You taught community college too?"

"Lackawanna County Community College. Not only was it the local community college, but a few blocks away was the University of Scranton. I couldn't get a job interview there, even with all the dirt I had on the Jesuit priests who ran it. Believe me, I tried."

"It's nice to know I'm not the only one."

"We all start somewhere, Orla. It's where we go from there that matters," Juliet said. Orla raised her Diet Coke to Juliet. They clinked glasses and drank to that.

"Babe, you're not gonna believe it!" Collin said as he rushed over to her.

"What?" she said, annoyed he had ruined her moment with the chair of her department.

"I'm gonna be a professor too!" he said.

"You're *what*?" Orla looked over to Juliet to make sure she heard that correctly.

"Not in my department," Juliet said.

"No," Collin said, "in Tisch. They need a new screenwriting professor. The Dean and I hit it off and she told me to come in on Monday to talk about the position and get paperwork started. Isn't that great?"

"I'm sorry. Are you telling me that after I spent more than a decade teaching community college and working my ass off to finally get a professorship at a real university, you got the same job after a cocktail and a conversation?"

"That's how I've gotten all my jobs. That's how Hollywood works," he said.

"This isn't Hollywood, it's academia!" Orla said.

"I thought you'd be happy?"

"I am happy!" she screamed.

"You don't sound happy," Juliet said.

Remembering that Juliet was there had a calming effect on Orla. She needed to let it go. Sure, a decade and a half of academic pursuits had led her to this night and Collin managed to obtain the same level of position through nothing more than charisma and a resumé. She was fine. She was not angry at the inherent unfairness. She was, however, going to take all of her non-existent rage and hormone dysregulation out on him in the bedroom tonight.

"Come with me," she said.

"Where are we going?" Collin said.

"We're going home and you're getting what you deserve," Orla watched as the recognition registered in Collin's eyes. He knew what mood she was in now and there was no way he was going to argue with her. He was starting to enjoy the pregnancy rules.

"Yes, professor," he said.

"See you in the office, Monday," Orla said with a wink to Juliet.

She led Collin away from the party in haste. Juliet stood and watched as the couple left.

"I really need to get laid," Juliet said, and downed her drink.

32
MINE NOW

O NE MONTH BEFORE Audrey and Noah's first wedding anniversary, they went to visit Orla and Collin in New York. They stayed in the nursery with Baby Rian. The experience helped them conclude that perhaps the adults had been right about waiting a little bit longer before they should have one of their own. Baby Rian cried most of the night, shit his pants often and with a formidable fragrance. But holy hell was he cute.

Noah and Audrey spent a beautiful fall morning having coffee in Greenwich before making their way over to NYU. Audrey wanted to visit the campus. She was still going to end up at Temple with Noah, but she wanted to give herself the illusion of choice. She was also going to make him record her skating around campus for content. They were going to meet Collin and Orla for lunch, then join a guided tour.

Collin convinced the drama department to put on one of Orla's new plays, with him overseeing the class production. After a brisk walk in the autumn city air, Noah and Audrey made their way to the theater to catch some of the rehearsal before their lunch date. They tried to sneak in unnoticed, but the door slammed behind them and the whole cast and crew, including Collin, shot bitter glances their way. They sheepishly waved their apology. As they took their seats, the cast went back to their ones.

On stage, one male and one female actor, both wearing yoga pants and tank tops, tried to find their blocking as they mimed holding documents and delivered their lines.

"I got in!" they both said, simultaneously, in an over the top, flamboyant, take.

Collin wanted to smash himself over the head with a brick. This was why he didn't direct.

Actors.

Actors are like children; they need constant reassurance, but you can't ever tell them what to do or they'll do exactly the opposite.

"Stop!"

The actors froze on stage as if they had been paused by a remote control. Collin wished he could rewind back to casting.

"Guys, that was just . . ." Collin took a deep breath. He stopped himself from telling the actors the truth. Never tell actors the truth, he remembered. Make them feel like it was their idea.

He heard the door open again, and saw that Orla was walking in with his son in a stroller. Just the distraction he was hoping for.

"Let's just take a lunch break, come back to it fresh after that."

The actors were released from the pause and moved freely through the fourth wall back to their real lives. They both pulled phones out of their butt pockets and walked backstage.

Collin pulled Baby Rian out of his stroller and held him under the armpits as high as he could before pretending to drop and catch him. The feeling of freefall delighted baby Rian and he giggled as his father held him close.

"Hiya, buddy," he said in a sing-song voice. "Hiya, sexy," he added with the same emphasis to Orla. He kissed her and pulled a ring out of his pocket. With his son in one arm, he knelt down and held the ring out with his free hand.

"Will you marry me now?"

Orla considered it for a moment.

"We've barely been dating a year. Too soon," she said in a sing-song voice to Rian.

"I'll try again tomorrow," he turned his attention to Rian and in an affected voice added "Yes, I will. Yes, I will. One day you won't be a bastard, buddy. I promise."

He kissed Rian all over his face until the baby exploded in a fit of giggles.

"Just get hitched already," Audrey heckled from the cheap seats.

"I'm hungry!" Noah followed up with.

"Come on, we're going to be late," Orla said.

"Yeah, well, these actors are ruining your play," Collin lamented.

"You're the one who wanted to produce it."

"I forgot about actors, all right?!"

"People ruin everything," Orla said.

Collin's phone rang in his pocket and he passed Rian back to Orla. She got him settled back in his stroller as Collin took the call.

Gene appeared on screen and was sitting in some kind of conference room. Gene was FaceTiming, which he only did when he had bad news. The room looked familiar to Collin, but he couldn't place it. Gene had his smug face on. Collin knew this as his *I told you so* face and thus prepared to be told his project was officially dead.

"You sick of directing art school trash off Broadway yet?"

"Rude!" Orla chimed in, bringing herself into frame.

"Sorry, Orla," Gene pretended to apologize.

"Hi, Gene," Orla said, genuinely happy to hear his voice. While the strike was in full swing, Orla and Gene had gotten close. They worked together to keep Collin from going into full on panic attacks as the weeks turned into months. Collin was a workaholic, he got that from his mother. This was the real reason he wanted to produce Orla's play. He needed to keep himself busy when he contractually couldn't write. Now that he could, he was reconsidering the play as a whole.

"It pays the bills," Collin said.

"Actually, it doesn't, at all. We're so hungry. All the time. Collin's been living on mac and cheese made with breast milk," Orla added. She was enrolled in Eliza's sarcasm class since having the baby, and improving at a rapid pace.

"It's delicious," Collin said.

"Gross," Gene dry heaved a little.

"But I'm happy," he added, looking at his little family.

"Well, get ready to be happy and rich enough to afford cow's milk. I'm just going to add the newly appointed Chairman and CEO of CBS."

Lana moved into frame.

Lana's break from the ranks made her a folk hero during the strike. It bought her better PR than any other executive. That, and the optics of doing it from the cancer ward forced the CBS brass's hands. She was untouchable now.

With her cancer in full remission, and her predecessor involved in a sex scandal, she found herself running the Columbia Broadcasting System. Lana had a large scar around the circumference of her head from surgery. It was healing well, and her hair was starting to grow back. Soon the hair—and good bangs—would cover the scar right up.

"Lana! You're not dead!" Collin jested.

"Kicked cancer's ass. But this development season kicked mine."

"Tell him!" Gene implored.

"We want to re-order *Daddy Issues*."

"Bullshit," Orla was shocked. "Sorry. Not my call." She took Rian and backed off.

"No bullshit. Full season, twenty-two episodes, writers' room and production in New York." Her voice was whimsical. Lana loved giving good news.

"Really?" Collin couldn't believe it.

"Honestly, you're the only writer we have a deal with who hasn't been outted as problematic during the studios' PR war against the writers. Mostly cause you're not famous enough yet. You don't have any weird sex stuff I need to know about, do you? Besides the breast milk?"

Orla winked at him, but knew better than to make a joke at his expense with the chairwoman of the network within earshot. She'd already spoken out of turn once.

"No. But I did punch a cop," Collin admitted.

"That's it? We can spin that if necessary."

"They're gonna do my show," he told Orla as if she hadn't overheard and been involved in the whole conversation. He was in a state of shock. The good kind.

"The show?" she played along. He nodded.

"So, you'll be making Hollywood money again?" He nodded again.

"Ask me," Orla said.

"What?"

"Ask me again!"

She was going to say yes!

Collin pulled the ring out. He got on his knee and looked at the woman he loved. This was it. No more living in sin. They were gonna do it. For real this time.

"Will you marry me?"

"Maybe in the fourth season," Orla deadpanned.

Lana, Gene, and an unidentified third voice laughed through the speaker. Even baby Rian laughed at his expense. Orla really had him thinking she was gonna say yes this time. Collin respected a good burn better than most.

"I love you," he said.

"I love you too."

They kissed.

"Ugh. Emotion. Gross," Lana interrupted. "Not to halt the tender moment, but I want to introduce you to our new VP. She'll be covering the day to day on your show."

Lana fumbled the phone and it fell on the table looking up at the ceiling. The face that entered the frame was familiar to Collin, but he couldn't place her. Where did he know her from?

Then he remembered. This was the skittish receptionist who used to work the front desk in the studio office.

"You're mine now . . ." she said.

KEEPING IT IN THE FAMILY TREE

ELIZA CASSIDY ——— ALLAN CASSIDY

BETH COUSINEAU ——— RIAN RUANE

JESSE COMSTOCK ——— SIOBHAN RUANE-COMSTOCK   ORLA RUANE

COLLIN CASSIDY   CASEY CASSIDY

KIP MONTIERO ——— VALERIE CASSIDY

AUDREY MONTIERO ——————————— NOAH COMSTOCK

TBD

Kevin P. Regan is an author, screenwriter, and former television development executive.

Regan received his MFA in Writing for Screen and Television from USC's School of Cinematic Arts. He was most recently a staff writer on *DAY ONES*, the half-hour dramedy from *Entourage* creator Doug Ellin and Matthew Vaughn's Marv Studios. He has developed television projects with producers from *Schitt's Creek* (Pop) and *Legit* (FX).

Previously, he was the Director of Television Development & Production for Yellow Brick Road, under a first look deal with NBC Universal, which produced *Gentefied* for Netflix.